THE SANDWICH GIRL

Recent Titles by Grace Thompson from Severn House

The Pendragon Island Series

CORNER OF A SMALL TOWN
THE WESTON WOMAN
UNLOCKING THE PAST
MAISIE'S WAY
A SHOP IN THE HIGH STREET
SOPHIE STREET

The Holidays at Home Series

WAIT TILL SUMMER
SWINGBOATS ON THE SAND
WAITING FOR YESTERDAY

THE SANDWICH GIRL

Grace Thompson

This first world edition published in Great Britain 2001 by
SEVERN HOUSE PUBLISHERS LTD of
9–15 High Street, Sutton, Surrey SM1 1DF.
This first world edition published in the USA 2002 by
SEVERN HOUSE PUBLISHERS INC of
595 Madison Avenue, New York, N.Y. 10022.

British Library Cataloguing in Publication Data

Thompson, Grace
The sandwich girl
1. Wales – Social life and customs – 20th century – Fiction
I. Title
823.9′14 [F]

ISBN 0-7278-5781-9

Except where actual historical events and characters are being described for the storyline of this novel, all situations in this publication are fictitious and any resemblance to living persons is purely coincidental.

Typeset by Palimpsest Book Production Ltd.,
Polmont, Stirlingshire, Scotland.
Printed and bound in Great Britain by
MPG Books Ltd., Bodmin, Cornwall.

One

After settling her Auntie Tilly for the morning and checking that the nurse was on the way, Roma Powell left for work. She lived near the office where she spent her day filing completed orders and dealing with estimates and stock control for a small firm of wholesale stationers. Although she was only a few minutes from her destination, by cutting along the lanes, she detoured to the railway station where she stopped to buy flowers from the stall at the approach. Mr Graham and Mr Pugh would probably insist they were relegated to the kitchen as usual, but today was her twenty-fourth birthday and she had to mark it somehow.

It was only five minutes to nine when she walked in, smiling. But the first words spoken to her on this special day were: 'Not in the office if you please, Miss Powell.'

'I – I only brought them in for you to see,' she said. How could she tell these grey old men that it was her birthday and she felt the need to celebrate?

'Very nice,' Mr Graham said. Then he looked pointedly at the large clock on the wall.

She placed the flowers in a bowl and hurriedly slipped out of her waterproof.

It was January, but the day was mild and she wore only a navy dress under the anorak. She used little makeup and the rather sombre colour drained her somewhat. Her grey eyes weren't helped either. She looked at herself in the mirror above the sink and frowned. If only she weren't so boring. Her father had been right: she hadn't inherited her mother's beauty. Perhaps she would go out and buy something a bit more colourful as a birthday treat? A new sweater in a soft blue? Or bright green or even red? Her friend Sylvia Davel would love to advise her. Then her shoulders slumped. She wouldn't be allowed to wear anything but grey or navy for work, and where else did she go?

Twenty-four and she hadn't moved on from a life of looking after her Auntie Tilly and working in this miserable office. Surely it was time for something new? But with Auntie Tilly, who was practically bedridden, to care for, how could there be?

'Miss Powell, there's a list of calls you have to make by nine thirty, remember,' Mr Pugh's thin voice called, and with a deep sigh and a last glance into the misty mirror at the face her father had called 'disappointingly ordinary', she began her day's work.

At ten forty-five, instead of a coffee break Roma was allowed to run home and check on her aunt. Grasping the flowers she ran along the lanes behind the rows of terraced houses which led her to forty-six Viking Street. There was a slight frown of concentration on her face as she thought of the short time she was allowed to dash home and attend to Auntie Tilly's wants. She was small and slim with her light brown hair short and unfashionably cut. Her clothes were unfashionable too, soberly sensible and far from new.

As she pushed open the door she heard voices and wondered who the visitor could be. The nurse would be long gone and few neighbours bothered to call anymore.

'Roma?' a deep masculine voice called, and she smiled as she opened the front-room door.

'Mal!' she said, as a tall, powerfully built man stood up to greet her. He seemed to fill the small, overcrowded room with his presence. Although only ten years her senior he was like a dearly loved uncle, and she was always pleased to see him.

She glanced round critically, checking that the living room, which now contained a bed, was as tidy as it could be. She gathered up the magazines that had slid to the floor from the bed and hurriedly pushed them into a cupboard.

She couldn't resist another quick glance in the hope of seeing a gaily wrapped parcel or two, but there was nothing in view except a few cards delivered by the second post.

'Coffee?' she enquired but Mal smiled and shook his head as he gently pushed her into a chair.

'The kettle's on, the filters are in place and I am going to make one for you,' he said as he strode towards the kitchen.

She had known Mal Parry for so many years she had lost count. A friend of her father's, until her father had moved away and left her, Mal was her only link with the past and a barely remembered childhood. Auntie Tilly had told her that even before her mother had died, Mal used to call in and talk to her father about his ideas and plans for the business he would one day own.

He was one of only four people who remembered her birthday, and also brought a gift on Christmas morning. Surely he hadn't forgotten? Auntie Tilly sometimes did, her memory was unreliable these days. There would be something from Sylvia, her closest friend, later on, so the day wouldn't go completely unnoticed.

Sylvia was a smart elegant young woman who always bought Roma some beautiful item of clothing which she never had the confidence to wear, but it was always a thrill to open the beautifully wrapped present. The other person who had remembered the previous year was the man she called Uncle Mick, who owned the Magpie, a public house just out of town towards the sea. But where was the present from Mal? Was she now, at twenty-four, too old to expect surprises?

Since her father had re-married and moved away from Bro Dawel she had been given into the care of her aunt. He made contact only very rarely. It was Mal and Uncle Mick who continued to keep in touch and checked to see that she was all right.

Apart from Auntie Tilly, they were the closest she had to a family; especially Mal, even though he sometimes treated her like a child.

Coffee was a rushed affair as she only had ten minutes before running back to Pugh and Graham, Stationers. She made her aunt comfortable, swallowed the coffee, then, leaving Mal to deal with the washing-up, ran back along the lanes to continue her morning's work. She was puzzled by his visit and by the absence of a birthday gift. If Mal had forgotten her, there was nothing to look forward to ever again. The thought made her feel a bit weepy and she coughed and blew her nose in an effort to disguise the fact.

The afternoon dragged on in the usual fashion: dealing with only a part of the process of taking orders. None of the tasks she was allotted gave her any pleasure because she never saw them through. She wasn't allowed to talk to customers, and she was given only one or two stages of each process before the order was handed back to one of the partners to complete. It was as though they were afraid she would learn too much about the business, or perhaps they simply didn't trust her. Whatever the reason, the method of working was very boring. She longed to find something more interesting, but there was no chance of that.

To her surprise, Mal was waiting for her when she stepped out of the office at five thirty that evening. Her first thought was that something was wrong at home.

'No, everything's all right and I have asked one of the neighbours to sit with Tilly while we talk,' he said.

He led her to his wine bar, Parry's Place, that he had started a couple of years before, and settled her at a corner table. It was empty, but there was a subdued bustle as the staff prepared for opening at six o'clock: bottles and dishes clashing, pans banging about on stoves, short bursts of conversations from the kitchen as the cook prepared the simple food for the menu displayed over the bar.

A young woman staggered through the room with a billboard on which the day's menu was written, and Mal stood and helped her take it outside where it might tempt passers-by to step inside.

'Although,' he admitted with a smile, 'I don't know why we bother as it's always the same. Chicken in a basket, scampi in a basket and assorted breads, cheeses and pâté!'

When they were seated again he handed her a small package. 'Today is your birthday, isn't it?'

Relief transformed her face into a wide smile.

'I might have known you wouldn't forget. Thank you. I almost forget it myself these days, life is so monotonous. It's nice that you remember.'

'It's fifteen years since I first gave you a birthday present. You were nine, I was nineteen and your mother had just died.'

'I remember. My father was horrified when I asked if I'd have a present that day. He told me I was greedy and wicked.'

'I know. That was why I made sure you had at least one.'

She opened the wrapping carefully, savouring the pleasure of revealing its secret, and gasped as she saw a gold chain and a pendant in the shape of a daffodil, also fashioned in gold.

'It's Welsh gold,' Mal told her. 'Small, but perfect.' He wanted to add, 'like you', but didn't. She still treated him like an uncle, a man of the same generation as her father, even though the age difference between them was not dauntingly large.

'What d'you think of the bar?' he asked, encompassing the room with a wave of his arm. 'I'm thinking of having it tarted up a bit.' Together they looked around the room with its dark chairs and tables, each lit with a low-wattage lamp. Customers could buy wine by the glass or by the bottle and sit and talk for as long as they wished. 'Any ideas?'

She looked thoughtful as she allowed her gaze to wander across the tables, the carpeted floor and the green and gold decor that, to her mind, seemed heavy and dull, then she looked back at him. Mal was darkly handsome with thick curly black hair and warm, deep-brown eyes. His skin had the glow associated with a Mediterranean sun rather than the Welsh valley town where he had been born.

'Sunshine,' she said, beginning one of the minimal-word conversations that were a kind of joke between them.

'How?'

'Italy,' she said finally.

'Explain,' he said.

'Give it an Italian setting. Paint the walls with scenes of Italy with a background colour of apricot or a washed-out tomato red. Light pine tables instead of these dark ones, or perhaps gingham cloths. And,' she added shyly, 'if you dressed more casually, you'd certainly look the part. You could pass for an Italian.'

'My grandmother was from Naples,' he reminded her.

'You could specialise in Italian wines,' she said as though thinking aloud, 'and you could even add pizzas to the menu. Some low music and the mood will be warm and welcoming.'

'You amaze me, Roma.'

She laughed. 'With a name like mine, what else could you expect?' Then she added, 'Don't worry, I won't expect you to do it, I was allowing my imagination to fly. Daydreams are the the only way I can escape from Viking Street, Auntie Tilly, and the glum brothers, Pugh and Graham.'

'You can't change the first two, but why don't you do something about the third? Leave Glum Pugh and Glum Graham and find a different job.'

'I can't. It's close to home and they allow me to pop in during the morning and afternoon to check on Auntie Tilly. What other employers would be that tolerant?'

'You could come and work for me.'

'Here? In a wine bar? I don't know the first thing about catering or the wine trade.'

'No one is born with the knowledge, Roma, it has to be learnt.'

'But I'd need to give a lot of my time to it, and caring for Auntie Tilly doesn't give me much free time.'

'At least think about it,' Mal said. Then he took her arm and added, 'I've got something to show you.' He led her upstairs to his flat where she had been several times before.

It was clearly a man's domain with low lighting, heavy curtains and few frills. But the few pieces of furniture were antique and glowed with the dull patina of many years. The flat was was orderly and beautifully cared for.

His possessions showed his interest in wines and beautiful things: a tantalus on a side table; crystal and old Welsh china in a glass-fronted cabinet; shelves neatly filled with books, many of them on wine; a cabinet full of records of classical music. It was a room in which she felt very comfortable.

Mal handed her a couple of books on the wine regions of France and Italy, and a huge tome on wines of the world. 'Look through and see if the subject gives you a buzz,' he said. 'You were quite interested in hearing about it when I was starting off, perhaps the enthusiasm isn't dead, just lying dormant.'

She was very thoughtful as she walked back to the house to relieve their neighbour and prepare a late supper.

She didn't discuss Mal's proposition with her aunt, Roma didn't want her to consider herself a nuisance. It was easy to explain that the visit to Mal's wine bar had been a birthday treat, and she showed Auntie Tilly the beautiful pendant necklace. But during the evening she studied the books and began to absorb the facinating world of wines. Mal had been right when he reminded her of her interest a couple of years ago, when he was starting the business and, once revived, she thought she might enjoy the subject.

Serving at the bar was impossible of course. He obviously intended her to be behind the scenes in the organisation. The girl who had taken the billboard outside was very glamorous, she could never compete with someone like that. Her friend Sylvia had tried to coax her into dressing more attractively but she didn't have the confidence.

Besides not looking the part, she knew she would need a very thorough understanding of the trade before she had enough confidence to deal with customers. But what was the point of even thinking about it? Bar work meant evenings and she couldn't leave Auntie Tilly alone until late at night. No, it was impossible, but she would talk it over with him though. After all, she thought, as a small hope continued to flicker, Mal was a friend and surely there couldn't be a better person to have as a boss?

The wine-bar licence meant Mal could serve drinks after hours with the meals he offered, and he could also sell beers but no spirits. It was the wines that she needed to understand and the more she read the more ignorant she felt.

Regretfully she put aside the thought of a change of employment – she would stick to what she knew: the wholesale stationers. It was just another disappointment in a string of many.

The following morning, the postman brought a card containing a five-pound note and an apology for its being late, from Uncle Mick. Then Sylvia arrived before Roma was ready for work with a silk blouse in a soft-peach colour that lightened Roma's features and added a glow to her skin.

'It's lovely, Sylvia, thank you but—'

'Don't you *dare* say you couldn't wear it!'

'But I don't go anywhere, except work and—'

'Wear it to work. Today. It flatters you and looks cheerful. It'll do you good!' Sylvia said in her forceful manner and Roma surrendered and put it on, hastily covering it with a navy cardigan. She hated the thought of being noticed, preferring to hide behind unobtrusive colours to match her 'disappointingly ordinary' face.

Sylvia ran a small fashion shop on the end of an arcade in

the town. Starting with financial help from her parents she had built up the business and was planning to expand into a second premises at the other side of Bro Dawel.

Roma thought sadly that it was because she was mousy, so unlike her friend, that Syvia and she had remained so close. There was no competition for Sylvia from her dowdy self, no fear of Roma out-doing her in anything. Sylvia could relax with her, unwind from the competitive streak that had made her such a success.

When she went home later that morning to make coffee and attend to Auntie Tilly, her aunt surprised her by handing her a small package wrapped in newspaper.

'This is for you. It was my mother's. Sorry I forgot your birthday.'

It was surprising to receive a gift from her aunt or for her to be aware of the fact that Roma had celebrated her birthday: Auntie Tilly was becoming more and more forgetful.

Signs of her deterioration were varied. Every Friday Roma gave her the money to pay the milkman, so she had been surprised when she met the milkman one day and he told her he hadn't been paid for several weeks. On another occasion she had gone home and found the milk stacked in the oven. For Auntie Tilly to have been aware of her birthday was an encouraging sign. Perhaps she would get better in spite of the gloomy predictions of the doctors?

She opened the untidily wrapped item with some trepidation, half expecting it to be something unpleasant like last Christmas when her aunt had cheerfully handed her a set of false teeth and wished her a Happy Easter.

To her surprise and delight she found a brooch which she had always admired, fashioned in a style popular in the Victorian period, beautifully designed with sapphires and diamonds and, she suspected, very valuable. Her twenty-fourth birthday hadn't changed her life but it had been more memorable than she had expected.

* * *

It was towards the end of January 1980 Roma began to suspect something was wrong with the firm of Graham and Pugh. The stocks were diminishing and no matter how often she reminded Mr Pugh that they needed to re-order, the stock levels continued to drop. More surprising than that, they actually reduced the price of certain items and sold them at a loss.

Presuming they were going to change their suppliers and maybe begin to stock items for the computers that in 1980 were becoming an important addition to offices, she didn't worry unduly about it.

February came with storms and icy weather and, apart from shopping and a weekly visit to the library to change her and her aunt's books, she didn't go anywhere. With her aunt, she struggled to play dominoes, draughts, ludo or card games, with Auntie Tilly getting confused about the rules.

'Which is trumps?' she asked on one occasion, when they were playing ludo. But even with the disappointment of her aunt's failing mental health, she was glad of the comfort of a fire and thick curtains to block out the inclement weather.

One day Auntie Tilly asked whether they could go into town. She didn't explain the reason, but just said she had something that ought to be seen to.

'Tell me what it is, Auntie, and I'll go in one Saturday and sort it for you,' Roma promised, but Tilly wasn't satisfied.

'You'll be all right you know. You'll have a home.'

For once her aunt seemed lucid and Roma calmed her and assured her that it wasn't the time to worry about such things.

'I want you to take a day off work, you have a couple of days' holiday left. We can organise a taxi and I can go and do what I have to do while you find us a nice place to have lunch.'

It had been months since her aunt had been well enough to go into town and Roma decided the best way was to humour her into a vague promise of, sometime soon.

'Once the stocktaking is over,' she said, 'I'll ask for a couple of days off and we can do your errand and order plants for the garden.'

'When?'

'After the end of March. It won't be long.'

Tilly frowned and touched her arm. 'I hope it won't be too late, dear,' she said, 'winter will be here before we know it.'

'Auntie, it's February.' Roma sighed.

Between periods of confused talk and muddled behaviour, they watched television, tried to play games and planned the flowers they would plant in the garden. They had light suppers and early nights. A gentle life, but Roma found herself becoming more and more restless. It was as if she were waiting for something to happen, but had no idea what it would be.

At the office her work consisted more and more of writing-down stock, devaluing damaged items and discarding out of date stationery. Monday, March the thirty-first was the end of the financial year, when that whole weekend would normally be spent stocktaking. This year the job would be done in half a day! The partners must be working towards a fresh start.

'Are we going to decorate before re-stocking?' she asked one day when she took down the last of what had once been a large selection of account ledgers, leaving the whole shelf empty.

'Why d'you ask, Miss Powell?' Mr Graham queried.

'I can't think of another reason to reduce the stock so much.'

'Can't you?'

'Well, not unless we're closing down.' She laughed.

'That's what we are doing,' the elderly man told her.

With a few days of holiday pay and a month's notice, Roma had achieved the change she craved, but not in the way she had imagined. She wasn't changing her job, she was unemployed and, with the responsibility for an ageing aunt, almost unemployable.

The resentful thought crept into her mind that if it weren't for Auntie Tilly she would have a wide choice, but the momentary ill-feeling was crushed. She owed it to her aunt to take care of her. She had been homeless when her father had remarried and moved away. Auntie Tilly had taken her in, given her a home, and treated her like a daughter.

'Treated you like an unpaid servant more like,' Sylvia said when they discussed the problem of a job.

'It isn't like that,' Roma protested. 'She's cared for me all these years when no one else would.'

'Just be warned that if you aren't very careful you'll end up a lonely woman with no hope of building a new life, having given the important years to a demanding old lady.'

'Rubbish, you don't understand,' Roma retorted.

Although Roma had only the small amount saved from her wages in the bank, Auntie Tilly pleaded with her not to rush to find another job.

'We'll manage nicely for a while, dear. You don't have to pay me any rent, just buy some of the food and if we're careful, we'll manage well for months.'

Roma browsed through the books lent to her by Mal. If only working for him were possible. The subject interested her and it would be a way of earning her living enjoyably.

When Mal called and offered her the job he had mentioned some weeks previously, Tilly became upset. When it was arranged that Roma went to spend a couple of evenings observing and learning what was involved, Tilly stopped her going by saying, 'I feel a bit queer, breathless, all hot and bothered.'

Roma phoned the doctor, apologised to Mal, and stayed at home. The following evening, Tilly called Roma back just as she was leaving the house and asked for some tea.

'I might get thirsty before you get home, dear. If you

could fill the flask with hot water and make a pot of tea I'll be fine.'

Glancing at the clock and rushing the small tasks, aware that once again she was going to let Mal down, Roma spilled the hot water and dropped and broke the flask. By the time she had re-made the tea and found and filled another flask, it seemed too late to go.

'Ring Mal, dear, he'll understand that you got delayed. Stay and share this tea with me.'

Mal wasn't angry about being let down twice, but he warned Roma about giving in too much. 'Don't let her take your life as well as her own,' he said the following morning when he called to enquire after the old lady's health.

'What d'you mean, take my life!' Roma demanded. 'I look after her because she looked after me.'

'She might have ten more years, and if you look after her to the exclusion of everything else, she'll have stolen those ten years of your life too.'

Roma was angry with him. He was as selfish as Sylvia. They didn't understand.

A trip to the cinema with Sylvia was cancelled when Tilly began to show signs of a chesty cold. Instead they both stayed at home and played draughts with her aunt. For a few minutes the old lady's mind cleared and she talked to Roma about her childhood. It was a happy time, re-living old memories; brief but satisfyingly pleasant. As she helped the old lady settle to sleep, she sat on the bed and asked, 'Auntie, why don't you want me to go out in the evenings? You know I'm never far away, and I never leave you for long.'

'Have I been that transparent? I'm sorry, dear, but I am nervous alone here after dark. I'll be fine when summer comes, and it won't be long, will it? We'll soon be having our trip into town. I won't be so nervous when it's light. Already we can have our tea without the electric light on.'

'Why didn't you say you were uneasy? I'd have arranged for Sylvia or one of the neighbours to come and sit with you.'

'You don't mind do you? It's only for a few months while the evenings are so dark.' She stared at Roma, a serious expression on her lined face and said, 'The trip to town. We must get that sorted as soon as we can. It's important. I'd forgotten, you see.'

'Auntie! What on earth is it that you have to do in town? I don't want you to tire yourself. I can deal with anything you need, can't I?'

'I want a coat,' Tilly said peevishly.

'Then I'll help you choose one from a catalogue, right?' Roma knew that it was unlikely that the old lady really wanted a coat. But what was it that she considered so important?

'But I need to go—'

'Don't worry about town. Let's deal with making you feel comfortable in your own home. That's more important surely?'

'And you won't go out and leave me after dark?'

'Not unless we make proper arrangements.'

Mal's words came into Roma's mind. Was she allowing her life to slip past? Twenty-four and there was plenty of time, but another ten years of holding back on her own life while helping Tilly enjoy her remaining years suddenly sounded frightening.

'Auntie, I do have to work. And I would like to try the job Mal is offering at the wine bar. I promise I won't leave you alone. I'll employ someone for the few hours I'm out. Will you agree?'

'You won't make much money doing that. Why bother? We manage all right and you've got a home. Plenty of time for gallivanting when I'm gone.'

'I dread the day I no longer have you, Auntie Tilly. You're the most important person in my life, but don't you see, I have to prepare for the time when I'm alone. This house won't run on air. Everything will still have to be paid for, and if I'm not trained to earn enough money, well, all your care would have been for nothing, wouldn't it?'

'All right, we'll give it a try. But not till summer.'

Roma went over and over the problem in her mind. There had to be a solution.

The following morning, Roma took a cup of tea to her aunt and found that she was still sleeping. She placed the tea and the solitary biscuit her aunt enjoyed on waking, on the bedside table and tiptoed away. After bathing and preparing herself to go and see Mal, she went back to see if her aunt had woken. Tilly was still exactly as before and, touching her, shaking her shoulder gently and then with more urgency, Roma realised that her aunt was dead.

Mal came soon after the doctor had been and began to make the arrangements. Neighbours called and the few friends Roma had came to see whether there was anything they could do. Sylvia came as soon as she heard and helped deal with the phone calls and the task of letting people know.

The following evening, the announcement appeared in the paper, leading to a steady flow of visitors and phone calls. Uncle Mick came and hugged her and told her she only had to ask for help and it would be forthcoming.

At nine o'clock, when she thought that the activity had stopped for the evening there was a knock at the door. Wearily she answered, expecting it to be someone else come to offer condolences. The man standing there was a stranger.

'Miss Powell?' he queried. 'Roma Powell?'

'Yes.'

'I'm from Bollam and Green, solicitors. Your aunt would have mentioned us?'

'I'm sorry, but no, she didn't mention any solicitors. Is it about the house?'

'Then you know about the house. That's good. It would have been an embarrassment for me if you hadn't been told.'

'Told what? The house is mine now my aunt has passed on, what else is there for me to know?'

'Oh dear.' He smiled, a friendly smile, and asked, 'Do you mind if I come in? This is rather difficult.'

He followed her into the living room where her aunt's bed still stood, now stripped of its bedding, in a corner near the window.

'Your aunt, Miss Matilda King, bequeathed this house to an organisation called Animal Home-finders. They specialise in finding new homes for unwanted pets. I'm afraid you will soon no longer have the right to be here.'

At last Roma knew what her aunt had needed to do in town. Her anxiety about changing her will had been thwarted by the heart attack that had ended her life.

Roma woke long before the six a.m. alarm sounded and began to prepare herself for her first day in Mal Parry's wine bar. She was nervous and, having washed, dressed and arranged her hair at least four different ways, she stared at the clock in disbelief – she had two whole hours to kill before leaving the small room where she had lived for only three weeks.

She dressed soberly, partly out of respect for the recent death of her aunt and partly because she felt safer in subdued clothes. She wore no jewellery apart from the daffodil pendant. The brooch her aunt had given her had turned out to be part of the bequest made to the animal charity.

Sylvia had styled her hair but it had at once fallen into untidy curls and overnight had collapsed into complete disarray. After all Roma's attempts to tidy it, it was nothing more than a wild mess.

If there had been a telephone in the bedsit, she would have telephoned Mal and told him she had changed her mind, but the one in the hall was out of order. With no experience, apart from working at the stationers, how could she cope with something as different as serving food and drink in a sophisticated wine bar? She must have been insane to believe she could.

The room she had rented was sparsely furnished with a

narrow bed, a dressing table and a tall single wardrobe that reminded her of her aunt's coffin. Her personal possessions were few. There were two photograph frames: one containing a picture of her parents and the other a picture of her aunt. For the first time in her twenty-four years she was free to do what she wanted, but the freedom hadn't brought any joy. She was ill-prepared by her solitary existence to step out into the world. The prospect of making a life for herself was terrifying.

She wondered vaguely, and without real hope of finding out, where her father and his new wife were. The last she had heard was when they moved into a small terrace house in Reading with their new daughter. The card had been signed 'Father, Morfedd and baby Catrin' and had borne no address. That had been five years ago and there had been nothing since.

A hasty move from Viking Street into the loneliness of a bedsit among strangers had been the worst moment of her life. Discovering that there was no inheritance to compensate her for the years as her aunt's companion had forced her to search for a job. When Mal Parry offered her a month's trial at the wine bar she had agreed, now she was wondering if she would last a single day.

Mal closed the door after the morning cleaner had gone and stared out at the street, wondering whether Roma would appear at nine o'clock, as arranged, for her first lesson in working at Parry's Place. He had closed the place for a month and now it had been redecorated on the lines suggested by Roma. He hadn't told her, but hoped the transformation would be a pleasant surprise. The walls were painted with scenes of Italy, the lamps shed a peachy glow and potted plants added to the illusion of exotic places.

A glance at the clock told him it was fifteen minutes to nine. Nervously he adjusted an ashtray and straightened a collection of shallow wicker baskets with their displays of fruits and nuts. She wouldn't come. He'd been foolish to imagine she would.

He couldn't remember the actual moment when he realised he loved her. After years of being an unofficial uncle, one-time friend of her cold, indifferent father, he had looked at her one day and saw, not a subdued child but a rather lovely woman. The thought of her working beside him both worried and excited him. He would have to be very careful not to frighten her away.

Opening a drawer, he busied himself checking through the lists of supplies due that day.

Roma Powell closed the door of her room and, taking a deep breath, set off for Harbour Road. She was far too early but she had decided to walk round the streets rather than sit and watch the clock. Instead, she turned off Park Street and went straight to the door of the wine bar. Might as well get it over with, she thought. How optimistic she had been to think she would last a day. She probably wouldn't last an hour.

The door bell gave a soft tinkle and she looked at the counter where Mal was working on a sheaf of papers. He looked up, smiled and came to greet her.

'Roma. You're nice and early. Marvellous. Now we can have a chat before I give you the grand tour and tell you the basics of working here.' He went to the coffee machine and poured two cups.

Roma half removed her coat, couldn't decide where to leave it and pulled it on again. She wondered whether the four-year-old black dress she had chosen to wear was suitable. Mal was wearing a boldly striped shirt and a red tie, with light, casual trousers. She had been wrong, she should have worn the beige. She looked dowdy and boring.

The room was quite dark with the blinds still covering the windows and only the light from a couple of wall lamps piercing the gloom. Then Mal switched on the central light. When she looked around her she gasped in delight.

The changes she had suggested had been implemented. She gazed in amazement, flattered that he had listened to her suggestions, as Mal had intended her to be.

'It's wonderful! Better than I imagined it. I didn't think through the details as carefully as you. It's – oh, Mal you are clever.'

'The ideas were all yours,' he reminded her, as he placed the coffee on a table. He took her coat and invited her to sit down, then disappeared, to return almost immediately with a red skirt and red and white blouse which he showed her.

'I hope you don't mind wearing a sort of uniform,' he explained. 'We all do, including my assistants, Ric and Susie, and me, so you won't feel conspicuous.'

She was shown the stock room. 'Although,' Mal reassured her, 'you won't be sent for replenishments, Ric or Susie will do that. I just want you to know where everything is so you understand how the system works.'

'The till looks terrifying,' she said at one point and he showed her several times and promised to be on hand if she made any mistakes. He couldn't have been kinder.

'Why are you bothering with me?' she asked after forgetting the price of the most popular line several times.

'Everyone has to start somewhere, and I've trained worse beginners than you.' He smiled, his dark eyes glittering in gentle teasing. 'Honestly, it's sometimes easier to train someone from scratch than take on an experienced person who refuses to do things my way.'

She thanked him and smiled, but didn't believe him. He was sorry for her and would soon have to admit his mistake.

The first day was exhausting. Serving customers without a good knowledge of the language of the wine trade seemed impossible, but after a week, things began to slot into place, the glamorous girl whom she now knew was Susie, helped her and she avoided the worst mistakes under her gentle guidance. After three weeks she had to admit to Mal that she was actually enjoying it. She didn't add that the worst part of her day was returning to the small, lonely bedsit.

Mal watched her blossom and grow in confidence in a way that might have seemed impossible a few short weeks before. The customers accepted her, teased her and eased her way into the complicated world of wining and dining. She applied for a course on wines of the world and bought more books to help her education.

Mal was attentive and always seemed to be there when a problem arose. She only had to frown a little and he appeared to sort out whatever bothered her. He never tired of answering her questions and seemed to take a pride in her progress. When customers flirted with her he smiled and nodded approval at her responses. When someone stepped over that invisible line towards the unacceptable, he came at once to defuse the situation. She thought she had never been happier.

In August when she had been working at Parry's Place for five months, he invited her out.

'Out?' she laughed. 'Out where? To a pub? Or wine bar?'

'That's the problem working at a place like this, where do you go to relax?' he said with a laugh.

'Walk?' she suggested.

'Cinema?'

'Walk!'

'Concert?'

'Walk!'

The following Sunday morning they drove out of town past the burgeoning splendor of the new marina, along the coast road which took them on a six-mile sweep round the bay, and parked overlooking a small beach near the coastguards' station. From there they walked, following the ancient footpath to the next bay and the next, stopping occasionally to watch the small fishing boats and the yachts with their colourful sails. The rowing club was out and the rhythmic calling of the coxwain could be heard below them. A school of canoeists shouted across to each other and their voices were crisp in the clean air. The schools were on holiday and the place was full of lively, laughing families having fun.

Mal and Roma didn't talk much, seemingly content in each other's company, He asked about the room she had rented, she asked about his plans. They walked arm in arm when the path allowed, single file when it did not. So it was a shock when Mal placed an arm across her shoulder and looked at her differently. Roma pulled away a little, not wanting to offend but not wanting to move that fraction closer, moving their friendship forward in a direction that might lead on to something for which she was not ready.

Mal was not the kind of man she imagined as a boyfriend. Then embarrassment flooded over her. How could she be so vain? How could she think for a moment that a rich, good-looking man like Mal would want her? That was even more crazy then her wanting him! She must have been mistaken in what she thought was an overture to greater affection. What a fool she was.

Fortunately they soon had to revert to solitary walking as people struggled to pass them on the narrow path, so the movement which might or might not have been an accident was forgotten.

He took her hand as they strolled back along the edge of the cliffs high above the sea; something he hadn't done since she was a child, and she found it alarming. It was wrong, it was madness. She was relieved when it became impossible to walk side by side with so many people using the path.

A narrow track ran up the hill to the top, where a parallel path led back to the car park. They went up and when they were out of sight, he pulled her close and kissed her. She was so surprised she didn't push him away, but when he released her she hurried on through the heather, bracken and brambles without a word.

When the path widened out and allowed them to walk side by side again, she determinedly kept ahead of him. What was he thinking of? He was a friend of her father for heaven's sake. How could he expect her to feel anything more than that?

They drove back to her bedsit in a silence that was no longer companionable.

She lay awake that night thinking about the change in Mal's attitude towards her. So that was why he had offered her a job. Not because he thought she'd be an asset to the business, or that he felt sorry for the daughter of a friend. It was so he could persuade her into an affair. She wondered how he could be so desperate. With women like the attractive Susie about, why would he bother with her?

Her father had taught her well when he had told her she was no beauty.

At three o'clock that morning, unable to sleep, she dressed and walked to Harbour Road and put a note through the door of Mal's flat telling her she would no longer be working for him. Getting back into bed she stared up at the cracked and stained ceiling and asked herself aloud, that with her aunt dead and Mal no longer a part of her life, what would happen now?

Two

Faced with having to find work, and fast, Roma went to the employment exchange prepared to do anything that would bring her in enough money to pay the rent and provide sufficient food. When she had woken the morning after the embarrassing interlude with Mal, it had been frightening to realise that she was alone in the world and practically penniless. But it was 1980, she wouldn't starve, it was idiotic to be alarmed.

The jobs offered were few, mainly because of her limited experience. There were barmaids wanted but the wine bar hadn't given her the right sort of experience and any office work needed a far wider knowledge than she had gathered working for Glum Pugh and Glum Graham. What a fool she had been to have stayed there, and put up with the little they offered.

She went to see Sylvia who suggested she might like to be a sales lady in her shop but Roma didn't think she would enjoy it.

After she left Sylvia, Roma wandered round town partly looking for something she thought she could do and partly so she wouldn't be in the bedsit if Mal called. She ate a sandwich for lunch in a small dingy cafe and later stopped for a cup of coffee in the busy market. At four o'clock, when the town was shining with falling rain and everyone was hurrying for home, she set off back to the bedsit in Carling Terrace. Head bent against the still-falling rain, she didn't look up until she was almost at the gate when, to her dismay, she saw Mal sitting in his car outside. He hadn't yet seen her, so regretting the unnecessary expense, she turned back and went to the pictures.

How had she been so unaware? Why hadn't she seen the signs? she asked herself as the film droned on without grabbing her attention. For Mal to kiss her like that he must have given some sign, yet she had seen nothing. I'm stupid as well as unattractive. She sighed. My father was right.

Mal sat outside the house where Roma lived and watched as an assortment of people went in and out. Students most of them, he surmised. Apart from going back to the wine bar once or twice to check that everything was running smoothly he had been there all day. He had telephoned from the box on the corner to get details on the houses and flats he owned and as two tenancies were due to end soon had hopes of offering Roma a flat before the end of the month. At nine o'clock he presumed she was staying with a friend and tried Sylvia's home.

'Sorry, Mal, but I haven't seen her for a couple of days,' she lied. 'I've no idea where she is.'

'I've been waiting for her all day, but I have to go back to the wine bar now. I can't leave the staff to manage alone. Will you tell her I called?'

'Why don't you leave her a note?' Sylvia suggested.

He went inside and Sylvia found him notepaper and left him in the kitchen to write it. He pushed the note through the front door at Carling Terrace and hoped that it would reach her.

But Roma was at home. Giving up on the film, she had walked back to Carling Terrace and to her relief had seen that Mal's car had gone. Still afraid he might be nearby watching for her light to reveal her presence, she sat in the dark and drank a can of Coke before undressing and slipping into bed.

The room she had found was so different from the quiet

respectability of Viking Road that she felt she was in an alien land. The noises had been confusing until she had begun to identify them: people coming and going at all hours; laughter; raised voices chattering or arguing or, on occasion, fiercely shouting. As well as the sounds of people in close proximity the plumbing had a cacophony of its own, while outside there were cars revving, doors slamming and brakes squealing.

Then there were the unacustomed smells. Trainers and socks and the ever present curries, had smells which crept through walls, and there was cooking going on at all hours of the day and night.

Roma avoided contact with the other residents who were just a few years younger than she but light years away in spirit and attitudes. She didn't use the kitchen, preferring to eat at one of the cheap local cafes.

Sleepless and miserable she began childishly to blame Mal for her misery as she lay in her narrow bed, and wished she had reacted in a more mature manner to his kiss.

When one of the other boarders handed her Mal's note the following morning she opened it at once. Their estrangement wasn't a lover's tiff nor had it been the result of a violent quarrel. She wanted to read his words and perhaps understand. A part of her blamed herself and she held her breath as she unfolded the pages, preparing for anger or criticism.

> Dear Roma,
> Please forgive me for yesterday. I was overwhelmed by a sudden and intense love for you.
>
> I so much admire your bravery during the many blows you've received and in the disappointments that fate has handed out.
>
> I don't regret my declaration of love – because that was what it was – but I wish I'd handled it better. Please don't cut me out of your life. I promise we can return to being the friends we have always been.

I need you to be there for me and want to be there for you.

Please phone me or call at the wine bar.

With affection and love

Mal

For the first time since the death of her aunt, she cried.

Mal was wealthy. Besides the wine bar in Harbour Road and two cafes in the older part of town, he owned three houses converted into bedsits and one converted into three flats. He also had a chain of laundrettes. He was selling the laundrettes and had intended to increase the number of student houses he owned, but something had changed his mind.

Starting out with a couple of student houses had been a very good move but he was aware of how difficult it was to keep up the standard of accommodation when tenants changed so frequently, and this, combined with having seen the small room that Roma was forced to call home, had decided him to go upmarket and change his properties into good-quality flats.

He wanted Roma to telephone. He wanted to know everything was all right between them and he wanted her to help plan the changes in the houses.

The morning after he had delivered the note he sat at one of the tables in the wine bar making phone calls. He had an office in his flat, but he preferred to sit in the silent cafe bar where he could look out and see people passing. Today he admitted he did this because he was lonely. He had plenty of friends and there was always a girl willing to provide company and laughter for an evening, but there was no one, he reflected sadly, with whom he came first and no one who he could care for and protect, which was what he wanted to do for Roma.

He had a life that many outsiders would envy. He had sufficient money to do what he wanted to do. He wore top-quality clothes, took holidays when he felt the need, but his hobbies and interests were few. Most of them needed to be shared. He enjoyed music of all kinds, belonged to a squash club and went swimming regularly. He had tried the popular holiday destinations including skiing but had no desire to go again. They too needed to be shared.

One day, he promised himself, I'll build a big, family house with a tennis court and swimming pool and be content. But that contentment seemed elusive. He wanted Roma to share his dream but there seemed little chance of that. He forced the gloomy thoughts aside and concentrated on the papers in front of him, deciding to accept the price for the laundrettes offered by a man who already had several. It was less than he had hoped for, but, he told himself, by accepting it he would be able to move on. That was what he wanted.

He had just put his flourishing signature on the final paper when there was a knock at the door. Not time for the staff already was it? He must have spent more time than he realised day-dreaming. He glanced at his watch. No, they weren't usually this early.

He released the blind and, as he saw his visitor, unhappiness fell from him like a great burden he'd been unaware of carrying.

'Roma!'

He was very formal in his welcome. He wanted to hug her and hold her but, although he couldn't prevent a smile from spreading and transforming his face, he held his arms rigidly at his sides.

'I want to say I'm sorry. I overreacted stupidly,' Roma said at once.

'I'm sorry, too, but let's make a pact never to mention it again, shall we? That way we can get on with being friends without any worries.' He led her to a chair and pointed to the coffee on the counter, tilting his head in question.

'Please,' she said, 'although, I'm awash with the stuff. I

was wandering round town yesterday trying to decide what I want to do.'

'You won't come back here?'

'No.'

He brought the cups to the table and said hesitantly. 'If I'm interfering, please tell me, but I do know of a job that might suit, temporarily at least. While you think about what you want to do with your life.'

'Another wine bar?' She laughed.

'Almost. It's Micky Richards at the Magpie. Uncle Mick. He wants someone to help out in the bar, mainly to deal with the bar food. You know, pies, Scotch eggs, bread rolls and crisps.'

'I don't know anything about—' she began.

He tilted his head again, this time as gentle reprimand.

'But, there, everyone has to start somewhere, don't they?' she finished.

'And you know a lot about wines. That will be helpful.'

'At the Magpie? From the little I've heard, the clientele are suspicious of everything that isn't called beer!'

'Not any more. People are beginning to ask for wines more and more these days, even in the Magpie.'

'He sent me a birthday card this year and last. Did you know?'

'He's sent one every year since you went to live with Tilly.'

'No, I haven't had one apart from the last two years.'

'Nevertheless, he sent them each year with money in them. Tilly thought it best you didn't receive them.'

'But, why?'

'She didn't consider him a suitable friend.'

Roma puzzled over this for a very long time, although Mal said no more.

When Mal phoned to tell Micky that Roma Powell was on her way as an applicant for the job at the pub, Micky felt a jolt almost of pain, if pain could be described as pleasurable. Roma working for him? Here, at the Magpie? It had long been a dream, but he had never dared suggest it. Certainly not while that aunt had been alive. She wouldn't have countenanced the idea for a moment!

If Roma would come here, learn the trade and help him build the business up, he would be content, even with his other problems hovering over him.

He hurriedly washed the kitchen floor and made sure everything was as neat as he could make it. Then he lit the fire in the main bar. Thank goodness the cleaner had come that morning to polish the brass and copper. The warming pans that adorned the chimney breast gleamed. The glasses and the windows sparkled. Roma mustn't be put off by any hint of laxness now she was thinking about it.

When everything was ready, he changed into a fresh shirt and trousers and stood at the door waiting for her.

Like Mal, Micky Richards had a gap in his life that needed filling. His loneliness was worsened by the fact that he had a son whom he rarely saw. His wife was dead and his feelings of guilt over her early death had prevented him from finding someone else.

What he wanted most was to have his son Leon back home, but that seemed a hopeless dream. His second wish was to see more of Roma, whom he had known since she was a baby. Her aunt had made sure he kept away from her until now, but perhaps his luck would change and she would come here and share the running of the pub that had been in his family for several generations. Then, if Leon made one of his rare visits she might persuade him to stay.

He shrugged the fanciful imaginings away from him. He was daydreaming like a child. But the dream didn't quite fade.

It was with some trepidation that Roma stepped off the bus from town and headed towards the Magpie. Auntie Tilly had strongly disapproved of Micky Richards, although she hadn't explained why. Roma had seen him only rarely, knowing her aunt didn't approve of him, and the last occasion had been at Auntie Tilly's funeral when everything was so confused she barely remembered him being there. Her aunt's attitude had encouraged her to imagine him resembling her father in age. So she unconsciously expected a sour-faced man whom she would dislike on sight.

When she saw a balding, slightly overweight man dressed in good quality casual clothes she felt relief. When he greeted her, his voice was soft and his eyes smiled in a way that made her warm to him immediately.

She was surprised to learn that he was expecting her, after a call from Mal.

'I hadn't even decided to come,' she told him as they shook hands.

'I wouldn't have wanted you to find me sleeping amid a pile of dirty glasses snoring like a pig in muck.' Micky grinned. 'I was glad of the warning, so I could tidy up.'

'Don't tease me.' Roma said. 'I bet it's always perfect.'

The pub had once been two cottages and the two main bars were at the front with a snug at the back alongside the kitchen. There was another room built on that Micky had intended to use as a preparation room for food, but when his wife died he had never bothered to develop the food side further than pies, sandwiches and crisps. So the trade had never grown sufficiently to justify completing it.

The cellars, which were whitewashed and spotlessly clean were reached from the kitchen. Upstairs were five bedrooms and two bathrooms.

'There's a bedroom and bathroom for you if you take the job,' Micky coaxed. 'You can take your pick of the three at the back along the passage. Mine's in the front above the door and the one next to it is for when Leon comes to visit.'

'Leon?' she queried.

'My son. He's what would have been called a hippy in the sixties, wandering about, working when he needs to and coming to see his old dad when he thinks of him. Which,' he added ruefully, 'isn't too often! He's just eight years younger than you,' he added.

To her surprise, she knew where the door in the back bedroom led to.

'That must be a staircase leading to the loft,' she said and Micky grinned.

'You remember? You came here often when you were a small child.'

She frowned and said, 'I don't think I remember it, I just presumed that was where it must lead.'

'Maybe. But memory is a strange thing. Your father and mother used to bring you here when you were very small.'

'You remember my mother?' At once it seemed right that she had come. She might learn something about the mother she only vaguely remembered.

'Oh yes,' he said with a smile. 'I remember your mother.'

'Most of my childhood was spent with Auntie Tilly,' she told him. 'My parents never seemed to have much time for me. I've often wondered why. Was my mother as clever and beautiful as my father always told me?'

'Yes, she was lovely,' he said.

'And I don't look anything like her, do I?'

'You're lovely too,' he said at once. 'You don't have to resemble your mother to be beautiful if that's what you're thinking. You're a person in your own right, not a shadow of someone else. Besides, no one could compare you to her unfavourably. No one.'

The compliment didn't register. He was so adamant, that she wondered if he had known her father well enough to understand the disapproval he had shown towards her. A bubble of excitement rose at the possibility of at last getting to know her parents through this man who had once been their friend.

'Look,' Micky said, rousing her from her thoughts. 'I might have a few photographs in the cupboard, I'll see if I can find some of your mother.'

'Thank you, Uncle – er – Mr Richards.'

'If you're going to work here, you'll call me Micky,' he said.

She took the job, partly because she liked Micky Richards and knew she could work with him, and partly in the hope that by working at the Magpie she would learn something about her parents. Small pieces of information to add to the fragile and probably false memories she had clung to, and perhaps help her understand her lonely childhood and the parents who had never cared for her.

She wondered too, at the eccentricities of fate that had led her into the licensed trade. Idle musing led to fears about her abilities and she lay awake all night wondering whether she could do it.

Micky Richards lay in his bed and hoped fervently that Roma would like working at the pub and stay with him. Guilt flooded over him as he thought of his wife Barbara and her suicide. He knew the fault was somehow his and he didn't deserve even the happiness of having Roma near. His wife had thought he'd been having an affair, and fear that he was going to leave her had turned her mind and caused her to take her own life. At least, that was what he had always believed, although Barbara hadn't left a suicide note.

That had been more than fifteen years ago, when Leon had been a baby, and since then he had concentrated on running the pub and building up a bank balance for the time when his son would settle down and come home. Leon, his only child, rarely visited and when he did never stayed more than a few hours. But Micky never gave up hope that one day he would walk through the door and announce he was home to stay.

Leon had run away from home once at eight and twice when he was nine. He had left again at twelve and again at thirteen. Since then he had defied the efforts of the police and social workers to make him return. An occasional postcard, untidily written and often without a stamp, was all Micky had to reassure him that his son, now sixteen, was alive. The last time Micky had heard, Leon was in Scotland working in a milk depot and staying with an unnamed friend.

After Roma had left, Micky went to a drawer and from behind the cutlery tray took out a shabby, well-thumbed collection of picture postcards. Seventeen in all. Not much to show the passing of the years but better than some fathers had. At least he did hear from Leon, he hadn't simply disappeared. If only there had once been an address so he could write back. He poured himself a beer and began reading them once again.

For the first few days Roma stayed in the kitchen as much as possible. She asked to buy fresh produce for the lunchtime trade, so instead of packets of pre-cooked meats, she added freshly cooked ham and pork to the choices. She made pasties and Scotch eggs instead of buying them in and added garnishes of salad to the filled bread rolls. The result was an increase in trade.

Being unfamiliar with the wide array of drinks offered she was slow to serve at the bar, afraid of looking foolish, especially as the locals had their own names for drinks. A 'mother-in-law' she learned to her amusement, was stout and bitter and there were several more like that.

Slowly she began to serve after endless lessons from a patient Micky. The first time she pulled a pint in full view, even though she had practised repeatedly, resulted in a glass of foam with very little liquid in it. The second one was better although accompanied by a slow hand-clapping from the regulars. Surprisingly, she quickly learned to cope with the teasing and instead of curling inward and pretending it wasn't happening, she began to enjoy it.

As Mal had been, Micky was remarkably patient, never

tiring of answering her questions. He desperately wanted her to stay. Cleaning up after the last customer had reluctantly left, they would chat about the session, laughing at some of the remarks made by the regulars and complaining mildly about Richie Talbot who was always the first to enter, having knocked on the door for at least five minutes before opening time.

Inevitably the conversations always turned to the subject of her parents as Roma tried to get every last fact and opinion about them from Micky.

When Mal came in she served him with growing confidence, discussing the beers and wines they had to offer. His dark eyes twinkled as he remarked to Micky, 'Roma is a natural.'

The uneasiness between them had faded away, a gossamer-thin memory that might never have been real. She looked forward to his visits and once accepted an invitation to see the house he was converting into flats.

'One could be for you if you want it,' he offered a few days later, as they walked into the neglected building with its peeling wallpaper and crumbling plaster. 'But please don't decide on the face of its present condition. When I've finished, it will be modern and elegant, especially if you'll help with the design.'

'Thanks, I'd love to be involved in the transformation if you really think I can help. Although I don't think I want to move out of the Magpie. It's handy living on the job and Micky has promised to teach me to drive so I can use the car to get into town.'

'I'm glad you're comfortable. I hated seeing you in that bedsit.'

'You didn't hate it more than I did.' She laughed.

'And you're happy now?'

'I love what I'm doing. It was a most unlikely choice though. My parents didn't drink, from what I've gathered.

I have the impression that my father strongly disapproved of public houses. I seem to remember being soundly lectured on the subject when I was too small to understand what he was telling me. And Auntie Tilly certainly didn't have more than a port and lemon at Christmas. She clearly disliked Micky too, for whatever reason. So it's odd that I've ended up behind a bar, isn't it?'

'Maybe,' he said mysteriously.

The house that Mal was converting into three flats had once been an impressive family home. The design was traditional with two large bay windows top and bottom at the front and a large porch over a wide front entrance. There were three living rooms and above, four bedrooms. The top floor, with dormer windows, had three rooms, one of which was a bathroom and one a kitchen. The whole building had been sadly neglected and it was Mal's intention to have the walls knocked back to the stone and replastered.

'But before that,' he told Roma, 'I want to decide on the staircase.'

'Two,' she said at once.

'Why?'

'The top flat would be less of a fire hazard with its own, and as a penthouse flat, it would fetch a higher rent.'

At once Mal took out the architect's plan and considered this. 'Damn it all, Roma, you're right!'

Smiling at his approval, she followed him through the house carefully, discussing the best places for storage and often disagreeing with the suggestions on the plan and revising the uses for odd corners and window seats.

The Magpie offered live entertainment every Saturday night. It was a world completely new to Roma and she found it exciting to see young hopefuls and sometimes not-so-young hopefuls, going on to the small stage, grabbing a microphone and singing their hearts out. Many were content to entertain the locals and become for a moment or two, someone of importance, someone with a talent that allowed them to rise a little above the rest.

There were others who saw the experience as a stepping stone to great things. As time passed, some faced the fact that this was it; they were living their dream and wouldn't get any further up the elusive ladder of success. But some would never give up.

One young man who came regularly and was given the slot just before the break at ten o'clock, was Frank Morgan. He called himself Fletch and, at twenty-eight, was a serious 'wannabe'. He did a patter act bringing members of the audience into his jokes and stories and he always ended with a sentimental song. After the first couple of weeks, Roma thought he was singing it especially for her. He would look at her, his head tilted on one side, the microphone leaning away from him, giving her an occasional wink and making sure the audience knew what he was doing. Aware of the looks she was receiving, as his performance became more obvious, she would disappear into the kitchen.

Another popular act was the Finks. May and Finks Johnson were in their fifties and Finks (Francis) played the guitar while they sang Country and Western songs. They also played a banjo and a fiddle, May played a mandolin and Fink played the ukulele and sang some of George Formby's songs. The instruments filled the small stage.

Fletch would sometimes stand at the bar after his act and, when Roma wasn't serving, he would talk to her about his dreams, ambitions, his successes and the times when he'd almost made the breakthrough. She listened and encouraged and felt a part of his excitement. Flattered and strongly attracted to him, she was soon counting the hours between Saturdays when he would make his entrance.

Most of the performers simply walked in, but some acts had their own kind of entrance. The Finks staggered in with their assorted instruments and a display board, banging against the door, struggling to get through until someone, usually

Micky, ran to hold the door open for them. Every week he demanded to know why they didn't bring the stuff in piece by piece instead of scratching his paintwork and every time, May would explain that it was too risky to leave valuable instruments outside in the van. Everyone laughed at the banter which seemed as much a part of Saturday nights as the singing.

Fletch didn't just walk in, but would throw open the door and, with arms wide, would shout, 'Roma, Micky, frrrriends, your favourite singer is here!' Everyone would laugh, drinks would be offered and then he would make his way to the bar and say a personal hello to Roma.

She would listen to his report on the past week's bookings and wonder if he would ever invite her out.

The cooking took a lot of Roma's time and she saw less than usual of Sylvia who was also busy, having opened her second shop.

After a few weeks at the Magpie Roma went to see it and was surprised at its smallness.

'Little more than a broom cupboard really.' Sylvia laughed as she invited her into the show area which measured less than twelve feet by eight. 'But the position is perfect; near the bus stop, with a car park only yards away. And besides, the customer feels it's exclusive; I only have one of each garment so she won't bump into someone wearing the same thing. I make sure they go out of here feeling very very special.'

One day Sylvia came to the the pub to tell Roma she was getting engaged to Daniel, a man whom she had known for several years. Their weekly meetings, which had fallen victim to Sylvia's new business and Roma's new job, now seemed likely to disappear altogether in the excitement of the engagement. Roma missed the confidential chats during which, over the years, they had shared so much. It was with Sylvia she had discussed her problems and moments of happiness. Sylvia to whom she had confided girlish secrets and first forays into the purchase and application of make-up. They had smoked a first – and last – cigarette together and had coughed and sputtered in the protection of Sylvia's father's garden shed, before deciding that money was best saved to buy records and lipstick.

The change in their relationship was disappointing but was only to be expected. Roma wondered whether they would lose touch altogether once Sylvia and Daniel were married.

So it was with delight that one evening, when the bar was rather quiet, she saw Sylvia enter with Daniel.

It was a hot evening in late September and there was that stillness in the air that hinted at the possibility of a storm. Roma served them drinks. Then, as there were no customers waiting to be served, she sat at the table with them to exchange news.

'We want to hold an engagement party here,' Daniel said at once and the rest of the conversation was about numbers, menus, costs and seating. When they left, still discussing their party, Roma felt deflated. So much had happened since Auntie Tilly had passed away, and she had learned such a lot since coming to work at the Magpie that she needed to talk to someone.

The next morning she rose early, completed the routine jobs in preparation for the lunchtime session and decided to go and see Mal.

Popping her head around Mick's living room to tell him she was leaving, she was startled to see him doubled over, coughing and obviously unwell.

'Micky?'

'Damned cigarettes,' he gasped.

'Micky,' she teased, 'you haven't smoked for years, or so you told me.'

'Don't worry. I'll be all right, it's just a bit of food that went down the wrong way. Go on, off you go.'

Doubtfully she took him at his word.

She couldn't find Mal at the wine bar and wandered off to where the work on the newly acquired house was in progress. Workmen were pulling out the staircase and knocking the plaster off the walls. It was a mess and out of the dusty doorway, a man emerged she did not at first recognise. His face was partly covered with a mask and his hair was white. When the figure raised a hand she hesitated. She approached quite close before she recognised Mal.

'Come and see the revised plans,' he said.

'What? I'm not walking down the road with you looking like the abominable snowman!' she joked.

'Come to the flat and I'll do a quick transformation.'

She waited in the empty wine bar while he went up to his flat to change. When he came down, he was carrying a sheaf of papers which he began to unfold. Before she began to look at them he tilted his head towards the coffee, a question in the quirked eyebrow, and she nodded. With cups of coffee beside them they studied the plans.

Having made a thorough study, Mal was able to explain the sketches to her and she quickly absorbed the ideas.

'It will be marvellous, Mal. I can imagine it all so clearly.' Then pointing to the artist's sketch of the grounds she went into one of their short sharp conversations.

'Get rid of the boundary wall.'

'Needed.'

'Take it down.'

'Why?'

'To see the sea!'

'Less secure.'

'A sea view.'

'Worth money?'

'A few pounds on the rent.'

'You're right.'

Like the friends they were, they burst out laughing.

As he drove her back to the Magpie she began telling him

about the people who came to the pub, some of whom he knew.

'I love the Finks,' he said. 'I've known them for years. They've struggled to survive on low-paid bookings at working men's clubs and dreamed of the London Palladium. I wonder how they can go on year after year, wandering round the country, performing miles from home, waking up in strange rooms and filling the time until their next train or the next performance.'

'It's an obsession,' Roma said. 'Disappointments are forgotten because the life gives them enough little bursts of hope and happiness to encourage them to go on.'

'So few make it, but I can understand them believing that the next discovery will be them.'

'Yes. Take Fletch,' she said, trying to sound casual as she spoke his name. 'He's so determined. He'll never give up.'

'At least he isn't married. I think it must be hell for the wives and the children with low wages and an absent father.'

'You don't have to tell me about absent fathers.'

'Sorry, Roma, I wasn't thinking.'

'Don't be sorry. It doesn't really hurt any more. Did you know that Micky used to know my parents really well? He and his wife used to be Mum and Dad's closest friends. A foursome.'

'Once,' he replied vaguely.

'Micky found me a few photographs and they all look so happy. Even my father was smiling, and in one he was holding a pint. He always warned me that drinking was evil. I wonder what happened to make him change from that relaxed, smiling man?'

'The death of your mother I suppose.'

'Maybe. But I don't think so. He never looked at me with love or affection. I squeeze my eyes tight and try to picture him looking kindly at me and I can never visualise him smiling, or talking to me without criticising me or giving me a lecture. He never held me, even when I fell over and needed comforting. It was Auntie Tilly, or you, who bathed my cut knees, mended my toys.'

'Forget him. Nothing can change the past. You've got a job you enjoy, you've got Micky and me as friends. Build on that.'

'Something happened to make him dislike me. Long before the death of my mother.' She frowned. 'Perhaps one day I'll find out what it was.'

The engagement party for Sylvia and Daniel took place on the last Saturday in September and when they were starting to decorate the bar with banners and balloons, Micky mentioned the need for the long stepladder. Without a thought, Roma went to the cupboard under the cellar steps. The door was hidden by boxes and she pushed them aside and reached in to drag the stepladder out. Then something stopped her and she stepped back as if frightened. Micky had followed her down and was looking at her strangely.

'How did you know the ladder was kept in there?' Micky asked.

'You must have shown me,' she said frowning deeply.

'I haven't used it since last Christmas. You've never had cause to go to that cupboard. So how did you know?'

'Micky, I don't know how I knew. But something about that cupboard frightens me.'

Micky took her arm and guided her back up the stairs. 'Then don't go there again. If you want anything from the cellar, I'll get it for you.'

She helped put up the banner and painted one with the names of her friends, but her heart was heavy and she didn't know why.

Three

One week after the engagement party, Sylvia called and asked Roma, 'When is your evening off? Still Thursday?'

'Yes, but why? Surely all your Thursdays are booked with Daniel now?'

'He had the damned cheek to suggest that I won't want to bother with any of my girlfriends now I've got him. If he thinks that being married to him means I forget everybody else, he's got a surprise coming. I fancy a good night out. So, are you on?'

'For me a good night out has usually meant a few hours off from looking after Aunt Tilly and then we usually ended up at the cinema. Forgive me if I don't sound excited!'

'Oh, I think we can do better than that. Daniel has introduced me to a few clubs that might be worth a visit.'

'A nightclub?'

'Hardly. Just a local where there's some entertainment a bit saucier than what you get at the Magpie.'

'I'm on!'

They went to a place overlooking the sea, where the clientele were unimpressed with the first act, a singer who had no volume and a poor sense of rhythm. The Finks came on next, singing Western songs, dressed in stagy cowboy clothes, and the reception was so rude that Roma wanted to drag them off the stage and hide them.

'The Finks deserve better treatment that that,' she said hotly.

'They chose the wrong songs for the audience,' Sylvia said. 'They should have known better after all their experience. You'll see what I mean when we see the other acts.'

'As for the rest, we get better than this at the Magpie,' Roma grumbled.

'Just wait. The saucier acts come later on.'

Sylvia was right; the acts grew more daring as the evening progressed and to Roma's surprise, the last but one was introduced as 'Fletch'.

'Is it the same Fletch that comes on Saturday nights?' she whispered. 'I think he's great.'

The act was slicker, the content more crude and the songs more sexually performed. Some of the girls screamed as he gyrated his way through the final number.

A couple of very gauche young men came across and invited Roma and Sylvia to join them at the bar for a drink. Fletch looked across and called to them jokingly, 'Leave my women alone, little boys!'

At once the two men began to heckle, but Fletch was too experienced to give them time to make themselves heard.

'Aw! Is mummy coming to pick you up, little lads?' Fletch jeered and the audience was with him. The girls screamed with laughter as he went on referring to the boys' youthfulness and Fletch accepted the screaming as a demand for an encore. He walked over with the mike and sang the song to Roma. He chose the Dr Hook song, 'When you're in love with a beautiful woman'.

She felt embarrassed, Sylvia laughed at her discomfort, but the audience loved it.

'Fletch usually sings sentimental songs,' Roma whispered as the audience applauded, 'and he always seems to find one about mothers.'

'That's what I meant about the Finks. Fletch has selected suitable material for his audience. They didn't.'

Sylvia considered the acts were moderately good but

disagreed with her friend when Roma said she thought Fletch was a star on his way to the top.

'Short climb and then a belly flop,' she predicted. 'But he's the type to keep on trying year after year, unable to believe he's not good enough. There are hundreds just like him. So if you fancy him, don't expect swish restaurants and diamonds. You'd have to settle for fish and chip suppers while you sit alone in a cheap bedsit waiting for him to come home.'

'A bedsit! Heaven forbid! I had enough of those after Auntie Tilly died.'

'Died and left you without a thank you for the years you'd given her. Catch me doing anything like that!' Sylvia said firmly. 'Stay away from people like Fletch or you'll spend the rest of your life looking after another emotional cripple!'

'Auntie Tilly wasn't intentionally unkind,' Roma protested. 'She made that will years ago and had intended to change it. She was on and on about going into town. I didn't know why, but perhaps she intended to change her will and maybe leave the house to me.'

'"Perhaps" and "maybe" don't get you far. Put yourself first, Roma, because if you don't, no one else will either! Stay away from losers like Frank Morgan or you'll find yourself in another Tilly situation and he isn't eighty! You'd be giving up on your whole life.'

It was after eleven and with the disagreement souring the evening, they were just beginning to think about leaving when Mal walked in with Susie, his assistant. Roma and he stared at each other in disbelief.

'Roma? I didn't imagine you visiting a place like this,' he said as he greeted her.

'I didn't expect you to be here either,' she replied. 'Shouldn't you be at Parry's Place?'

'We're spying out the opposition,' he whispered as he pulled up chairs to join them.

Roma and Sylvia didn't stay much longer and, although they talked and laughed easily among themselves, for Roma, the evening was spoilt. The warning from Sylvia about Fletch, then seeing Mal with Susie on his arm had destroyed the happy atmosphere.

She was surprised at the sensation of jealousy which had been aroused on seeing Mal walk in with the attractive Susie. How could that be? Although she tried to deny it, the edginess and the disapppointment wouldn't go away. What was the matter with her? She had no feelings for Mal other than affection for a big brother, so why did it bother her seeing him so attentive to Susie?

It was after her visit to the nightclub that Frank invited Roma out. She had brushed aside Sylvia's warning and was ecstatic at the thought of a date with him.

Taking her small savings, she went to Dorcas, Sylvia's fashion shop, and bought herself a cheerful blue, purple and jade dress. She didn't even want to try it on when Sylvia held it up but once on, she saw how it improved her looks; her hair seemed less mousey and her eyes appeared larger and more intensely blue. Even with a discount it was frighteningly expensive but she bought it, plus a blue and jade jacket and went home happy, excited and broke.

She had one full day off each week and, as Sylvia had remembered, usually chose Thursday. It was October and the air was crisp and clean. The trees had given their last colourful display and leaves were falling to carpet the ground in the last extravaganza of the year. There was the occasional smell of a bonfire as gardeners tidied everything up for winter, but this too was a clean scent, very much a part of the glorious season.

Roma went by bus into town to where she and Fletch had planned to meet at the entrance to the Hotel Unicorn where they were to have dinner. Fletch wasn't there and after a while Roma went inside and sat in the foyer and pretended to look at a magazine she had bought.

After an hour had passed and she had drunk a cup of coffee

and read the magazine from cover to cover, Roma was about to leave when Fletch burst in, his face glowing, his coat flying about his slim figure, and she gasped at the sight of him, he looked so man of the world and so handsome.

There was no apology. Instead he led her out of the hotel and into the street telling her about the audition he'd been promised. He went through every detail of his act, even humming a few bars of the songs he planned to sing. There was no mention of the dinner she had been promised. He seemed to have forgotten they had arranged to meet and was acting as though they had met by chance and he was glad to have someone to talk to.

'Should I break with tradition and start with a song?' he asked. When she said that a slick gag might grab their attention better, he shook his head as though talking to a very stupid child.

'You don't understand, I want to be different. I want to make them laugh but I want them to warm to me and there's nothing like a good, sentimental song for that. Well sung it can make everyone there believe I'm singing for them.'

Her heart raced as she remembered him singing to her. She offered a few suggestions but soon realised that although he asked questions, he didn't really expect or want any answers. She was there to be a listener, someone with whom he could talk out his ideas. She felt immensely flattered at first, but when he kept saying the same things, prodding for approval, agreement and admiration, she began to tire.

After more than an hour of his excited chatter, she began to find it difficult to keep her mind on what he was saying. Her high-heeled shoes – borrowed from Sylvia – were hurting, and she was hungry. When she could stop him talking without offending him by her interruption, she asked if he fancied some fish and chips. They had just passed a chip shop and the smell was tormentingly good.

He agreed and leaned against the wall outside, jotting down ideas in a notebook, while she bought them. Then, as they ate, still going over his plans for the audition, they continued to wander.

Once her hunger was satisfied, Roma felt slightly better but her feet felt as though they were tied up in wooden boxes. She wondered where he had left the car. They had been walking around the streets for more than two hours when she said, 'Fletch, I have to get home.'

'Okay,' he said. 'If we can just go through the routine once more so I have it clear in my mind. Then I can hone it during the night. I won't sleep much.'

'Neither will I if I don't get home soon,' she said pointedly. 'I have to be up at six.'

They walked past two car parks and headed for the bus station. He must have parked in the multi-storey behind the department store. But no. To her surprise he led her to the bay from where her buses left.

She was hurt, confused and not a little angry. What was he thinking of? This wasn't the evening out she had been promised.

'You needn't wait,' she said hiding her humiliation under an attempt to appear indifferent. Surely he wouldn't agree to that? He couldn't be that unkind. But he did.

'Thanks for being so understanding. Not many girls would realise how important this is for me. I'll see you at the Magpie, eh? And we can go out and really celebrate.'

'Lovely.' Her voice sounded lifeless even to her, but he was oblivious to her disenchantment.

He turned her to face him, his arms slid round her and after staring deeply into her eyes for a moment, he kissed her.

Foolishly, trying – and failing – to remember the disasters of the evening, she glowed with happiness all the way home.

The next day, at lunchtime when she was serving customers and the queue of people who came regularly to buy takeaway lunches for their colleagues in the offices and shops near the pub, Fletch walked in.

This time there was no jokey entrance. He came and sat on a bar stool and dropped his chin into his cupped hands, looking a picture of despair.

'Fletch?' she asked.

'A double poison please.'

'Has the audition been cancelled?' she asked diplomatically.

'No such luck. I was awful. But it was a set-up. The pianist they gave me was rubbish, I went on as the third of the four comedian/singers and they talked all the way through my act. It was decided before I went on. No consideration for an artiste's time.'

'Perhaps there are just too many doing an act similar to yours,' she suggested, handing him a double whisky.

'What d'you mean?'

'I mean you might try something a bit different.'

'What d'you know about it?'

'I've been here long enough to have an idea when someone is . . .' she hesitated. She knew how touchy he was and how easily he could misunderstand and take offence. 'I know when someone highly talented isn't using that talent in the best way.'

'Are you trying to teach me my profession?'

'Can't you play guitar? If you have to depend on pianists you're bound to get an unsympathetic one now and again. A guitar would avoid that problem.'

'You don't understand. You wouldn't like me to copy the pathetic Finks would you and sing out-of-date songs, wearing ridiculous fancy dress?'

'May and Finks Johnson are good at what they do,' she said defending them.

'And I'm not?'

She thought it best not to reply and was thankful when someone wanted serving.

Afterwards, Micky told her to be careful.

'Most entertainers are fantastic people, kind, generous, and the sort who make good friends, but you get some who are so egocentric they live in a bubble of selfishness. They can't help it, but you can help yourself – by staying clear.'

'It's all right, Micky. I'm not so smitten that I'll give up on my life to support his talent. Sylvia has warned me that I could lose the best years of my life on him, like when I was looking after Auntie Tilly. I didn't agree with her, but talking to Fletch for hours on end, I can understand what she meant.'

'Just be careful.'

'I will,' she promised, but when she was alone in her room, her imagination soared with thoughts of her supporting Fletch in his rise to the very top. She understood his need to fight for what he wanted: after all that was surely how Sylvia had found success. But Roma felt she had to be certain that her own feet were firmly enough fastened to the ground to be able to cope, without giving up everything to help Fletch achieve his dream. Dreams aren't for one. The best dreams include two, she reminded herself confidently.

Sylvia Davel was so different from her friend Roma it was difficult for outsiders to see what they had in common. But their differences were what kept them together. Each admired a part of the other's personality: Roma longed for a bit of the confidence Sylvia showed; Sylvia frequently wished for Roma's calmness and patient understanding.

Roma accepted that certain things would never be hers and she lived vicariously through Sylvia's exploits. Telling Roma about her adventures and victories was important to Sylvia, and when they met there was never a lull in the conversation. In all the years they had known each other they rarely ran out of things to say.

For Sylvia, life was a fight for survival, and survival for her meant an easy life with sufficient money and all the comforts she could dream up. She set her sights high and never accepted second best. Whoever had to pay for it, doting parents or doting Daniel, she always managed to get whatever it was she desired.

She had borrowed money from her parents, which they got by raising a mortgage on their house, to start a small fashion business. Selling good-quality separates for women, first on a market stall then in a small shop, she had recently expanded the business to include exotic underwear, nightwear and impractical slippers. The second shop was small and carried only a few expensive lines, but looked to be a real winner. She was negotiating with a manufacturer to start a range of clothing under the name of her shop, Dorcas.

Sylvia was attractive with small, perfectly proportioned features, pale skin, dark-blue eyes set in thick lashes. Her shiny black hair was cut fashionably short like a pixy cap on her small round head. Always dressed to impress, she looked stunning. Her customers came because they hoped to look as devastating as she.

Roma, who hadn't changed her hair style since school, and wore mostly black and navy, admired her and never tried to compete; she knew she never could.

'I've always aimed higher than I can afford. It's the only way to get on. Take these flats Daniel insisted on considering,' Sylvia said as the two friends sat in the bar during a lull. 'I told him we should buy a house. A flat, I said, would have to have a decent hall, a proper dining room and at least two bedrooms. But would he listen? You should have seen the one he dragged me to see this morning!'

'It was too small?' Roma coaxed.

'Two bedrooms? Cupboards more like! I told him he could forget poky places like that or forget marrying me.'

'What did he say?' Roma couldn't imagine talking to anyone she loved in that way.

'He said, we'll look at houses!' Sylvia screamed. 'Isn't it fab?'

After describing the fitted carpets and the made-to-measure curtains she wanted and the king-sized bed and the new kitchen, Sylvia suddenly remembered about the date Roma had had with Fletch, and demanded to hear every detail.

'Oh, it didn't go very well,' Roma told her. 'In fact it all went wrong.' With the time that had passed, the humiliation had faded and she was ruefully able to make a joke of it all. Sylvia and she laughed as she described the awfulness of Fletch's behaviour.

'That's it then. He won't be seeing you again, will he? You're worth a dozen of him, Roma. Don't forget it.'

'Well,' Roma said hesitantly, 'I'm seeing him tomorrow.'

'You're a martyr! First that aunt, then, as soon as you're free of her you find yourself another blood-sucking monster.'

Laughing away the outburst from Sylvia, Roma insisted that this time it would be different.

'Oh yeah? How? This time you take yourself to the bus stop?'

Even Roma had promised herself that this would be the last chance she gave Frank – or Fletch, as he insisted on calling himself. She knew she was being foolish agreeing to meet him again after the treatment she had received last time, but there was so little in her personal life to enjoy and he was excitingly different, and her body did funny things when she remembered that kiss.

She had refused to wait at the Hotel Unicorn again. And he had agreed to pick her up from the Magpie at eight. He came in carrying a huge bouquet of flowers which he handed to her in front of the regulars with a deep bow. She walked out blushing with embarrassment. In the car, he gave her a small box which contained a pair of earrings. Each a small daffodil because, he said, he knew how much she liked the pendant she so often wore.

'I hope it wasn't bought for you by another admirer,' he teased.

She didn't explain that it had been from Mal. Fletch knew very little about Mal, only that he was an older man, a friend of her father's. She hadn't told Mal about her date with Fletch either.

Dinner at the Hotel Unicorn was superb. She wasn't allowed to order for herself, Fletch had been in earlier and had selected from the menu. 'So we don't have to concentrate on anything else but each other,' he explained, reaching for her hand.

He took her home but stopped the car some distance from the pub and wrapped his arms round her. She sank willingly into his kisses but tensed when his hands began to search in her clothing, intent on more intense love-making.

He was quite good natured about it. 'I know, you have to get up at six,' he whispered against her ear. 'But one day, my lovely Roma, one day . . .'

When she walked through the now empty bar into the kitchen to make a cup of tea she was floating. What had she done to deserve someone like Fletch?

Fletch returned his father's car and let himself into his parents' house. Such a tiny, mean little house in a mean little street. He couldn't wait to be free from it. Living with his parents at his age was crazy. Just as soon as he'd saved a thousand pounds he'd be off and they wouldn't see him again.

Helping himself to a slice of cake and a pint of milk, he wondered vaguely and without much concern, how he was going to return the latest fifty pounds he had borrowed from his mother. Soon he'd be a real success, then he wouldn't have to bother his parents for anything. He went up to bed, remembering that it was Thursday. Good. Mam always changed his bed on Thursday. Crisp clean bedlinen always made him feel good.

Mal called in to the Magpie most weeks to see how Roma

was getting on. She was always glad to see him and happily talked about her work and the characters in the pub who now accepted her as part of the fixtures.

'It's as though I've been here for years,' she told him. 'In fact, I sometimes get flashes of memory about the place and Micky says it's because I was often here as a child.'

'That's right, but you were very young, it's surprising that you remember.'

'I don't really, but occasionally something's on the very edge of memory. Sometimes these impressions are happy, sometimes hauntingly sad.' There were others that frightened her but she said nothing of these.

'You get on well with the customers?' Mal asked.

'Oh, yes. They were marvellous when I first started. They teased of course, and kept threatening me with having to sing a song on Saturday night, but they're a great bunch and I'm happier than I thought I'd be. Although I still find it strange to be working in a pub, especially when I remember how my father disapproved of drink – and everything else,' she added wryly.

'I'll have to come one Saturday to hear the entertainment, although it's difficult, that's one of the busiest nights at the wine bar. Are any of them any good?'

'Well, I like the Finks. May and Finks have been entertainers since they were children and although they only have small parts in panto and a small circuit of regular spots, I don't think they will ever retire. Then there's Frank Morgan. Fletch, he calls himself.'

'God 'elp! *He* isn't still trying to convince someone he's got talent, is he?' Mal groaned.

'He's good enough to do better than he's doing at present,' Roma said. 'You have to be determined. The ones who persevere are the ones who make it to the top, the ones who believe in themselves.'

'Don't confuse talent and a belief in yourself with pure vanity. In Frank's case his parents have supported him in this impossible dream for too long. Time he stopped wasting his time and their money and started paying them back.'

She didn't reply. How could she tell him that she was half in love with Fletch and desperately wanted him to succeed?

'Did I tell you I'm applying for a full licence so I can develop the wine bar into a restaurant?' Mal said then, and for the rest of his stay they discussed the possibilities of the project.

'Talking about Frank, were you?' Micky asked when Mal had gone. 'I don't think he'd be pleased to know you're going out with that loser, Roma.'

'He isn't a loser, he just needs a bit of luck, that's all.'

'Did you know he borrowed fifty pounds from his parents to take you out the other week? Owes them hundreds he does, living there without paying a penny for all this time. He should be ashamed.'

'Sylvia's parents helped financially when she got started, why don't you criticise her?'

'Because she knew what she was doing and she repaid the loan as soon as she was able. Principles, that's the difference.'

'What's it to do with you, anyway?' she protested angrily.

Micky stared at her for a long moment then said quietly, 'Nothing, Roma. Nothing at all.'

Fletch guessed she was upset when he called to take her out later that day. She had a few hours off and was going into town. Fletch had offered her a lift.

'Something wrong, love?'

'Oh, it's just Micky, interfering as if he were my father or something. What with him and Mal watching my every move, I feel like a child. I think I'll put my hair into pigtails!'

'And wear a gymslip?' he whispered with a wink.

She blushed and turned away from the suggestive remark.

'Sorry, love. I forgot who I was talking to. Forgive me?'

'No need,' she replied, wishing her face would cool down.

'I'm not such a sheltered violet that you have to watch every word.'

'What have they been saying?' Then he guessed from her silence that he had been the subject of the disagreement. 'Me, is it? They don't approve of me. Surprise. No one approves of someone trying to achieve success in the world of entertainment, then when you do make it big they're all over you, boasting about knowing you and full of anecdotes about the chumminess they shared as children. I've seen it so often. Half the people in the Rhondda swear they were a friend of Tom Jones!' He kissed her and asked, 'What did they say?'

'That you should give up, get a proper job and look after your parents, you know the sort of thing. People don't understand.'

'My parents don't support me like people think. They do nothing but criticise me even when I hand over the contents of my wallet after a successful few weeks. They grab anything I offer and at the same time tell me how useless I am. Believe me, they have never helped except by the occasional loan but that's all counted up and repaid. I cover up for them of course. I never tell people what they're really like. I'm too proud to admit it. I sing sweet songs and dedicate them to Mam and Dad, and tell everyone what wonderful parents they are.'

'That's so kind, Fletch.'

'Anyway,' he went on, 'Micky isn't in a position to criticise me. He drove his wife to suicide. I've never done anything that terrible.'

'Suicide?'

'Hardly in a position to tell me how to live, is he? Or you for that matter. A man who made his wife so unhappy that she killed herself rather than live with him. There isn't a worse rejection that that, is there? Forget him, Roma, love, he's only your employer.'

By Christmas, even Frank's optimism was showing signs

of exhaustion. He needed money and with nothing booked before the New Year he was desperate. He had failed to get a pantomime booking and even the few spots at small clubs and parties he'd been given had been cancelled. He realised that he had to get work, any kind of work, to earn some money to see him through until after the pantomime season, when theatres returned to weekly shows and plays. But what could he do without losing face? He didn't want to go away, not with Roma promising better things to come.

On several occasions he had worked in a bar, when he had been away from home and without any bookings. He had never told his parents or any of his friends about this. Any money acquired, he insisted had been earned on stage. Now, he thought he had to try for something locally and bar work was the only qualification he had.

Smiling optimistically he headed for the Magpie.

Micky wasn't keen. He didn't like the man and only tolerated him because of the Saturday-night entertainment when, for some reason, he was popular. Roma overheard Frank asking for work as he had intended she should, and she later pleaded his case with Micky.

'We'll need extra help over the Christmas and New Year. We've got several parties remember. Better to start him now so he can get used to our way of doing things.'

'There's Matthew Rolands, he's always looking for extra work. We'll manage.'

'Fletch will be more popular,' she argued.

Micky couldn't disagree. Matthew Rolands was a forty-year-old part-time barman, not very popular with the customers but very efficient. Besides dealing with customers he would do whatever job was necessary, replenishing stock without waiting to be asked, making sure the glasses were always collected and washed. Micky used him from time to time when they were extra busy. A widower, Matthew was often to be seen frequenting the betting shops and this,

Micky guessed, was the reason he was always looking for extra hours.

Giving in to Roma's pleading, albeit with reluctance, Micky took Fletch on part time and for the holiday period only. 'After that, we'll have to see,' he said.

'Thanks, Micky,' Fletch said when he was told, 'but I don't think I'll be available after the holiday anyway. I've sacked my agent, see, and the new one will take a little while to get things started. 1981 should be a good year though. Fresh start, eh?'

'I don't believe a word of it,' Micky grumbled to Roma.

Roma was delighted that Fletch was coming to work alongside her. Now Mal would get to know him and surely to like him. There would no longer be any need to hide from Mal the growing affection and love between her and Fletch.

On her next day off, Roma didn't arrange anything with Fletch. There was something she wanted to do. She went into town and spent several hours at the library looking through old newspapers.

She found it in January 1965. She would have been just nine years old.

The report was not very long, just telling of the discovery of a body left in a car with the engine running. Then, on the next day was a follow-up giving the woman's name as Barbara Helen Richards, aged twenty-eight. She hadn't left a note, but friends told the police she had described her life as pointless, as her husband no longer loved her and was going to leave her for another woman.

Roma sat and thought about it for a long time. How could someone become so desperate that they couldn't face another day? Her anger against Micky was short lived. Even if he had had an affair, it was a terrible punishment to have to live with the death of his wife on his conscience.

For no particular reason, she continued looking through the papers. Each binder contained six months of copies and she relaxed and was amused at some of the court cases that, after so long seemed rather tame. The advertisements too were funny and the prices were surprising. She wondered idly whether Fletch could use them in a comedy sketch.

A picture caught her eye. It looked a bit like one given to her by Micky, showing her parents. It was in the last newspaper for June 1965. She was nine and Leon would have been about two years old. As she looked vaguely at it thinking of the resemblance to her parents, a name leapt out of the page at her. A small piece in an inside page reported the death by drowning, of Mary Anne Powell. Her mother's name.

She looked away from the paper, unable to read on, wanting to run away from it. It couldn't be her mother. There must be plenty with the name Powell. Her mother had died in a road accident. Her father and Mal had been over and over it when she was younger and needed repetition to convince her that her mother would never come back.

It was several minutes before her heart slowed from the reaction to finding the reference to her mother. Then she slowly scanned the page and looked at the item. She turned her head and looked at the page with a slanting view, as if sneaking up to reassure herself it wasn't true. She tried to read the item but the connection between her eye and brain couldn't be persuaded to concentrate. She wanted to know with half of her mind but the other half refused to co-operate.

A body had been taken from the river Tawe the previous night and had been identified as that of Mrs Mary Anne Powell, she eventually understood. She read and re-read the report, still disbelieving it. Yet the address was the same and it even mentioned herself, the nine-year-old Roma, who was being cared for by an aunt.

How could it be true when her father and Mal had always said her mother had died in a road accident? Her first impulse was to run to a phone and talk to Mal, but she didn't. Instead she collected the next set of newspapers and looked for a follow-up to the story.

The next item was much longer and described the investigation into the cause of death. The body had been half submerged, held down by weighted sacks, but death was not due to drowning. She felt the shock creating shivers of horror as she read on. Her father had obviously been a suspect. He was questioned but finally released. It was several weeks before they allowed her mother to be buried.

Apparently there had been a severe blow to the back of her head and although this hadn't killed her outright, death had occurred within hours and she had received no medical treatment.

Roma was shaking when she stood up to leave. Her muscles were so weak she couldn't carry the heavy binder back to the counter. She could hardly lift her handbag. In the last piece she had found, there was still no explanation for the head injury and no suspect for the murder, except her father.

Murder. The word went through and through her mind, a chant of mind-numbing fear. Her mother murdered? Why? And by whom?

She tried to imagine how her father must have felt, losing his wife then being accused of murdering her. Tears filled her eyes as she thought that even at such a dreadful time, her father didn't want her around for comfort. She had lived mostly with Auntie Tilly up until that point, and had then been sent to live with her permanently, and subsequently her father had abandoned her.

She went to the wine bar, but Parry's Place was closed and she changed her mind about calling at Mal's private door. Perhaps it would be better to wait and absorb this terrible story before asking him to explain. For the first time in many months she wondered where her father and his new wife and child were, and whether he still relived the nightmare of that terrible time.

She hardly remembered him, but she sent out a wave of sympathy and hoped he was happy.

Four

Roma didn't tell Mal or Micky what she had discovered. They had both lied to her and she needed time to think about why. It was understandable when she was a child of nine but why, in all the years since, hadn't she been told the truth? She went to the house where Sylvia lived with her parents and told her.

'I don't understand why you weren't told either,' Sylvia said when she had read the copy Roma had made of the newspaper items. 'I can understand them keeping it from you when you were a child, but you're twenty-four. Why haven't they said something before this?'

'My thoughts exactly. Perhaps they had intended to tell me but haven't found the right moment. Perhaps my father was ashamed in some way of the manner in which Mam died. He really is a very stiff and formal man and I think I can understand how the publicity might have upset him.'

'You think he suffered more from embarrassment than grief?'

'He's very conscious of the impression he gives to others and even sadness at her death wouldn't have completely prevented his embarrassment at so public a death as murder.'

'Too embarrassed to show grief?' Sylvia repeated.

'Yes, I could believe that of him.'

'Sorry, Roma, but I think it was a good thing you spent most of your life with Auntie Tilly. With your father's selfish attitude you could have turned out even less confident than you are. Although,' she said in an effort to take her friend's mind off her startling discovery, 'I must say that Fletch has brought you out more than a bit. Happy with him are you?'

'Very. I hope he and Mal will grow to like each other, then I'll be content.'

'Mal works hard to achieve what he wants, Fletch waits for some elusive bit of luck, so I can't imagine those two ever being friends!'

'Perhaps not, but they might learn to accept that I love them both.'

The next person Roma told about the manner of her mother's death, was Fletch. It was late November, the night was chill, but he drove her out to sit under the stars in a secluded part of the cliffs and, protected from the night air by his blankets from the car, his coat and the undulating dunes, he asked her what was wrong.

She thought she was calm and had accepted the fact of her mother's murder, but when she began to tell him about the shock of recognising the photograph and reading the news item, she broke down. It was as if the grief which she had been too young to feel when her mother died, and when her father abandoned her, had been pent up and waiting for release.

He held her and caressed her and soon her tears dried up and the magic of his hands and seduction of his lips began to make her forget her sadness and, with growing awareness, she began to respond to his love-making. Ignoring or even unaware of the coldness of the sea-touched air, they undressed and slowly explored each other's bodies. Then, as she fought to forget the sorrow of her discovery, Roma lay back and allowed passion to overwhelm her. An hour later, arms round each other, relishing the touch of their responsive bodies as they held each other close, they strolled back to the car, whispering of their love.

Because they worked together, it was impossible to hide the change in their relationship. Roma's appearance altered, her face took on a special glow as her love grew. Her eyes shone brightly with her wakened spirit. She had her hair styled and relaxed her choice of clothes, no longer feeling the need to hide her attractive figure under dull, ill-fitting dark dresses. She was easier with the customers. She bloomed, and everyone saw and smiled at their own memories. The teasing began, as customers noticed the happiness she and Fletch shared. Their faces showed unmistakable signs of their new-found joy, and only Micky showed no pleasure in it.

Fletch went home one night and found his father was waiting up for him. As usual, Fletch ignored him and went to find himself something to eat and drink in the kitchen. His father followed him.

'Frank, your mother and I have decided it's time for you to leave.'

'Pity, because I haven't.'

'You're almost twenty-nine and we've supported you most of your life. Well, now it has to stop.'

'You promised—'

'We promised to give you a year or two to try and get a break, but now we want you to get out. I'm retiring next week and your mother and I want to travel a bit, see something of the world and we can't afford it if you're still here.'

'How can you be so selfish!' Fletch gasped. 'I've got a few things lined up for January and it's only a matter of time before I'm spotted and pushed up the ladder.'

'Selfish is it?' His father shook his head sadly. 'Selfish I'd be if I allowed your mother to go on looking after you as if you were still at school. This is our time, Frank, and we want to enjoy it. You don't have to leave before Christmas, January will do, but that's it – no more excuses to delay. January and you're out. Right?'

'That's not a problem. There are plenty of places I can go.'

He watched his father walk up the stairs and guessed his

mother had been listening from the landing. 'Proud you'll be of me one day, mind. And guilty too for not helping your son when he needed it.'

There was no reply.

He sat in the quiet kitchen for a long time, wondering what was the best way to persuade Roma to move in to a flat with him and pay the rent and food. Surely he had sufficient charm to achieve that?

He went to the Magpie at lunchtime the following day and showed her a cutting from the local paper.

'How does this grab you, Roma, love?' he whispered. 'A flat for you and me to share.'

'What? You want me to leave the pub and move in with you? Fletch, I couldn't do that!'

'Not leave the job, just the room. I don't earn much at present but I'll chip in what I can and I'll soon be earning enough to keep us both. Until then we could live quite cheaply.'

Roma had always imagined living with someone only after a traditional wedding. 'No, Fletch. I don't want to do things that way. I'd rather wait.'

'Wait for what? Just think, we'd be together, partners, working towards a wonderful future. Oh, Roma, I can just imagine it, when I'm working I'll be dreaming of going home to you.'

'It isn't what I want, Fletch. I know this is the eighties and things are changing, but I want to be proud when we tell the world we're together, not avoid questions and face sly looks and unkind remarks.'

'Marriage you mean?' He touched her cheek with his lips, sliding down to kiss her neck. 'Don't you think I want that too? I love you Roma, you know that. You're the best thing that's happened to me, ever. I want to be a part of your life. I want that so badly. The marriage will come, but not until I can afford to give you the best. I want our wedding to be the biggest and most splendid the town's ever seen, but only when I can pay for it. I have my pride you know.'

'I don't know, Fletch. What would Mal say?'

'Don't tell him. Just come and have a look at this flat, it's reasonably priced and not far away.'

'I'm still not sure,' she said hesitantly.

'Come and look at it. If you'd share it with me I'd be so happy. I know I'd succeed if I had you to support me, I'd work harder than ever. You, my love, are my inspiration.'

Although common sense should have warned her, Roma had been thinking of a flat like the ones Mal owned, and when she saw the peeling paint on the front of the run-down property to which Fletch had taken her, she couldn't believe that it contained the flat he had in mind.

'Now,' he warned playfully, 'I know it needs decorating, but don't let that put you off. I've done a bit of painting in my time, actors and entertainers have usually done a variety of jobs while resting, and I'll have it looking good in a couple of weeks. Picture it in sunshine colours. Here we go.'

Inside it was even more run down than Roma had expected. Damp had loosened the wallpaper in the kitchen, the floors were covered with oddments of carpet and the windows were draped with torn nets. The toilet smelled worse than any she had encountered and the washbasin was coming away from the wall. Buckled and rusted, the cooker might have spent months out in the rain and looked ready to explode.

Looking at her face, Fletch said encouragingly, 'I'll get it cleaned up before you set foot in it, right? I'll get the walls freshened up and we can probably find carpets in the local ads. What d'you think?'

'I think you must take me for a fool!' She ran from the building and had reached the corner before Fletch caught her up and held her against him.

'It isn't what I want for you, my darling, but I can't start us off in debt. I want this to be my side of things, I want to pay for our first home, even though it isn't anything like you deserve.'

On the firm promise that the place would be cleaned and decorated by Christmas, she reluctantly agreed. Having a flat of her own for the first time in her life was so tempting that it distorted her thinking.

News got out among the regulars at the pub and their attitude was mixed. Most thought she was mad, a few who found Fletch attractive envied her and it was these to whom she listened.

When Mal called to see her she took him aside so he didn't become involved in the jokes and innuendoes. But before she told him about moving in with Fletch, she had to give him one more chance to talk about her mother's death.

'It was summertime when my mother died, wasn't it, Mal?'

'Yes. Fifteen years ago last June. Why?'

'Talk to me about her.'

'She was lively and had a wicked sense of fun. She used to torment your father, play tricks on him, then tell him he had no sense of humour. Laughing and full of life, that's how I remember your mother, although I was only nineteen when she died. Remember,' he added with a smile, 'I'm ten years older than you, that's all.'

'How did she die?'

'You know how. I've told you the story so often. She ran across the road without looking where she was going. I think she saw your father and ran to greet him and was killed by a lorry.' He turned her face to look at him and said softly, 'Don't you think you should forget how and when she died? It's about time you started thinking about your own life. Your future.' He spread his arms, encompassing the bar room. 'Are you going to settle for this for ever? Or are you going to make a start building something better for yourself?'

'I'm content here for a while, then, who knows?'

'As long as your future doesn't include Fletch.'

'He's not that dreadful, Mal. I like him a lot.'

'He's a scrounger and he'll let you down.'

She didn't argue. Her mind was on the way he had perpetuated the myth of her mother's death. It was clear he never intended her to know the truth. A momentary thought that her father might have been guilty was brushed quickly aside. Her father a murderer? Never. He was so afraid of doing anything improper, it was impossible that he could ever be violent. Correctness and honesty were his main characteristics; she remembered that much about him.

'Roma, it's only four weeks to Christmas and five to the end of the year. A time for new beginnings, a time to step out and, sometimes, to leave things behind.'

'You think I should shed things like trying to know my mother?'

'That and other things. Forget plans that aren't going to work, and relationships that aren't going anywhere.'

'Fletch and me you mean?' When he nodded she said, 'It's a bit late to tell me that. He and I will be moving into a flat together in the New Year.'

His reaction was startlingly fierce.

'Don't do this! The man will drain you of every spark of personality. He won't allow you to grow and develop. Everything will revolve round him! All you are, all you could achieve will be ground down and fed to his ambition, and it's an ambition propped up by ego, not talent, so you'd be giving up everything for no reward. He'll end up leaving you and blaming you for his failure. Please, Roma, reconsider. Don't do this I beg you.'

She was startled by the vehemence of his response and said nothing for several seconds. Then she murmured, 'Sorry Mal, but it's already done. We move into Crown Street in January.'

'January. That's when his parents have told him to be out of their house. Did he tell you that? And did he tell you why they don't want him there any more? That they are sick of him scrounging from them and borrowing money he never returns? Did he tell you that?'

'Of course he told me,' she lied. There was no point telling him Fletch's version. He wouldn't believe it.

'You're a fool,' was his parting shot.

She told Fletch what Mal had said and he admitted that his parents had told him to leave. 'They let me stay when I have money,' he said sadly, 'but when I hit a bad patch they won't help. I didn't tell you, because I'm ashamed. I need support but they don't give it. I pay them back every penny when I'm earning but when things get a bit rough they turn me away. And they tell people I'm still in their debt.'

She built up a picture of two hard, unkind people and knew that if she ever met them she would dislike them on sight.

At the approach to Christmas, the pub was extra busy. There were several office parties and two retirement do's in early December and Roma provided the food and Micky dealt with the drinks. They worked well together, although she occasionally had to battle to persuade him to change the fillings of the sandwiches and rolls they offered. He seemed to think that a choice of ham or cheese was sufficient.

Some of the girls who came to collect lunches each day began to place orders for different fillings the day before. This worked quite well, but occasionally someone asked for a sandwich prepared for someone else, or an order was changed and Roma was rushed trying to make extra in the small kitchen while the queue waited, with growing impatience, to be served. She began to wonder whether there was a better way to do things.

Fletch was still chasing round looking for bookings, hoping that a replacement was needed for someone taken ill or unable to perform for some other reason, but he had no luck. The imaginary agent was blamed for his inability to find a job.

The entertainment at the Magpie was still a regular feature of Saturday nights but Micky no longer added Fletch to the list of performers. He didn't want to help Fletch any further now he knew that Roma was planning to move in with him. He thought it was a serious mistake, and he wasn't going to help her make it. But one evening the compère failed to turn up. Pleading that he would do a good job, Fletch asked for a chance to show how capable he was of holding the evening's acts together.

When Roma added her plea to Fletch's, Micky knew he had to agree; if he drove Roma away from the Magpie he might never get her back.

Fletch secretly thought the job was beneath him and that he was doing them a favour offering his professional services to what was little more than an amateur night. A price was agreed and at nine o'clock he stood up on the small stage and addressed the crowded room with a confidence that surprised Roma and made Micky breathe a sigh of relief.

He played himself down, offering only a few gags to connect the acts and stood back from performing himself. Tonight he was a compère and that was what he would do. Although, he admitted silently, he was hoping someone would ask him to sing. After all, he had a finer voice than anyone there. As the evening wore on with the Finks the most popular act, he began to think no one would 'persuade' or even invite him to sing. He would close with a few words and a final joke, take his money and sod the lot of them.

Still with the intention of pleasing Roma, it was Micky who asked him to sing and hand claps from Fletch's friends encouraged him to accept. He did his best, imagining he was at an audition, and he came off the stage to considerable applause.

Roma was thrilled at his reception, forgetting that he had been a regular there for many months and that loyalty was strong among the regulars. To her it was a great success and she promised herself that she would concentrate on giving him the support he needed. Mal was wrong: Fletch did have talent and she would be happy to remain in his shadow, cushioning his disappointments and lifting him up by her belief in him.

On the following Monday, Fletch bought brushes and paint and prepared to make a start cleaning up the flat in Crown Street. When he got home there was a letter waiting for him and, to his delight, it offered him three evenings at the nightclub, Top Hat, in a town about eight miles away. The money was the same as Micky had paid him, hardly worth the travel, but he wrote straight away and accepted.

For the rest of the day he worked on honing his script and learning it. He practised in front of a mirror, and his parents heard him and sighed. They had hoped that by withdrawing their support he would have given up and looked for a more stable job. Having heard of his friendship with Roma Powell, they had both hoped he would stop dreaming and settle down.

He only remembered to tell Roma about the booking the evening before the first performance.

'Pity you can't come, love. I'd work better if I could see you there. I'd perform just for you and forget the other people.'

A young girl, who looked about seventeen, watched him all through his act and he found himself working to her and during the final song, he moved among the audience and stopped in front of her and sang in a sexy way, just for her. Walking her home wasn't a big deal, he had to be available to his fans. Roma would understand that he belonged to the people and could never be tied to one particular person, that wouldn't be fair. Thus convinced, he stayed with the girl, whose name he discovered the next morning was Dawn, until lunchtime the next day.

'That bloody car,' he complained, when he saw Roma, 'only broke down again, didn't it! I'll have to get something better as soon as we're on our feet.' That the car was his father's, and, as usual, he had taken it without asking, he didn't bother to explain.

'I think I'll stay overnight as I'm on so late,' he said as he set off a few hours later for his second performance. To his delight the girl turned up at the next two gigs and he stayed an extra night having phoned Roma to tell her he had been offered an extra spot.

On New Year's Eve when the Magpie provided an 'Anyone Welcome' party in the bar, Dawn arrived and went straight to Fletch and kissed him.

Roma's heart sank. Was this what she could expect as he climbed higher and higher? Forcing a smile, she went to be introduced.

'Who's the flighty tart with Fletch?' Sylvia asked as she and Daniel came to the bar later.

'Some smitten admirer,' Roma said. 'There are always plenty of those around when Fletch performs, but he can manage them. Flatters them a bit then gradually eases away.'

'Plenty of flattery going on, but no sign of him easing her away,' Sylvia said sharply. 'She's practically eating him! I'd go over there if I were you, or, better idea, tell the pair of them to get lost!'

At closing time, as midnight struck and the new year of 1981 began, Fletch sang 'Auld Lang Syne' with the rest, then told Roma he was giving the girl a lift as her friend hadn't turned up to take her home. 'We can't allow a young kid like her to find her own way at this time of night, can we?'

She had to agree. 'I'll be here for at least a couple of hours,' she told him. 'We can't leave all this mess for tomorrow, so come back and we'll have a new year drink together.'

As Fletch left, ushering the girl in front of him, she saw his hand go around her shoulders. She remembered Mal's furious voice, and his words echoed in her head, 'You are a fool!'

*   *   *

Fletch didn't come back that night and Roma didn't see him the following day. As Saturday, the third day of the year, passed with the usual crowd and rather more subdued entertainment, she wondered whether the move to the flat was still a reality.

On Sunday morning as she was sorting out her belongings she realised with a sudden lowering of her spirits that she had hardly anything of her own. Her worldly possessions fitted into four cardboard boxes. What a waste of twenty-four years: working for a low wage for a firm who had treated her with such indifference and she had been grateful to them for the few moments they had allowed her to go home and check on an elderly aunt; an aunt who had provided a home and a way of life suitable for herself and not allowed a moment's frivolity for her young companion. Her spirits plummeted further as she faced the fact that it was her own fault it had been like that. No point blaming anyone else, she was the one who had allowed it to happen.

Looking at the clothes and one or two ornaments, the record player and a small stack of records Micky had given her, she thought of how barren her life had been so far, and wondered whether her next move would bring more of the same. Could she face a life of propping up a wannabe?

Leaving the packing she went to find Micky, who was in the cellar polishing the pipes and checking that everything was in order.

She was hesitant about going down there, something in a clouded memory holding her back. Then, calling herself a cowardly idiot, she went down the steps, superstitiously crossing her fingers hoping that the lights wouldn't fail and not looking at the cupboard that gave her such a frightening feeling. She heard Micky coughing and found him bent over, holding his chest and looking exhausted.

'Micky? What is it? Are you ill? Shall I get the doctor?' she asked in concern. She drew a glass of water, handed it to him and waited while he caught his breath, his eyes streaming with the effort of controlling the spasm.

'I'm all right,' he assured her. 'I was chewing some nuts and one went the wrong way.'

She watched him doubtfully for a moment or two, but he seemed recovered.

'Micky, how did my mother really die?'

He guessed she had found out the truth and said, 'We think she was killed by someone in a panic after seeing something she shouldn't have seen. She was just in the wrong place at the wrong time. There isn't any other explanation.'

'She didn't do anything to make someone hate her?'

'She wasn't killed by someone who knew her. It was coldly done, after that first violence. No one who knew her could have done that.'

'Not my father then.'

'No. He was never violent. He loved your mother. Not in the right way perhaps. He wanted to hide her away, not let her have any friends, not let her smile at anyone but him. But, oh yes, he loved her.'

'Violence is in most of us though and a moment's anger . . .' she persisted.

'No,' he replied firmly.

'Thanks for being honest with me – at last.'

'At first, Mal and I intended to tell you – we knew your father wouldn't – but as the years passed it seemed unnecessarily cruel. So we allowed the lie to remain, hoping you'd never find out.'

'I think I can understand that.'

'How did you find out?'

She didn't want to tell him she had been looking for details of his wife's suicide so she just said, 'Oh, something someone said added to one or two other details, you know how it is.'

A few moments passed then Micky asked, 'Roma, you are sure about what you're doing, are you? Moving in with Frank?'

'It's Fletch, and yes, I'm sure.'

He turned away and went on with his work. 'When is Frank – er – Fletch, coming to pick you up?' he asked, polishing the last pipe.

'I don't know. I think I'll get a taxi and go now, then I can spend an hour or two unpacking and getting straight.'

'I'll give you a lift,' he offered. He didn't want her to go, but was afraid that if he protested too much she would leave the job as well. He didn't want that.

'Thanks, Micky, but I think I'd rather go in a taxi, it's something about making a fresh start and—'

'Leaving something behind?'

'I'm not leaving the Magpie, just living out instead of in.' She smiled and he hugged her then, awkwardly and embarrassed.

'As you wish. But if you want to come back. If . . .' He didn't say 'If it doesn't work out' but the words hung in the air between them. 'Well, you know there's always a place here. I'd be glad to have you back, just remember that.'

The taxi driver helped lug the boxes as far as the front door and when she found the key she began to carry them up the fifteen stairs to flat three. On her fourth journey, Fletch arrived.

'Roma, love, you shouldn't be doing this. Here, let me.' Taking the last of the boxes he went up the stairs, stopping at the top and dropping his burden. He held out his arms for her, insisting he carried her over the threshold. Kissing her, he took her to the bedroom and put her down on the pillows. She was aware of the scent of perfume and wondered, with a stab of dismay, whether it belonged to Dawn. Then she forced herself to brighten up. Of course it wasn't Dawn's perfume lingering here. How could it be? It was she, Roma Powell, who was here, in his arms, she was the one he came home to, not some silly little stage-struck child.

As he released her and she looked around she saw with dismay that the room hadn't been touched. The bed on which they both lay wasn't even made up with the bedding she had provided.

'Fletch! You promised!' she wailed. 'We can't live in this mess and I've got to get back to the Magpie! How could you leave it in this state?'

'I've been busy, you know that. I love you and I wanted to get it perfect but I can't be in two places at once. Come on, let's go out and eat, then we'll come back and tackle it together.'

'I'm working in less than an hour. You'll have to do it.'

'All right, I'll give you a lift back to the pub and then it's straight back here to get it comfortable.'

'I'll get a taxi,' she said, guessing that he would stay at the Magpie or go somewhere else to spend the hours she was behind the bar.

When she returned at three o'clock, the bedroom floor had been partly covered with a fresh piece of carpet, scrounged from his parents, and the bed was made up with crisp new sheets. They made love and she lay on the bed looking up at the stained ceiling and wondered why she was continuing to accept second best. Later as she sat on the couch, which had been spread with the blanket from the car, she was again aware of perfume. Grabbing the blanket, she pushed it into the bath and washed it vigorously.

It took a week of her spare time to get the place moderately comfortable and as a result, all the money she had managed to save was gone. She had painted the walls a cheerful primrose and the windows were hung with pale-green curtains and frilly nets. Superficially it looked fine. She would have to train herself not to notice the flaking of the new paint where damp was insidiously doing its best to destroy her efforts.

Fletch was out when, on her day off, there was a knock at the door. She was painting the kitchen walls, and wore a pair of jogging pants and a too-large sweater. Who could it be? She didn't want Sylvia to see her in this state. Or that silly little Dawn. She brushed her hair back ineffectually and opened the door. To her dismay it was Mal.

'What the hell are you doing in a place like this?' he demanded. 'I have properties, why didn't you ask me?'

'Because I knew you wouldn't approve,' she said, putting her brush down and reaching for the white spirit to clean her hands.

'Let him go, Roma. You can't be so desperate for someone that you can accept this.'

'You don't understand. Fletch needs someone to support him. Everyone lets him down and I'm determined not to.'

'Everyone including his parents?'

'They won't help. He protects them by pretending they support him, but they don't. He's allowed to live there when he has money, but as soon as he hits a bit of a lull they throw him out.'

'Come with me,' he said firmly. She protested but he insisted, taking the paint tin, closing it, throwing the brush into the rubbish bin and handing her soap and towel.

'Where are you taking me? I don't want to look at one of your flats. Fletch can't afford it and he wants to pay the rent.'

'And has he?' He looked at her as she dried her hands. 'Has he paid the rent?'

'I paid the deposit and the first month – but—' Mal took her by the shoulders and shook her.

'For God's sake, Roma. Wake up!'

Hurting her with the strength of his anger, he pulled her roughly from the flat and down the stairs. She thought of her conversation with Micky about everyone being capable of violence, if only momentarily, given the right situation. She looked at Mal, tense and unmistakably angry, but there was nothing in his expression to make her think he would hurt her.

He drove to a small, neat terrace not far from the centre

of the town. Knocking on the door, he looked down at Roma as if wanting to shake her again. She looked away from him, seeing love and disappointment in his dark eyes.

The door was opened by a neatly dressed man of about sixty. Behind him was a woman of a similar age. They smiled when they saw their visitor and invited them both inside.

'This is Roma Powell,' Mal said, then, staring at her in a half-accusing way, he added, 'This is Mr and Mrs Morgan, Roma, Frank's parents.'

She said nothing but listened as Mal asked about the latest news of their son, and it was soon clear that Fletch's story about their indifference and lack of support was nonsense.

'We've tried,' Mrs Morgan told her tearfully. 'We've kept him all these years and we haven't seen a penny. When he's working he stays away and when there's no money left he comes home.'

'We aren't going to do it any longer,' Mr Morgan said gruffly. 'We haven't had a holiday, you know, not since Frank was fifteen. Now we want to spend the rest of our lives doing some of the things we've missed.'

Fletch's mother looked at Roma and said, 'We know we shouldn't talk bad about our son, but we don't want you making the same mistakes as we did. We hoped that for you he'd make an effort, but we were wrong. You're young and he could take everything you have and demand more. Frank's like that. It's the dream of big success that ruined him. A talent competition in Butlins, that's when it started. Can you believe that a holiday could have ruined his life?'

'My wife is right, young lady. Don't give him your life too.'

'Where shall I drop you?' Mal asked when they returned to the car.

'The Magpie,' she whispered.

Mal said nothing as he drove her back to the pub.

'I'll see that your things are brought back,' he said as he dropped her off. 'Leave everything to me.'

She went into her room, which was exactly as she had left it just a couple of weeks before, and Micky acted as though she had never left. She looked around at the comfortable furniture and the pleasant view across the gardens, listened to the subdued sounds as Micky got ready to open the bar and felt the warmth of a homecoming. The lack of a family wasn't a disease for which she had to grab someone, anyone, to fill the void.

She didn't have to paper over the stains and hide the sordid truth. She was twenty-four and free and she was going to start again without the need for a crutch. Fletch was worse than Auntie Tilly, greedy and selfish and incapable of real love. She had been too full of romantic nonsense to see it. Today she had at last grown up.

Five

Just after Christmas, Micky had given Roma driving lessons as a twenty-fifth birthday present and offered her the use of his van whenever she needed it. Taking advantage of every spare moment with either Micky or Mal beside her, she concentrated on developing her driving skills. To her delight she found it came naturally to her and she was soon anticipating the freedom that it promised. To give her more time, Matthew Rolands helped out in the pub occasionally.

She was surprised and touched when, on her actual birthday she received small gifts and cards from many of the regulars, including the usually complaining Richie Talbot. It was a day during which she thought long and hard about what she wanted to do with the rest of her life.

In February, after passing her driving test, she finally made up her mind. Saying nothing to either Micky or Mal she began to make enquiries and visited the bank to discuss a business loan.

Life continued as normal at the Magpie as winter gripped the country. The few hours of daylight were reduced by dark clouds, and icy winds and occasional snow flurries persuaded many of the regulars to stay at home. Roma added bowls of soup, chilli con carne and baked potatoes to the menu, and soon new faces were coming regularly for a warming lunch. The pub food grew into a successful sideline.

In March, when the worst of the winter was behind them

and the newly emerging leaves promised an early spring, Roma told Micky she was leaving.

'But I thought you were happy here,' he said, aghast. 'Please, Roma, think about it and if there's anything I can do to make you more comfortable just tell me. What if I cut your hours?' He looked very distressed and she felt unkind. 'I should have thought of it before,' he went on, 'I know you've worked very hard this winter, what with the extra food as well as the rest.'

'It isn't the work, Micky. I love it here, but I want to start a business of my own and what I have in mind would overlap yours.'

'Explain.'

'So many of the offices and shops send out for sandwiches and rolls at lunchtime that I thought I might start a delivery round.'

'Make them and go out with a selection you mean? I'll agree to that. You can use the kitchen and—'

'I want it to be my business, not the Magpie's and it wouldn't be fair to work from here, I'd be taking some of your customers. So I thought of finding a premises some distance away and building up from scratch.'

'Look, Roma, if you leave I wouldn't have time to deal with food anyway. Go ahead, use the kitchen and start up on your own. If you can still find some time to work in the bar I'd be pleased, but treat this place as your base, your home, whatever you decide.'

'You've done enough already. It's thanks to you I can drive and without that I wouldn't be able to think of doing this.'

'You've more than repaid me for the little I've done. Just having you here has made life better for me. I'd hate you to leave.'

'You're very generous, but I couldn't just take your customers. I have to start on my own then it would really be mine.'

As if changing the subject, Micky said, 'It was your

twenty-fifth birthday in January. Twenty-five, that's quite a milestone, we should have celebrated with a party. So, what if we give one now, both as a belated birthday bash and to wish you luck in your new venture?'

She wasn't keen, she was still not happy being the centre of attention, but the look on Micky's face made it impossible not to be pleased.

'Wonderful. Thank you,' she replied, giving him a gentle hug.

'And you'll stay?'

'I'll think about it,' she promised.

Using her spare time she looked round the estate agents for suitable premises to rent, where she could live and do the catering. She was flattered and touched by Micky's generosity but didn't feel she could accept. Starting her own business meant just that, not building on something she had stolen from Micky. Finding somewhere was not as easy as she had hoped, all the places she looked at were either too run down or too far from where she planned to operate.

She discussed it with Sylvia who had plenty of advice, having been in business on her own for several years.

'Take Micky's offer,' she urged. 'The first year is crucial and you need every bit of support you can get. Even after the first year a new business is still precarious, so thank him and take it.'

Roma also went to see Mal and told him what she had in mind.

'Want any help?' he asked.

'Some,' she replied.

'Premises?'

'Please.'

'Advice?'

'Definitely!'

They laughed at the brief conversation and Mal said, 'Advice first. Take Micky's offer and when you get too big, move on. Leave him with the business as before, but train someone up before you go, then you wouldn't be stealing, only borrowing.'

'You've been talking to Micky.'

'I have.'

'He wants me to stay.'

'He does.'

At the party which Micky had insisted on giving to mark the beginning of her enterprise there were three gifts to unwrap. One was from Sylvia and Daniel, a very expensive food mixer to prepare some of the sandwich fillings she planned to offer. From Mal there was a Gucci watch to make sure she was never late for an appointment and from Micky there was an envelope which she presumed contained only a card, as the party was her gift from him. Inside she found a hand-made but pseudo-legal document which officially handed his lunchtime customers into her tender care!

After she had read it and hugged him, he handed her another small envelope. 'And this is my real good-luck card, is it?' she asked as she slit the seal.

Inside the card was a cheque for five hundred pounds. 'And no, it isn't to persuade you to stay,' Micky said as her eyes widened in surprise. 'It's to give you a bit of help while you build up this business of yours and to say we all wish you luck.'

'We?' she queried.

'The regulars all contributed, and Mal and I, as your closest friends, topped it up.'

There were other cards, each filled with good wishes for her venture but nothing from Fletch. She still felt a twinge of disappointment even though she told herself she was over him.

At his own expense, Micky modernised the small back room to be used as a kitchen and had the health and safety people check it over and approve. On 20 April 1981, Roma began her delivery rounds.

Before the actual day, she spent every spare hour canvassing orders from firms nearby and already had thirty calls booked, so it wasn't with a feeling of complete newness that she set out that Monday morning. She knew many of her customers well, others she had only met once or twice when she had approached them and asked if they would like to be included.

As her scheme was obviously quicker than sending someone round the staff to take orders, waiting for a list to be prepared, money collected and a junior sent to the Magpie, many companies agreed to give the idea a try.

By the end of June, the customer list had grown to forty-eight calls and she had employed a girl to help for a few hours each morning.

It meant a very early start as she didn't want to risk delivering stale food. Before five thirty each morning she collected together the ingredients and started work. Sometimes, when Micky came down an hour later, he helped. He was very interested in her venture and anxious for it to succeed.

One morning the post arrived just as she was packing the food into the van and Micky handed her a postcard. His smile was wider than she had ever seen, and she guessed the name of the sender at once.

'From Leon?' she asked.

'Look at the postmark,' he said. It had been posted in town on the previous day and, as she read the few words, he added, 'Perhaps he's coming home.'

When she returned, as Micky was opening the bar for the lunchtime session, she asked whether there had been a visitor. Micky shook his head. She stared at him him closely, noticing with shock that he had lost weight. Afraid to ask, she wondered whether he was ill and felt guilty at her plans to leave, even though she would never lose touch. The thought of losing Micky frightened her. He had become very important to her in a way she didn't really understand. Perhaps it was because of his link with her mother, someone who had been there and who knew everything that had happened at the time of her mother's death. She knew she hadn't been told the full story.

Leon didn't appear that day or in the days that followed.

'As he's so near, why don't we go out and look for him?' Roma suggested one afternoon. 'We don't reopen until six, we have a few hours. Come on, we'll go and visit some of his friends to see if he's been in touch.'

Without much hope they set off, each armed with a list of possible addresses.

On Micky's list, after the few of Leon's friends he still remembered, were three semi-derelict places where homeless people sometimes gathered. One was the old Saunders' farm outside the town. He shuddered at the thought of his son frequenting such places.

Roma went first to the house of Dai Jackson, but there was nothing known of his one-time friend. Neither Tony Lewis nor Harry Price had heard from Leon Richards for years. Tommy Thomas suggested Leon might be at the Saunders' old place as he had stayed there in the past. Unaware that Micky was also heading there, she went to find it.

As she was sitting in the car outside Tommy Thomas's home studying her map, someone knocked on the window and she looked up into the smiling face of Fletch.

'Roma? What are you doing here?'

'I'm helping Micky visit some of his son's friends. He thinks he might be in the area and he wants to see him so badly.'

'I've been to see a bedsit,' he said with a reproachful look. 'I couldn't afford to keep the flat on my own.'

'Are you working?' she asked, ignoring the jibe.

'I've got a few bookings. I had an interview for a play last week, thought I'd spread myself a bit. I haven't heard officially, but I think I've got it. Things are looking good.'

Although she didn't believe him, she wanted to. 'I'm glad,' she said.

'Mind you, if there's ever a job going at the Magpie I wouldn't say no. I could work round my bookings, couldn't I?' He fumbled in his pocket and handed her a piece of paper. 'That's my address if you hear of anything.' He blew her a kiss and sauntered off, an insouciance in his walk, an optimism in his voice that was fading from his eyes.

Leaving the town behind, she drove along roads with fewer and fewer houses on them, then went up a lonely lane to where a stone-built house stood amid the debris of demolished or collapsed outhouses and barns.

There were still smells reminiscent of farm animals lingering on the air, but from the look of the place, many years had passed since it had been inhabited. The windows were mostly intact but there was a hole in the roof, and the chimney stack had fallen down in one of the winter gales and taken the guttering with it. Broken fences, rusted wire, rotting wood and patches of stinging nettles filled the yard. Barns, their doors long gone, were caves that threatened with unseen eyes.

What looked like the remains of a bonfire were visible near the entrance. A pile of sawn logs, many covered with a carpet of moss, had been disturbed by whoever had taken pleasure in the comfort of a warm fire. It wasn't the kind of place she'd have chosen for a picnic, she thought with a shudder.

She was plucking up courage to get out of her car, wondering whether it was wise to investigate alone, when Micky drew up. Seeing her car he hurried across.

'Roma, leave this to me. If there's someone there they might think we're from the police and get nasty.' Making sure she was locked in her van, he went inside.

Roma waited five minutes then, arming herself with a heavy torch, she followed.

The walls were wet with condensation and various moulds had created strange patterns in the old plaster. The smell of decay and death filled her nostrils. Surely no one could live in such a place? Even in winter the fresh icy night air would be preferable. Now, with the warmth of summer making frost unlikely, nothing would have persuaded her to stay inside.

'Micky?' she whispered, as if afraid to disturb sleeping ghosts.

There was a crunching sound as Micky walked on fallen masonry and when she looked up he emerged from an upstairs room and looked over the banister.

'It's empty,' he reported, 'but someone is using the place. There are cans of food and a small stove. It's filthy and sordid and – hell, how could anyone be reduced to living like this?'

'Keep back from the banisters, they don't look safe,' she warned.

He grasped the once lovingly polished handrail and shook it experimentally, then leaned over and grinned at her. 'The walls might be crumbling but I bet the wood in this house will last for ever.'

She waited while he went into the remaining rooms, some of which were down a long passageway, in what had obviously been an extension at one time. She heard him walking back, his feet loud in the hollowness of the building. Then he stood at the top of the stairs and leaned over.

'I think I'll just look up in the loft. They might have heard me coming and hidden up there, there's a ladder leading up to the roof.'

'Use your son's name. Call to let them know who you are, they might be dangerous,' she whispered.

The house felt eerie and she glanced round her at the rubble-strewn floor imagining some irate landlord creeping up, about to spring. Half-empty tins of food lay abandoned, rotting fruit, several chunks of bread discoloured by mould. A door had been removed and part of it had been used as firewood in a grate spilling out ashes and scorched metal. There was the unmistakable sight of rat droppings. The silence was oppresive. She moved to the staircase; she wanted to get out of there.

'Come on, Micky, he isn't here. Your son wouldn't live like this with a home only a mile or two away.'

Footsteps sounded above her and she heard Micky retreat back down the ladder. It was a relief to see him lean over the banister and say, 'You're right, Leon wouldn't accept this.'

He was starting down the stairs and Roma had turned away towards the door when a voice called, 'Dad?'

A dishevelled figure came out of a back room where he had been hiding behind the door. Micky stared for a moment, then with a groan he ran back up the stairs to greet his son.

'Leon, what the hell are you doing here? Why didn't you come home, son?'

Roma moved up a few stairs as father and son embraced, unwittingly wanting to share the moment. They were on the landing and in his distraction and joy, Micky leaned back against the banister, hugging his son to him. There was a loud cracking sound as masonry began to shower down on her and Micky's shouts mingled with the groaning of torn wood and the crashing of plaster and stones.

The two figures appeared to be leaning on nothing but air as they struggled to find a hand hold on something solid. The place was filled with pattering and thumps and then they were falling, twisting, arms flaying in an effort to grab something and slow their fall. A terrifying ballet with only one outcome. The crunch and the expending of breath when they landed awkwardly on the stairs was a sound she would never forget. For a long moment they remained as though frozen as plaster continued to drift down on them. She reached out to them to tell them they would be all right, and was relieved to see that their eyes were open and they were grimacing in pain.

'I'm all right, love,' Micky gasped, 'but you'd better fetch an ambulance for Leon.'

'Try not to move, Micky. Either of you,' she instructed. 'I'll fetch help straight away.'

Micky ignored her and got up and, with his arms round the filthy figure of his son, prepared to wait.

With an outward calmness she did not feel, she made sure Leon was breathing properly and that neither of them would slip any further down the stairs if they lost consciousness and cause more injuries to themselves. Covering Leon with her coat, with the squeamish resolution that she would afterwards throw it away, she ran to the van and drove to the first house she could find where she dialled 999 and reported the accident.

Within two hours Leon was assessed as having a broken arm, broken collar bone and severe bruising and put to recover in a hospital bed, with Micky, Mal and Roma in anxious attendance.

Accepting the lecture given to him by Mal for going into such a place and for putting Roma at risk, Micky wondered how the Magpie would cope without him for the few days. This was an opportunity for him to spend time with Leon, an opportunity he might never get again.

'I'm staying with Leon,' he told Roma, 'can you manage for a while?'

Understanding clearly the need for Micky to be with his son, she nodded enthusiastically, grateful for the chance to help him.

'Of course you must stay. I'll get some help. You don't have to worry about a thing.'

'The order comes tomorrow and you'll need to get the empties ready,' he said. Other problems occurred to him as he realised what it would mean to be away from the Magpie for several days and he began to list them.

'I'll see to it,' Roma promised each time he voiced another of his fears, 'you know I'll manage.' She appeared cheerfully confident but inside she wondered how on earth she could run the pub and continue with her sandwich round. Both were important, and if it meant an eighteen or twenty-hour day she would do it.

Then she remembered Fletch and decided that as she needed help, she would be foolish to ignore his offer. She said nothing to Mal or Micky – best they didn't know beforehand or they'd object. She smiled to herself. Dishonest or diplomatic, she was learning fast!

There was no phone number with the address Fletch had given her so she drove to the house and knocked on the door. A young woman opened the door and from upstairs she heard the sound of singing. A Carpenter's number, 'Solitaire' – one of Fletch's favourites. Smiling, she gestured up the stairs behind the woman and said, 'I was going to ask if Fletch is in, but I can hear that he is, could I have a word, please?'

'Fletch? You're wanted,' the woman shouted without moving from the door. The singing stopped and Fletch appeared at the top of the stairs before running down to greet her.

'Roma! What a wonderful surprise! Come in, meet Valerie, I'll get us a coffee . . .'

'There's a job at the pub if you want it,' she said crisply, trying not to notice the exciting and needful ache his nearness gave her. 'It's only temporary, mind. Micky's son is in hospital for a few days, he had a fall.'

'Start tonight, shall I?'

It was a shock to realise that 'tonight' was only fifteen minutes away and she had done nothing towards preparing for opening. Telling him to come as soon as he could, she hurried back to the pub, her mind racing with what she had to do.

The food in the evening was easy. Sandwiches left from her rounds, pies, pasties and crisps. Thank goodness there was nothing more needed there. But what about all the things Micky dealt with? How could she find time to attend to those?

As she reached the door she realised that the lights were on and then Mal's reassuring presence filled the doorway and she sighed with relief. It would be all right.

Everything was prepared for opening. The tables and chairs in place, the floor washed, the tables and counters wiped and ashtrays set out. Cloths had been removed from the pumps and in his hand Mal held a beer which he had drawn to test that everything was in order. He had even found time to replace a light bulb that had failed.

'Mal. Thank you. I've been arranging temporary help in the bar for a few days. D'you think Leon will be kept in for very long? Micky did look shaken, didn't he? I hope he's all right.' She was talking fast, hoping to avoid Mal enquiring about who she had employed.

'I can stay for this evening,' he said, to her relief. 'Susie Quinn will manage the wine bar. Then tomorrow there are one or two ex-employees who might be glad of temporary work.'

'There's no need, but I might have known you wouldn't let me down,' she said, taking up a duster and unnecessarily polishing the bar counter.

'You haven't asked Fletch, I hope!'

'Well, yes. He's coming as soon as he can. I didn't have time to look for anyone else and I happened to see him when I was on the way to Saunders' farm.'

'Micky won't like it.'

'It's the best I could do. Now, any chance of a quick cuppa before we get crowded?'

She unlocked the doors in answer to some irate banging which she knew before she opened would be Richie Talbot, and the evening began.

Fletch came within the hour and settled into the job with ease. The customers knew him and were soon chatting to him like old friends. He put on his entertainer act, relating stories about the famous and giving the impression he was one of them, or at least knew them personally.

'Laughter follows him like a breath of summer.' Roma smiled.

'Cloying and choking,' Mal retorted.

At closing time Mal told Fletch he could leave and stayed to help Roma clear up.

'Your assistant must be very capable if you can leave her in charge,' Roma said as they put the last of the glasses in their place.

'Susie's experienced and, yes, very capable. I've seen the wine bar through its first years and now I'm leaving her to manage it while I go on to other things.'

'I must meet her again,' Roma said. 'Perhaps I can learn a thing or two.'

Although she had no feelings for Mal beyond friendship, some perverse side of her was resentful of someone else being his close associate. She couldn't ask outright whether Susie was married, but she hoped she was. And happily so!

Micky had no serious bruising. Somehow he had managed to fall less awkwardly than his son and he refused to be given more than a very cursory check-up. One of the doctors tried to persuade him to at least have an X-ray of his wrist, which was rather painful.

'It's my son you want to take care of,' Micky said.

'You could ask for something for your cough,' Roma whispered when she was visiting and overheard one of these exchanges. Micky shook his head.

'I'll see to that later. Now, I want to spend every moment with Leon. There's no telling how long he'll be persuaded to stay. I've got to make the most of it.'

Leon was in hospital for three days, after which time the sister told him he was free to go home on the following day after a final visit from the doctor.

'But you'll have to come back for check-ups, young man,' Leon was told firmly. 'There'll be further treatment on that arm, and you'll need some physiotherapy no doubt.'

Roma knew Micky would be delighted that the boy would have to stay for a while longer. She had managed to go in to the hospital each day and report on the previous day's business. On the day Leon was told he could go home, she said, 'I expect Mal has told you that I've employed Fletch temporarily. I know you don't like him but I had to make a decision quickly.'

'I left the decisions to you, love, I can't do that then tell you what not to do, can I?'

'It's only until you're out of here.'

'I'm coming out today,' Leon said, 'and if they refuse, I'll sign myself off, wrap these blankets round me and walk home!'

'You'll do as you're told and wait till tomorrow,' Roma said sharply and to her and Micky's surprise, he agreed.

On the day Leon returned from hospital, Micky's first action was to pay Fletch and tell him he was no longer needed. Now he no longer spent the days at the hospital, he was determined to do without him. He'd rather delay his own recovery by weeks if the alternative was watching that creep working his way into Roma's life again.

He helped in the bar when necessary but spent most of the opening hours in the back room with Leon. Roma was extremely weary, but forced herself not to mind. This was the best chance Micky would have to talk to Leon and perhaps to reach an understanding.

Mal turned up every evening in time to help clear the bar and at half past eleven she fell into bed after setting the alarm for five a.m. She wondered how long she could cope with an eighteen-hour day, aware that her hours would be even longer if Mal didn't come to help.

Micky had not completely avoided injury when he fell down the stairs. He was pale and weaker than he admitted, and the muscles damaged in the fall were very tender. He didn't get up as early as usual and sat dosing in an armchair for a couple of hours while Roma finished her sandwich round. Then he would brighten up and try to hide his tiredness and discomfort.

The first person to walk in each day was still Richie Talbot, a childless widower whose only social life was what the Magpie had to offer. If the Magpie didn't open precisely on time, he would bang monotonously on the door until it did.

But tonight, on Leon's first day home, he was beaten by a young man who looked as though he'd been living rough for a long time.

Roma looked with distaste as the boy came to the counter. His skin was scaly with the dirt of months, his hair was matted and smelled strongly and he was in dire need of a wash. His clothes looked so much a part of him, he must have been wearing them for as long as he had needed a bath – months in her estimation.

'Can we get you anything?' she asked, and nudged Micky, expecting him to tell the boy to leave. But by the expression on Micky's face when he looked up, she guessed that he felt sympathy for a young man living as miserable a life as his son.

'Came to ask about Leo the lion,' the boy said and Micky smiled and called his son.

The two young men greeted each other, called each other 'man' a lot and began discussing their most recent adventures. After a moment or two Micky and Roma were introduced to Joe, and Micky asked if he could offer him some food.

'What do you want first, a bath or food?' Leon asked, while Roma shuddered at the thought of this apparition using a bathroom and towels. Thank goodness she had her own. Micky was so obviously pleased at being able to help one of his son's friends that she said, 'I'll run a bath, shall I? And while you're washing I'll get some hot food.' Stopping only to draw Richie's first pint, she went to do as she promised.

Sitting down to pie and chips, his face cleaned of the worst of the neglect, wearing clothes borrowed from those Micky kept for Leon, the boy looked very different from the scarecrow who had walked in. Younger more vulnerable – Roma felt a sympathy almost as strong as Micky's.

While Joe and Leon talked, Micky listened, asking questions and gradually drawing out of them a picture of their strange life. They moved around sleeping in squats or, when they had money, in bedsits. They existed on the edge of society, shunned and ignored or showered with abuse, drifting in a casual life that was dictated by weather and the amount of money they owned.

Joe told them his father had left and then, after struggling for a while, his mother had left too. He and his younger sister had been taken into care.

'I ran away though. Hated it. Then I bumped into Leon and we've been together ever since.'

'Haven't you tried to find your father or mother?' Roma asked.

'What's the point? Strangers they'd be. Last thing they'd want would be me turning up and expecting a kiss, eh?'

Roma dealt with a bar that was thankfully quiet. At nine o'clock she found a moment to phone Mal. A female voice answered on his private line and when she asked to speak to Mal, she was told that he was not available and would she call in the morning.

'Will you tell him Roma phoned,' Roma said politely, but the response was the same.

'Please call in the morning.' There was a breathlessness in the woman's voice that barely registered.

Customers demanded her attention and as the place filled up she had to put aside her irritation with the over-efficient Miss Susie Quinn, for she guessed who it was, and deal with them.

An hour later, Mal arrived, looking as though he had hurriedly thrown on his coat. She felt a jarring pain in her chest as she realised that he and Susie Quinn had probably been disturbed from an intimate moment. She continued to serve without looking at him, for surely the embarrassment, for that's what he must feel, would show in his eyes? And her own.

A party of seven arrived, wanting drinks and sandwiches, and she was thankful when Mal came round the counter and began helping. Still she didn't speak. He had been there for half an hour before she managed to tell him that Leon was home and that his friend had turned up.

'Wonderful!' He left her to serve the dwindling crowd and went to find Micky. For the rest of the evening she was alone. At closing time, Mal reappeared and began helping with the clearing up.

'I can help if you like,' Leon's friend Joe, said.

Thanking him, Roma gave him a few small tasks to do and said to Mal, 'Sorry if I interrupted your – evening – but I thought you'd want to know Leon is home.'

'You didn't interrupt anything, why did you think that?' He smiled. 'Susie and I were—'

'I don't want to know,' she broke in. 'What you and Susie Quinn get up to is your business and no one else's.'

'Get up to?' He frowned, then a half smile appeared, wrinkling his dark eyes.

'I won't ring you at the flat in the evenings again,' she said pompously.

'But Roma!' he protested, still with that smile.

'I'm only here temporarily.' Leon's friend Joe spoke loudly. 'I'm not staying. But if you show me where the rubbish goes, I'll sort it and get rid of it.'

'Why did you come now?' Mal asked the boy. 'Did you know Leon was injured?'

'News gets round, someone saw him go off in an ambulance and passed the word.'

A week later with his arm still in plaster, and the bruises very visible, Leon announced that he and Joe were leaving the following day. Micky tried to persuade them to stay but they were anxious to be off. He explained to Roma that his son could never stay in one place very long.

'Before we turn soft,' Leon said to Roma in confidence. 'Makes it hard for a while if we get too soft.'

'When you go, will you try and leave a contact number, where we can find you if we need to? I think your father would be much happier if he knew he could get in touch sometimes,' Roma said.

'Depends,' Leon said. 'I don't want him bothering people on my behalf. They'd soon get bored with anyone who fussed.'

'I'm sure he'd appreciate it.'

'By the way,' Leon said, 'can't you do something about that bedroom?'

Roma had made up Leon's bed and he had groaned when he saw that the room was still much as he had left it. 'I wish he'd accept that I won't be coming back,' he said. 'And if I did, I won't want to play with Action Man and Thunderbird Two!'

'I don't think he ever will accept it. So let him keep the room for you, use it when you can and he'll be better able to face the loneliness.'

'Lonely? My dad? Does he really blame *me* for that? How can he complain about loneliness when that's what he inflicted on me all through my childhood? He never had time for me, you know. Always working, and did he share what precious free time he did have with me? No, he didn't! I was ignored, unloved. All I had was money to go to the pictures or buy a new toy. It's only now, as he's getting older that he wants to have a son. He certainly didn't want one when I was a child.'

Roma talked to him for a very long time. As they shared stories about their miserable childhood, a companionship grew in hours that might have taken years. When she went to bed, after taking both Joe and Leon a cup of hot milk and some biscuits, she hoped that when she finished her sandwich round the following morning, he would still be there.

In fact, he rose soon after her, neatly dressed in clothes

that Micky obviously kept for him. The garments were new and Roma wondered whether Micky bought things at regular intervals and discarded them when he judged they would no longer be likely to fit.

After ostentatiously scrubbing his hands, Leon began to help her. Going with her in the van, he carried the baskets of food to each of her calls and in between they chatted like old friends.

'Wasn't it scary, running away from home when you were so young?' she asked at one stage. 'Specially at night?'

'Very, but I think I stuck it to worry Dad, to get some sort of reaction to show he loved me. Pathetic, eh?'

'I can understand,' Roma said sadly.

'At first I used to hide in the garden. D'you know, once I hid in the garden all day and it wasn't till nine o'clock that night that he missed me and came to look for me?'

'Give him a chance to make it up to you,' she pleaded. 'I'd love the chance to get to know my father, but I don't even know where he is. Somewhere in Reading is all I know.'

At their final call, Leon went in alone while Roma counted the remaining stock to decide what she would need to add for the sessions at the Magpie. There was still plenty of choice, just a few more Scotch eggs would be needed. She was meticulous about selling to Micky, and made sure the profits were his.

Leon came out of the insurance offices smiling and said with a wink, 'Him in there, Jason something or other, he fancies you something rotten.'

'In that case you'd better stay another day.' She laughed. 'I can't have any distractions or my business will suffer.'

He looked at her for a moment then said, 'Right then, I'll stay another day. The fact is, I've enjoyed helping you.'

'I've enjoyed it too,' she assured him truthfully.

Six

By daily coaxing, Roma persuaded Leon and Joe to stay another week. A rapport had grown between the seventeen-year-old Leon and Roma Powell by the time they prepared to leave.

The revelations of a similar childhood began it, but they found they had the same sense of humour, and they worked together like a practised team when the sandwiches were made and delivered. Roma would be sorry to see him go, but knew she had to forget her own disappointment and concentrate on cheering Micky who had hoped that this time his son would stay.

Wearing new clothes, which looked somehow incongruous on the young long-haired boys, and carrying the rucksacks with which they had arrived, they waved cheerily to Roma and Micky, who stood together and watched them get on the coach that would take them to Devon where, Leon told them, they intended to spend the rest of the summer.

The day following his son's departure was wet and cold, and Micky's melancholy at Leon's leaving him, matched the weather.

'Pity Leon didn't stay.' Micky sighed. 'He really took a liking to you, didn't he?'

'Yes, he did. But not enough to persuade him to give up the life he enjoys.'

'Does he enjoy it? Being so uncomfortable and not having decent food?'

'It doesn't seem to bother him. He's young I suppose.'

'He didn't say "no" to much while he was here!' Micky said, and Roma laughed, relieved when Micky joined in.

'I could just see you two managing the Magpie one day,' Micky said as they prepared for opening.

'Dream on, Micky. I don't think your son would settle down that much! A job maybe, but not a pension scheme and a long-term commitment.' She turned to him then and noticed how tired he looked. Afraid to face the fact that he might be ill, she said, trying to reassure herself as much as Micky, 'You're feeling low because of the fall you had. You'll be fine once the last of your aches and pains are gone.'

'Would you consider taking this place on?'

'Me? Well, I'll always want to help you. You've been unbelievably kind, even allowing me to steal your lunchtime customers. Not many bosses would do that. But, taking it on, that's different. I don't think it's a job for a single woman. Not this woman anyway. It needs two people really and preferably one with muscle.'

'Think about it. If you and Leon would work together – and from what I've seen this past week, that isn't such a wild hope – then I'd feel I was leaving it in safe hands.'

'Leaving it, Micky? What's all this gloom and doom? You had a fall, you recovered, so why talk as though you were wearing your last clean shirt?'

She looked anxiously at him and he grinned apologetically. 'All right, so I'm feeling low. But I've always imagined you running this place and sharing the work with Leon. That's why I was so pleased when you came here to work. Dreams do come true you know.'

'Why me? There must be dozens who'd do as good a job as I would. Better, in fact.'

'It would be so – right. There's no one more fitting to take on the Magpie after me than you and Leon.'

He didn't explain why and she decided he was suffering serious thoughts on his mortality after the fall had reminded him of how quickly things could change. It had hardly been a brush with death but, together with Leon's visit, serious enough to warrant some thoughts on the future.

Richie Talbot began banging, and when Micky let him in he was closely followed by Mal.

'Are you feeling better, Micky? Is everything all right?' he asked, glancing around to see who was there.

'Yes, I'm fine. Missing Leon though. I'd hoped that this time he'd have stayed.'

'Is it back to you and Roma, or have you taken on extra staff?' was Mal's next question, as he continued to look round.

'Matthew Rolands will be in later,' Micky told him. 'He's broke as usual, and glad of the extra shifts.'

Roma thought it was obvious that Mal had come prepared to face Fletch, and probably to tell him to go. A mischievous part of her wished she had asked him, but with Micky still sore from the accident and unhappy about his son, she wouldn't have done anything to upset him. Mal, maybe, but not Micky.

While Micky was in the cellar, she mentioned his low spirits to Mal.

'The fall shook him I think. That and the visit from Leon. And he's still bothered by the cough. He's been talking about who will run the Magpie after his time, would you believe!'

'I think we all have thought about death, especially when something reminds us of it, like that accident. He'll soon forget it.'

Micky came out of the cellar and while Roma served, Mal asked him how he was feeling.

'Dejected and a complete failure,' Micky replied. 'I can't think what I've done to deserve this. My son can't stay in the same house as me for more than a week or two, even with his arm in plaster.'

'Come on, at least Roma is staying.'

'Yes, if she left I don't think I'd cope at all.'

'Rubbish. Give Leon a few more years to get this rebellion out of his system and he'll be back.'

'A few more years, and then a few more. Time passes, Mal, and takes with it a lot of enthusiasm and a lot of hope.'

At Roma's last call on her round, the man who Leon had said fancied her was obviously pleased to see her. 'I thought you were avoiding me,' he said with a smile, holding the door as she struggled through with her basket. 'Sending Leon instead of coming yourself.'

'Leon is Mr Richards' son and was helping for a week or so. He's gone now, unfortunately. I miss him.'

When she called on the following morning, he invited her out.

'Sorry, Jason, but it's absolutely impossible. Very bad timing. Mr Richards is unwell and I'm doing two jobs: besides getting up at half five to start making and delivering my sandwiches, I'm doing part of his job as well as mine at the pub. Thanks anyway.'

'Don't you get a day off? No one works all day every day.'

'I do. I really do, but if you don't change your mind, perhaps when Micky – Mr Richards – is back to full strength, I'd love to go out with you.'

'Make it soon,' he said as she gathered up her depleted basket to leave.

Jason was an accountant working for an insurance firm. He wore a smart three-piece suit in a pale-grey and shoes that shone like glass. His long, fair hair was never out of place and she had always imagined that he rarely went over the doorstep without umbrella and waterproof, he appeared so in control. So it was a surprise to learn through their brief conversations, that his hobbies were walking, horse riding and on occasion, rock climbing.

'People are never what they seem,' she told Sylvia when her friend called one evening.

'What's he like?' Sylvia demanded to know.

'Well, if I'd thought about him at all, I'd have said finicky and over-fussy about his appearance. He wears formal suits and his hair looks as if it's been put in place by a designer. But it turns out he's very much an outdoor man. Horse riding would you believe, and rock climbing.'

'Worth cultivating?' Sylvia asked.

'I hadn't taken much notice of him before Leon's remark, but now, I hope that once Micky's back in harness, he'll invite me out again. This time I'll accept.'

'Come to Dorcas and I'll pick you out an outfit that'll dazzle him. And I'll go with you to my hairdresser and get your hair re-styled.'

'Steady on, I'm not that excited by Mr Jason Stevens.'

'Maybe not, but I'll guarantee he'll be excited by you, and that's much more fun, believe me!'

Calling at Dorcas one afternoon, the shop was taken over by Sylvia's determination that Roma should look her best. As it was summer, they decided on a flowing dress in bold colours that at first, typically, Roma refused even to try on. Once she had, adding simple white sandals to wear with it, she knew it was the right choice.

Feeling good, she took a couple of hours off one Monday evening, having employed a temporary assistant to help Micky, and met Jason.

They went for a meal and he was attentive, amusing and the evening was a success. But she knew immediately that Jason would never be important to her. Promising to repeat the experience, they parted with a light kiss and, although she had no strong feelings of excitement, she was glowing with the pleasure of a good night out with an attractive young man. Her eyes sparkled when she walked back into the pub as they were about to close. Mal was there and she was aware of a tenseness in him as he asked whether she had enjoyed herself.

'Wonderful,' she said. 'Absolutely wonderful.' She wasn't sure why she had exaggerated, or why she was gratified to see a look of disappointment on his face.

Fletch had given up the bedsit he had rented and moved in with a friend in London. The arrangement didn't last long. Without money his friend swiftly grew tired of him. He found others willing to accommodate him for a few weeks, but he wore out friends at a fair old rate as he scrounged and begged and promised to repay them.

He tramped round looking for work, refusing anything other than stage work. Ignoring the truth that even the greatest had been forced on occasions to do menial tasks, he insisted on the stage or nothing. He met several hopefuls and laughed when they told him they would do anything to earn money to give them longer in the city with its hope of a lucky break.

'I won't lower my standards and work in a chippy or a pub,' he said, denying the times he had done just those things to survive another week, in other towns. 'I can honestly say at interview that I'm a singer, comedian and actor and I've survived without doing anything else.'

Whether anyone believed his lies he neither knew nor cared. It was his image and he would polish it in the way he wished. By scrounging off this one and that and even resorting to occasional shop lifting, he survived for one more day, one more week, one more month . . .

Then he met Fiona Roslyn and thought his best moments were upon him. She was only eighteen and very lovely. With blonde, naturally curly hair, enormous blue eyes and a figure most women would kill for, she took his breath away.

She had a job in the chorus of a London musical but for some reason she ignored the many exciting young men gathered round her and fell for Fletch. Within days of their meeting, he was sharing her flat, going with her to the theatre and he quickly became well known among her group of friends. Vicariously, he lived the life of a working actor. With the chatter and the esoteric language of the young, which he quickly absorbed and used, he was accepted as one of them.

Luck smiled on him briefly and he got a small part in the chorus of a six-week run of a new musical. Unfortunately, it flopped dramatically and after three weeks he was back on the dole. But it was enough to add to his background knowledge and his stories.

When Fiona's run ended and she was also unemployed, she had to go home for a while, until she found something else. He was utterly dejected and wrote or phoned her several times each week begging her to come back and share his tiny room and his bed.

He pretended to be employed in a chorus line again and didn't tell her that to pay the rent he had found employment in a cafe a few miles away and often had to walk home.

Micky was still subdued and when September came with its darker mornings, Roma was struggling to get up at five a.m. each day and get out on her rounds. She continued to help Micky in the bar until late evening and as she grew more and more weary she knew she had to find some way of easing her work load.

If only Leon would come back, she thought. Besides cheering Micky out of his depressed mood, she would be glad of his help and his cheerfulness.

Accepting that he was still feeling the effects of his fall and the loss of his son, Roma was persuaded by Micky to stay at the Magpie for a few more months, 'Just until Christmas', but all the time she was searching for new premises. The sandwich round had grown so much she needed to split it, and to do that she had to find an assistant. Although she had tried several young women and men, none had stayed longer than a couple of weeks. So when Ruby Gorse, a forty-five-year-old widow asked for the job, Roma willingly agreed to give her a month's trial. Ruby fitted in so easily that after the first week Roma wondered how she had managed without her. Instead of having to tell her what was needed, Ruby seemed to understand exactly what she had to do. She came with fresh ideas and added to the list of sandwich fillings, she made cakes in the large rectangular trays and they were always of the same quality and appearance.

'We have to make them the same size,' Roma had warned her but Ruby said, 'It's simple!' She pointed to the permanent marks she had made on the sides of the tin and, with a length of smoothed wood made for her by a local craftsman for a ruler, she cut the cakes into identically measured pieces.

On Roma's rare free evenings, when Mal came in to give her a break, the temptation was simply to go to bed early, but occasionally she met Jason – Jay – Stevens. He was pleasant company, but he didn't reach her heart and he gave up trying to persuade her into an affair and accepted they would never be more than friends.

Jason had other friends but it was rare for a week to pass without him meeting Roma and at least having a drink together, sometimes in Parry's Place, where Mal would usually join them. They were affectionate friends, but both knew they were marking time until someone else intervened and ended it.

Mal seemed to like Jay, but Micky was almost as suspicious of him as he had been of Fletch.

'Micky treats me like a daughter,' Roma confided to Mal one evening when she had called in to the wine bar to see him. 'Honestly, any moment he'll come out with some line like, "There isn't a man in the town who's good enough for you"!'

'He's already said that to me!' Mal told her. 'And he means it!'

'When Leo the Lion comes home – did you know that was what Joe calls Leon? When Leon comes home it will be different. Then Micky will give all his affection and love to his son, and that's how it should be.'

'I'm not too sure. I think he'll always want to have you around.'

'Why?'

'Why not? You're lovely, kind and generous, hardworking and loyal, and I never want you out of my life either.' He kissed her lightly on the forehead and went to settle a query at the counter.

It was Mal who found the property. Taking Roma to a place not far from the wine bar, he led her to an empty shop. One of the downstairs rooms had been cleared of shop fittings, the floor made good and freshly tiled and the walls and ceiling had been replastered. Mal showed her a simple plan for turning the double-sized room into a kitchen. Above was a two-bedroom flat.

'Living room, bathroom and kitchen with the second bedroom fitted out as an office. Do you think it would suit?' he asked.

'It would be perfect,' she breathed, then a slight frown creased her brow.

Studying her face, Mal quirked a questioning eyebrow and asked softly, 'But . . . ?'

'But will I afford it and how will I tell Micky?'

'Tell him straight away. It will take a few weeks to get the work done and that will give him time to get used to the idea and take on an assistant.'

'I know he isn't a relation or anything but he'll miss me and I'll miss him.'

'This is Harbour Road not southern Australia!' Mal laughed. 'You can still visit Micky, you have free time most afternoons and you don't work at weekends, why not agree to stay on but with fewer hours? Besides, from what you say, Ruby Gorse is as good as a partner, so you can leave a lot of it to her.'

'And I can still give him the sandwiches I have left so he keeps the little bit of business I left him with,' she added.

'He doesn't mind about that. He couldn't have done the food without you anyway.'

Micky went to see the proposed kitchen, and gave his approval to the scheme, and Roma negotiated for the purchase of 2, Harbour Road. Between them, Micky and Mal arranged for builders to go in and begin the conversion.

By the middle of February 1982, the place was up and running and the business, which she had named The Kitchen, had widened to provide a takeaway counter for casual passers-by as well as the delivery service. Roma had three part-time staff, and as the business showed signs of rapid increase, she would soon need more.

As Mal had suggested, Roma continued to serve at the Magpie in the evenings and at weekends. When the takeaway counter closed at two o'clock on Saturday she would go to join Micky and, after catching up on the latest gossip, she would work in the bar, where the Finks and several other acts still entertained. Sometimes she wondered about Fletch and the memory of him was still painfully raw.

In June, 1982, as the British flag rose again after the Argentinian war, and Prince Charles's first child was born, Fletch went back home.

The house was silent and had the look of abandonment. Perhaps his parents were away? He walked round to the back lane and looked over the fence. The car had gone, but they might simply be out shopping. Irritated that they weren't there to offer food and a night's sleep, he went to the Magpie.

As he walked he began inventing the stories he planned to tell them about the time he'd been away: the time he was on the West End stage; the way that youngsters looked up to him and begged for help before they attended auditions. By the time he stood outside the door of the pub, he almost believed it all himself.

Walking in, he glanced quickly around to make sure there

were enough of the regulars there to remember him, then he burst wide the doors and stood, one knee bent, arms wide and said, 'He's back! Your favourite performer and mine, Fletch is here!'

Seeing Roma behind the bar, he felt a superior glow as he said, 'You still here, Roma? Same place? Same job? Poor love, you should have travelled with me.'

He bought drinks for a few people, just enough for them to start buying for him. He listened to the Finks and applauded in a way that might have been construed as condescending, before being persuaded, without much effort, to sing. He sang the Nilsson number from 1971, 'Without You', looking at Roma as he did so.

Then, without relinquishing the microphone to others who waited to go on, he began telling a few jokes and some anecdotes about his time in London. Without actually lying, he implied a close friendship with a few famous people. Without actually saying so, he left his audience with the impression that he had been invited to parties by Tommy Steele, Cliff Richard, Wayne Sleep and many other famous performers, by using their first names, and talking about them as though they were personal friends. That some of the locals were impressed was obvious by the expressions on the faces.

At closing time he went out, waving a flapping hand to the few remaining customers. To Roma, he blew a kiss.

'Meet me tomorrow, love, there's lots to tell you. When I go back next week, I could be persuaded to take you with me, show you what it's like to be working with the greats.'

He had been hoping to wait until Mal had gone, then persuade Roma to let him stay the night. If his parents were away for the night, he had no key and didn't want to risk the embarrassment of being caught breaking in. But Mal seemed in no hurry to leave.

Outside, Fletch stopped and nodded to the others as they left. When he looked back he saw Roma on her own at the bar and slipped back inside.

'Roma, love. Mam and Dad will be asleep by now. I don't want to disturb them. Any chance of a bed for the night? Yours'll do,' he said jokingly.

Micky appeared in the doorway of the back room and said, 'I don't think so.' Coming around the counter, he grabbed Fletch by the shoulder and frog-marched him out. 'Keep away from Roma. Understand? She isn't taken in by your fantasies, neither are most of the people who listened to you with more politeness than you deserve. Get out and stay out.'

'Who the hell d'you think you are, her father? What gives you that right to decide who she sees and when?'

'Just go before I call the police.'

'All right, I'm going! I didn't want to disturb Mam, that's all. Don't start a war!'

'Your parents? Seen them have you?'

'Of course I have. And I've wrtten regularly. They're expecting me back for supper.'

'That's strange. They left a few days ago and don't intend returning for a month.'

'Oh, that holiday. I'd forgotten! Got their number have you?'

'No chance. They've taken their caravan so you can't get in touch to bother them. Sense at last, wouldn't you say?'

Hurrying back to the house, Fletch eased open a window, went inside, poured himself a drink, flopped comfortably in an armchair and phoned Fiona.

'Fiona, my darling girl, I've found us somewhere to live for at least three weeks. Who's a clever boy then?'

Roma's thoughts repeatedly returned to her mother's death. She wondered about her father, about how he had coped with it, and how often he thought about her now. She mentioned it to Sylvia when her friend called at The Kitchen one Saturday lunchtime to see her.

Sylvia arrived as Roma was packing the left-over sandwiches

into one of the large wicker baskets she used on her rounds. Seeing a rather sad expression on Roma's face, Sylvia asked, 'What's up, the business not going well?'

'Business is fine,' Roma assured her.

'Then why the sad face?'

'I was thinking sad thoughts, that's all. Day-dreaming I suppose.'

'About Jason?'

'No, about my father. I don't even know where he lives, apart from the fact that he's in Reading, and I don't know his wife. They have a daughter, my half-sister whom I've never even seen.'

'Perhaps the child will seek you out one day, when she's old enough to be curious.'

'Perhaps. I hope he's kinder to her than he was to me, gives her more attention, tells her she's loved.' Covering the packs of sandwiches and cakes with a gingham cloth, she put it ready to take to the Magpie. 'Was it my mother's murder that turned him against me?'

'How could that be! You didn't cause her death!' Sylvia sighed. 'Look, Roma, forget it. You can't change anything, there's no way you can help your father deal with it even if you knew where to find him. It's far too long ago. It's pointless dwelling on it, it's over and a part of history. She's dead, and that's all you need to know.'

Something in her friend's expression made Roma catch her breath. 'You know something, don't you?'

'No. No, I don't.'

'Your mother would, and she's told you something, hasn't she?'

'I'm not going to ask her. Forget it. Listen,' she added in an attempt to change the subject, 'come and see the new stock we had in yesterday. There's a range in burnt orange and a gingery brown, perfect for your colouring.'

For a few minutes they talked about clothes, Sylvia enthusiastically and Roma at a superficial level, her mind still wrestling with the mystery of her father's rejection and her mother's sad and cruel death.

It might have been the thoughts of her father and the memories brought back after reading the truth of her mother's death but whatever the cause, Roma felt very much alone. So when Fletch came into the Magpie a few days later, with a stunningly beautiful Fiona Roslyn on his arm, she felt a strong pang of jealousy. She had Mal and Micky but no one who loved her in the way she desperately wanted someone to love her and seeing Fletch with this devastating girl was a painful blow.

In an inexplicable way she wanted to hurt herself, give herself a reason to feel this pain that was without a physical reason.

Without waiting to be invited, Fletch launched into the usual stream of anecdotes about singers, comedians and musicians, wearing the condescending expression of being kind to the peasants, that Micky found so irritating.

'Somebody ought to warn that kid,' he said to Roma, gesturing with a nod towards where Fiona sat watching Fletch perform. 'She's young enough to learn by her own mistakes, but youth is too good to waste on the likes of him.'

Roma was unable to reply. She feared her voice would let her down. But silently, she wished that the girl would see sense, if that was what it took for her to leave Fletch. Each time she thought she was over him, something happened to pull on her deepest emotions, reminding her that she still knew no one else who could make her happy.

It had been a mistake to move into that grotty flat with him so soon. If she had only waited, she might have been able to make it work. Regrets made her impatient with customers and Micky wondered if she were unwell. Guessing the cause, Mal watched and worried.

Two weeks into the three that Fletch thought he had in which to make free with his parents' house, he and Fiona were still blissfully happy. They lived comfortably, using the phone each day to ring agents and producers in the hope of work and not worrying too much when nothing was offered. Money was short, but the freezer had been filled with food and they gradually emptied it, eventually laughing at the odd combinations of food they prepared and called a meal.

Then Fiona was offered work. There was a three-week run in a theatre outside London and she took it. Jubilantly she put on a tape and danced round, doing some of the steps she had learned for a previous show. Fletch joined in, improvising and laughing when he made a mistake, and crashed into her, hugging and holding her and finally falling with her on to the couch, breathless and happy.

'We'll get a room near the theatre and when your run finishes we'll go back to London and try and find something together. We'll be the new Astaire and Ginger, the new Sonny and Cher, we'll be the best, my darling girl, the best.'

'No, Fletch, I'm going on my own.'

'What?'

'There won't be enough money to keep us both. I'll share with a couple of the girls. That way it's cheaper, and I'll be able to save some of my wages.'

'But, love, we're together, aren't we?'

'When you've got work, ring me. You can reach me via my parents.'

He stared in utter disbelief as she packed her suitcase, rang for a taxi and left.

He looked round the untidy room and wandered through the house where they had left a trail of used beds, unwashed dishes, empty cupboards and freezer. If his parents returned, how could he explain? Hurriedly, he began to gather the bedding, intending to take it to the launderette, then he remembered the cost of it and, dejected, he sat down amid the mess and wallowed in self-pity.

Guilt made him take a tenner from his seriously depleted

funds, which he placed under a milk jug. Then he closed the house and left, taking his sports bag containing all he owned in the world.

Being an optimist, he quickly shrugged off his misery and decided he couldn't leave without trying once more to talk to Roma. He had seen clearly that he still attracted her. If she would help him, tide him over his present difficulties he'd soon be on top again. He called at the Magpie and when he was told Roma wasn't there, he went to find her at The Kitchen.

Putting on a lugubrious expression, he went to the counter, where she was serving a couple of shoppers with sandwiches and a drink, and said, 'Just called to say goodbye, love.'

'Fletch? What's happened?'

'Fiona's left, taking most of my money. I had enough to pay my parents for the few bits and pieces we used while we stayed there, but I'm wiped right out.'

'D'you want to borrow—' she began, but he shook his head, the picture of a beaten man.

'I'm giving up, Roma, love. I can't go on. This has finished me. I'll find a room, get a job cleaning up in a supermarket or something.'

'Giving up on show business? You can't!'

'I have to. I'd need so much money to get me back to London, revive my contacts, get a flat. I've let everything go, see. Fiona told me she needed a rest, a break after the strenuous season she's had and, well, I agreed to come here for a couple of weeks. You've no idea of the chances I let slide. And now, well, it's time to accept defeat.'

'Look, you can stay here for a week or two, I won't charge rent. And you can use the phone, get a few auditions lined up, then, when you go back you'll have something positive to build on.'

'Roma! You darling! Would you really do this?'

'You share the flat but not my bed.'

'Pity,' he said with a wink. 'All right, if you insist.'

'I do!'

'I wish you'd said that a couple of years ago, and in a church,' he said in a hoarse, emotional whisper. 'My problems would have been solved if you'd stayed with me. I'd have worked for you, succeeded for you.'

'You'd better get your things upstairs,' she said, turning away, her eyes filling with regretful tears.

Roma said nothing to either Mal or Micky about accommodating Fletch. But the news reached them in less than two days. Within hours of arriving, Fletch had persuaded Roma to give up her occasional outings with Jason, and he had told Mal that Fletch was back on the scene.

'What the hell's the matter with you?' Mal demanded when he burst into The Kitchen one morning as she was about to set off on her rounds. Ruby Gorse, who was washing the last of the baking tins, removed her rubber gloves and left the room.

'This is about my offering a few days' accommodation to Fletch I suppose,' she shouted back.

'Did you know his parents are back and he and that tart of his have emptied the house of everything edible and used every bed and probably left telephone bills they might not be able to pay?'

'That was Fiona,' she said defending him. 'Fletch had the money to replace everything he used but she went off with his money and he couldn't do anything.'

'Richie Talbot's son is a taxi driver and he took Fiona Roslyn to the station. She told him a different story.'

'She would, wouldn't she!'

'Roma, for goodness' sake, if you are going to help the man at least face the facts!'

'I am! It's you who are determined to think the worst of him. He can't be as wicked as you make out. You exaggerate to try and convince me and that's almost as bad as lying, isn't it?'

'He's a devious, cheating liar and if you think I am too, then there's nothing more to say, is there!'

Roma was tearful when she set out on her deliveries next morning and Ruby Gorse called her back and asked her to wait. Without explaining, she ran upstairs to where Fletch was sleeping on the couch in the small living room and demanded that he get up.

'Come on, get up now, this minute. Roma's had a row with Mal and she's upset. And it's your fault! I'm going with her on the deliveries and you, young man, are going to look after the counter.' She pushed a bag of change at him and added, 'The prices are on every item and I know exactly what's in stock, right?' Without waiting for a reply, she ran back down the stairs. At the bottom, she called, 'I'm leaving the place open, mind, so you'd better be down here and ready to serve in less than a minute!'

She was very angry and had to pause a moment to calm herself before catching up with Roma and telling her what she was doing. She sympathised with Mal, and agreed with him that helping a useless scrounger like Fletch was insane.

That evening Roma didn't go to the Magpie. She asked Ruby to deliver the food and stayed at home talking to Fletch. She was confused by warnings from her brain that Mal was right and urges from her body that told her it didn't matter. Fletch was here, now, and she desperately needed to be loved.

Fletch pretended to sympathise with Mal's point of view. He sat close to Roma with an arm round her shoulders and, gently stroking her, told her he would leave.

'It's for the best. For you, anyway. I still have a few friends in London where I can stay for a couple of days while I sort myself out,' he said sadly. 'I'll be all right and you've done enough, my love.'

More distressed than she had ever imagined at the quarrel with Mal, Roma was feeling bereft. It was always easy to convince herself that no one loved her or cared for her. Mal was protective and Micky needed her, but love, physical human contact and love, she had only found with Fletch.

Seeing her distress, he took advantage and hugged her, holding her close, pressing her pliant body against his own, and sang softly, 'Can't live, if living is without you . . .' She stifled a sob and he whispered, 'My dearest love, I've missed you. Why did we part?' Kissing her hair and her cheek, he moved down and down until he was opening her blouse and letting his lips wander, without resistance. He knew there was a chance and was ready to take it. He stared deep into her eyes, seeing the longing and need of his love, and slowly, he lifted her, his lips performing their magic, and carried her to her bed.

Seven

The time when Fletch came to stay was the happiest Roma had known. Fletch melted into her life like a dream, waking with her and helping with the early morning preparations, attending to the takeaway counter while she and Ruby delivered to the customers. He was there each evening and had often even started to prepare a meal by the time she had taken her left-over food to the Magpie for a rather surly Micky to sell.

She didn't allow Micky's obvious disapproval to dampen her spirits. She was so happy she floated through the days and thought she would never return to earth.

Taking the opportunity of Fletch's help, she and Ruby canvassed several firms and increased their business satisfyingly. They took on more part-time staff, even finding someone willing to start work at five a.m. and help with the preparation. Roma bought a mini-van with the aid of a bank loan which displayed their logo, consisting of a profiled smiling face and a hand offering a plate of food.

Jason was pleasant and helpful, showing no anger at the tapering off of their friendship. In fact, by late summer he, too, managed to find her a few more orders and Roma and Ruby were kept so busy making cakes, pasties and Scotch eggs they sometimes thought they could never eat a single mouthful of food themselves. But going home to where Fletch had begun to cook a curry or a spaghetti Bolognaise or a casserole of chicken, she quickly changed her mind.

'It's such a perfect end to a busy day, going home to Fletch,' she told Ruby.

'Make the most of it, love,' the down-to-earth Ruby Gorse sighed, 'it won't last. Nothing does.'

Roma smiled, she knew it would. There wasn't a thing that could happen to spoil it. There had been no word from the selfish Fiona, and Fletch had showed no sign of wanting to get back to London. There was no need to ask whether he had given up on his ambition, she just knew he had.

Perhaps one day soon he would either agree to work with her full time, or find work locally. The flat was small, but they managed, and they were so busy they were hardly in it long enough to find it cramped. Perhaps they could look for something larger in a year or so. She was too happy to think far into the future. They were in love and utterly happy. Now was the time to enjoy, tomorrow there would be plenty of time to discuss serious things.

There were a few mild disasters of course. One morning, in heavy rain, she was leaving one of the offices, quite early in her delivery round, when she saw Mal standing, just staring at her. They had hardly spoken since Fletch had returned and she was uneasy, feeling the waves of disapproval emanating from his once friendly countenance.

Self-consciously she waved, hoping the frown would leave his face and she tripped over an uneven paving stone and lost her grip on the basket. Before Ruby could reach out and help, the packets of sandwiches and cakes slid out and landed in a deep, muddy puddle. They were protected by their wrappings but completely unsaleable and she stared at them in horror.

'Now what shall I do!' She glared at Mal as though he were to blame, which, in a way he was.

He came over and began gathering the unsavoury packages. 'Let Ruby go on with the deliveries while you go back and make more?' he suggested amiably.

'How can I get back to The Kitchen from here? Ruby will

need the van,' Roma wailed. 'Besides there's no one there to help, the early morning girls will have gone home.'

'Oh, dear, you are in a bad way, aren't you? Not able to work out something as simple as this? I take you back, help you make the replacement food, then bring you back to join Ruby.'

'Would you, Mal?'

'I would.'

'Now?

'Immediately.

'Thanks'

'All right.'

They looked at each other edgily, a desperate need to end the separation apparent to them both. A half smile on his face encouraged one on her own and they were no longer the enemies they had recently become but long-term, loving friends. Roma was aware of a lifting of her spirits. She hadn't realised just how much she had missed Mal and needed his approval.

After a brief discussion about where they would meet, Ruby went off with the rest of the sandwiches while Roma got into Mal's car with the spoilt stock and headed back to The Kitchen.

Fletch was serving a couple of young women with pasties and he smiled when he saw Roma, kissed her affectionately, to the amusement of his customers, and ignored Mal completely.

'I've got a new order for you, love. These two ladies are having a hen party next week, marrying brothers they are and I said you'd give them a good price for supplying the food.'

Mal turned away and set about making replacements for the lost sandwiches, while Roma and Fletch discussed the party arangements with the prospective customers. They agreed that the Magpie was the place to hold it and the snacks would be provided by Roma's kitchen. Mal said nothing. Roma later discovered that the party had been booked elsewhere but, on being persuaded by Fletch to give Roma a chance, they had cancelled it. It was Micky who told her the previous booking had been at Parry's Place.

'Did you know?' she asked Fletch when she realised the truth.

'Of course I knew. Why d'you think I did it? Couldn't resist it once they told me they were having it at Parry's Place, could I? Specially when Mal turned up and was standing there glowering while I succeeded in persuading them. Brilliant it was! He dislikes me, and for no other reason than I love you. Why shouldn't I take the opportunity to get a bit of owns back?'

'So you were persuading those girls to have their party, not at Mal's wine bar but at the Magpie, while Mal was here, helping me after I'd dropped a basketful of food?'

'Yeah. Good wasn't it?'

He grinned unrepentantly and her disapproval faded, softening into a smile. He loved her, and why shouldn't he put her interests first? The kiss that followed and the eventual love making was as satisfying as any they had shared. It was only on the following day that sanity returned and she felt ashamed.

As soon as she was able, she went to see Mal to apologise.

'I didn't know what was happening, Mal, you must believe me.'

'Fletch did. He deliberately persuaded them to change from my wine bar to the Magpie, with you doing the catering.'

'What shall we do? Shall I go and see them, explain that there's been a mix up?'

'No. It wouldn't be fair to mess up the arrangement again. That way we'd both lose a customer. Go ahead. But, Roma,' he paused and she knew there was a criticism of Fletch coming.

Bracing herself to take it and not retaliate, she watched his face while he gathered the words. He must have seen the slight tightening of her jaw, the protectiveness in her expression, because he turned away and only said, 'Be careful, Roma. Fletch gets what Fletch wants. And only for as long as Fletch wants it.'

She didn't reply.

A few weeks later, Fletch announced another party booking.

'Not at the Magpie, not at Parry's Place, but in a village about an hour away on a Saturday night two weeks from now. Want it, do you?'

After a quick check to make sure they had nothing else on, she nodded. 'Give me the address and I'll talk to them, find out what they want and give them a quote.'

A phone call was followed by a meeting with eight people at a public house called the Sugar Loaf. They were planning a surprise party to celebrate their parents' golden wedding. An agreement was more or less made. The four couples knew exactly what they wanted and, having sought advice on wines from Micky, Roma was able to give them prices there and then. She was excited by the booking. This was an area in to which she could expand.

To her disappointment they rang the following morning and told her they had been given a better price. Lowering the price by a few pounds was getting close to the risk category, but she offered the revised total, convinced it couldn't be bettered.

'My prices are fair,' she assured them. 'I don't expect you'll find anywhere else as good. So, I hope to see you in a couple of days to get it underway.'

To her surprise she had a letter telling her that they had received a better offer. Free venue, and a reduction of a pound per head. Straight away she wrote back offering a further reduction of fifty pence and half-a-dozen extra bottles of wine. It would be tight, in fact she'd be lucky to come out of it without losing and there certainly wouldn't be any money left over. But catering for parties and, eventually, weddings, was a part of the business she wanted to develop. Better to lose profit on one or two events and create a reputation for good food, reasonable prices and reliability.

'You don't know who the other contenders are then?' Fletch asked.

'Fletch! It isn't Mal again, is it?'

'Out-of-town catering? He doesn't have the staff to consider it. No, it's probably some small firm prepared to take a cut to get a few bookings.'

'Like me!' she said. 'I can't make anything on the prices I've agreed, I'm treating it as an advertising scheme. Recommendations by word of mouth could be better value than a few newspaper ads.'

She had to take a further twenty pence off each person catered for but eventually it went ahead. But from the moment the decision was made, things went wrong. Firstly, her reliable support, Ruby, was unwell.

'Thank goodness you're here, Fletch.' Roma sighed as she replaced the phone on a migraine-suffering Ruby. He smiled and assured her that all would be well. Then the suppliers were late delivering and they had to stand around waiting to begin work while the clock ticked closer and closer to the time they had to leave.

It had been arranged that Fletch would stay and deal with the last couple of hours of the takeaway business while Roma drove to the venue with one of the young assistants in plenty of time to get the food displayed and the wine sorted. With Ruby ill, Roma was a little concerned that beside being later than planned she was having to depend on an inexperienced stand-in.

After a mild panic, they finished the preparations only twenty minutes later than planned. Roma set off with the mini-van loaded with food and drinks for seventy people.

She was unworried by traffic. It was a Saturday and there were the usual shoppers on the roads going to and from the cities, but with the absence of the heavy lorries she thought she would have a free run. Then the engine on the van began to fade out and she looked round wondering whether to persevere or leave the main road and look for a garage. A glance at her watch – the Gucci watch Mal had bought for her twenty-fifth birthday – and she decided to take a chance and push on. No matter what she tried, the normally reliable vehicle finally stopped in a country lane about seven miles from her destination and indicated that there it was going to stay.

'Why didn't I stop at the first sign of trouble, while there was a hope of finding a garage!' she moaned, with a shrug of impatience. The young girl looked at her and repeated the shrug. It wasn't her problem and she wasn't in the least worried, she would be paid for her time whatever happened.

There were a few cottages not far away and Roma left her guarding the food and went hopefully to ask to use a telephone. The first three she tried were empty.

Walking more than a mile back the way she had come, she finally saw a telephone box. She'd phone the AA and explain the urgency and they'd soon be here. She stepped into the kiosk with a sigh of relief. Then a glance revealed that the telephone was damaged and useless.

Fully aware of the danger, she walked back in the direction she had originally been heading in the van and tried to thumb a lift. A young man stopped for her and had a look at the van but failed to improve matters, and offered to drive her to the Sugar Loaf. Unfortunately they couldn't find it. Somehow they had taken a wrong turning and were now twelve miles from where she ought to be.

They finally found a phone that was working and her first call was to tell her customers about the problem. She was about to ask whether someone could tow her in, when there was a tirade of abuse during which she was told that her services were not required. Before she could explain, the phone was slammed down.

She rang the AA and the good-natured young man drove her back to the van to sit and wait.

'At least you won't starve,' he said cheerfully.

Ruefully, she offered him some sandwiches and pasties which he took with a wide smile and a 'Good luck, love,' before driving off.

It wasn't until that evening at the Magpie, as she unpacked the huge order of unwanted food, that she told Micky about the disastrous day. He looked at her oddly when she said she had no idea who the rival had been, but wished she'd let them have it.

'You really don't know who the other caterer was?'

When she learnt who her rival had been for the cut-price booking, she couldn't believe what she heard.

'It was Mal? But, Micky, it couldn't have been! How could he deal with an out-of-town booking? He hasn't the staff or the facilities. You must be wrong. You must be.'

Micky shook his head and she was horrified. Cutting her prices to the bone in a determination to grind down the competition and all the time it had been Mal.

'I wouldn't even have tried to get the job if I'd known Mal was involved, you do believe that? But I don't understand. Why was he competing for an out-of-town party? And at such an abysmally low price? That isn't his thing at all. Are you quite sure?'

'The family are friends of Mal's and he gave them a low price as a contribution to the celebrations. They were going to hold it in Parry's Place.'

'Then why—'

'Your Fletch of course!' Micky spat the name out angrily. 'He told them that by having it in their local pub and you doing the catering they wouldn't need to hire a coach or worry about drink-driving. Everyone would be close enough to home to walk there.'

She was trembling as she sat down on a bar stool. How could such a mess have happened? Around her on the bar counter were mountains of food which there was no possibility of selling. Besides the platefuls of sandwiches, carefully displayed and covered with cling-film, there were quiches, gateaux, trifles and fresh-fruit salads. She and Fletch and a part-timer had been up half the night preparing it all.

'How do I tell Mal and make him believe I didn't know?'

'Don't try.' Mal came into the bar from Micky's back room. His face was closed and he was white with anger. 'You've made your decision about loyalty, Roma. I just hope you don't regret it.'

He walked through the bar and was going out of the door when she ran across and stopped him. 'Mal, I'm terribly sorry. I really didn't know.' He continued to glare at her coldly and angrily. 'Is there any way you can take this food to the Sugar Loaf for me? No charge of course. I'd rather give it to them than see it all wasted.'

He continued to look at her but didn't reply. Not waiting to see whether he would do what she suggested, she ran up to the back room that had once been hers. Opening the curtains, she stood there as the car engine was gunned into life and Mal drove off down the road.

Fletch was unrepentant and laughed at her dismay.

'But love,' he said reasonably, 'how was I to know they were friends of Mal's? Even you wouldn't have expected him to be involved in such an arrangement, would you? Catering for a party of old dears? Not his scene at all, he likes glamorous girls with long legs and—' He stopped when he saw he wasn't convincing her. Then he went on, 'I overheard them talking about what they were planning and I recommended you, my brilliantly talented love. But I must admit I'm not sorry you messed up Mal's plans and upset his friends.'

Sometimes seriously, sometimes with laughter, he gradually coaxed her out of her misery and shame. She understood why he was antagonistic towards Mal, whom he saw as a threat to their relationship. 'But,' she warned him, 'next time you choose to torment him, please don't involve me!'

Mal didn't go back to his flat. Even music wouldn't calm his temper. He drove to the Sugar Loaf and tried to make amends for the mess-up over the party. It was soon clear that the family blamed themselves for being persuaded that they could get the catering done more cheaply by someone else. This made Mal feel worse, and he didn't stay.

He had been persuaded by Micky to take a couple of boxes of food but decided that, as they had managed to deal with the last-minute rearrangements themselves, he would just leave them in the pub kitchen for them to find. Handing the anniversary couple a gift he had brought, he left.

It was on impulse that he stopped at Jason's house and knocked on the door. On a Saturday night, it was unlikely he would be in, but Jason opened the door, poured Mal a drink, and sat and listened to the trail of troubles that had led him there.

'D'you think Roma would get over Fletch if he went back to playing the the clubs?' Jason asked. 'Only there's this bloke I know, Gunther Brooks, calls himself an impresario. He acts as an agent and books small-time acts for small-time venues and he's often looking for people to fill a programme. I could talk to him if you like.'

The knowledge that Mal was no longer her friend, caused Roma great distress which she tried to hide from Fletch – he wouldn't understand. She wanted to phone Mal but each time she lifted the receiver to do so she couldn't think what to say that would persuade him to listen. Eventually she wrote him a brief note explaining that she had had no idea of his involvement. She also wrote to the family whose party she had all but ruined. Time passed and things settled back into the usual routine, although Mal rarely spoke to her.

*   *   *

When the letter came for Fletch, Roma guessed what it contained. The advertising on the envelope left her in no doubt, and for a brief moment she was tempted to throw it away before Fletch read it. But that would show a lack of trust and a lack of confidence. Of course he should see it, then they would discuss it, he'd reject it and they would be able to talk everything through, make plans, real plans for their future, together.

She watched as he read it and her heart shrank like a squeezed orange. His face was so lit up with excitement, his smile so wide he was a stranger.

'This could be it, Roma love,' he said, without looking at her. 'A letter out of the blue, isn't it just what happens? You think all doors are closed then, suddenly, someone remembers you and wants you, and you're off up that ladder of fame. Baby! This could be *it*!'

'You'll take it?' she said, wondering how her voice could sound so normal. 'I thought you were happy working with me, building our business together?'

'You'll keep everything going while I'm away, won't you? And I'll be back every week. Well, probably,' he added with reservation. 'And I'll soon be able to repay you for what you've done for me. You've supported me and believed in me when no one else did. Roma, you're wonderful!' He still hadn't looked at her.

Without even wondering how she would manage without the help he had given her and which she had become to expect and depend on, he threw a few clothes into a suitcase and left on the mid-morning train. She had left him in her flat, eating toast and drinking coffee at nine thirty and when she and Ruby returned from their deliveries at one thirty, he was gone.

'I know I'm not supposed to say it, but I'm going to anyway. Told you so!' Ruby remarked as she tidied the kitchen and opened the takeaway counter that Fletch had regularly manned at nine thirty. 'Only four hours late with the takeaway counter. What will you do, get a part-timer to run the takeaway?'

She was so matter-of-fact, Roma could half believe that Fletch's departure wasn't true, that it wasn't the end of her dream. She could pretend he was only out for an hour or two, perhaps for something as mundane as a haircut, and not on a train taking him to another town and another life. A life in which there was no place for her.

'It's only for a few weeks,' she said eventually.

'Oh yeah?' Ruby said, handing out packs of sandwiches and taking money from two young girls.

'Where's Fletch today then?' one of the customers asked.

'Gone fishing!' Ruby replied abruptly. Then, turning to Roma with a softer, kinder expression, she asked, 'Have you decided what excuse you'll give for his disappearance? Better get a story sorted, love.'

'It's only for a couple of weeks,' Roma insisted.

'If you say so. But we'll tell everyone you persuaded him to go, shall we?'

Tears falling, Roma could only nod agreement. What did it matter how she excused him? Mal and Micky would know the truth and they were the only ones she cared about.

Fletch's booking was short-lived and poorly paid but he didn't go back to Roma. Instead he went to see Fiona, lied about the way he had been forced to help out a friend in need and let his career slide, and moved into her bedsit. They both found a small part in a pantomime and for the present, that was enough. He was on stage and could tell his parents he was a success. Fiona had a little money saved and had an invitation for both of them to join her family for Christmas. That was as far ahead as Fletch wanted to look.

Mal and Micky said nothing to Roma about Fletch's leaving her. Mal, because he felt guilty at his part in it, having phoned Gunther Brooks and persuaded him to offer a booking to

Fletch. Micky didn't mention Fletch's leaving because he didn't want to rub her face in the humiliation she was feeling.

Roma took to staying at the Magpie on Saturday nights after helping out in the bar and enjoying the usual entertainment. If some of the youthful wannabes reminded her of Fletch, and added to her misery, she didn't show it.

There hadn't even been a postcard. And as she hadn't taken the addresses of any of the bookings from the letter, she couldn't contact him. She had left him that morning, as he sat hugging the letter offering the bookings, presuming that there would be a chance later on in the day to discuss keeping in touch. Now, all she could do was wait for him to write or phone, and, he did neither.

At the beginning of December she realised that the calendar was giving its fatal warning. She was pregnant. At first she pretended the dates were wrong and checked and double checked in her diary. Then she tried to convince herself that there were other reasons for her body to depart from its orderly pattern.

One Saturday night, after a party for Richie Talbot's seventy-fifth birthday had exhausted her, she went up to her room and fell into bed. This was tiredness like she'd never known. It shut off all thoughts, all worries. Her body seemed to melt with relief into the soft mattress, her brain no longer having problems to solve, muscles having no further need to keep her upright, she gave in completely to a self-indulgent wallow.

She relaxed into that pleasant state when sleep hovers, and takes you away from the room you inhabit on an effortless mood journey, and allows thoughts and imaginings to blend, and hopes for the future and past successes meet in peace. She was comfortable and grateful not to have had to drive back to the flat, that so empty flat, above The Kitchen. Easily pushing thoughts of Fletch aside, allowing nothing to spoil the dreamy moment, she felt her eyelids grow heavy and sleep began to bring down its blanket to shut out every attempt to think.

When she heard someone moving about, she wasn't even irritated. She thought idly that Micky was going down to make a cup of tea as he sometimes did at night when sleep wouldn't come. In her semi-conscious state she felt sorry for him and his inability to enjoy the pleasure of fatigue-induced sleep. Then she realised he was being sick.

Sleep fell from her and reaching for her dressing gown she ran down to the bathroom he used and knocked on the door.

'Micky? Are you all right?'

'Go back to bed, Roma love, it's all right. I ate too much supper, that's all.'

She remembered with a chill of fear that he had hardly touched the meal she had cooked for him. She went down and put the kettle on, surprised to see that it was almost six clock. She had not realised so many hours had passed since she had locked the door after Richie and his friends.

She made a pot of tea, and as she was stirring sugar into the cup she suddenly felt queasy. Could it have been something they had eaten? Surely it was too much of a coincidence otherwise? Rushing up to her bathroom, she turned on the tap to mask the sound of her retching, but when she came out, pale-faced and weak, Micky was standing there waiting for her.

'Must have been something we ate, eh?' he said as he helped her downstairs.

She couldn't drink any tea but watched as Micky did. She was aware of how thin he had become. Why hadn't she seen it before? Had she been so selfishly wrapped up in her own life she no longer noticed him?

'Micky, I don't think your supper caused this. Your appetite isn't good and to say you over-ate, well, it sounds to me that you're hiding something.'

'You were sick too,' he said.

'That's a common symptom of pregnancy,' she said quietly.

He looked at her, the disappointment and sadness in his eyes making her want to cry.

'Don't say anything, Micky,' she whispered, fighting back tears.

'I don't know *what* to say,' he replied.

'I haven't had it confirmed, but I'm sure. What I haven't decided is what I'm going to do.'

'That's up to you and him.'

'Fletch doesn't know and I don't want him to know. Not until I decide what I want.'

It was too late to go back to bed and enjoy a brief Sunday lie-in. Roma was wide awake and they sat there for a long time, Micky drinking tea and choking on it occasionally while Roma persuaded him to see a doctor and Micky tried to help her think out the choices she had.

'Whatever you do decide, remember that there's a home for you here, with or without the baby,' Micky said as he went up to shower.

'What have I done to deserve you?' she said as tears began to overflow.

'I've cared about what happens to you ever since you were born,' he said. 'Lonely little thing you were, with a father who never had time.'

'Lonely little thing with a father who never had time,' Roma repeated when she met Sylvia later that day. 'How much worse for my baby if I continue with the pregnancy. She wouldn't have a father at all, not even a disinterested one who called her "disappointingly ordinary".'

'You're sure Fletch wouldn't help?'

'I can't imagine Fletch accepting responsibility for our mistake, can you?'

'By "accepting responsibility", you mean giving up on showbiz and settling down to being a loving parent?'

'Neither of us wants this baby, but what can I do? She's here, she's a fact, not a what if – Oh Sylvia, what a mess. What can I do?'

'You have thought about abortion,' Sylvia murmured. 'Don't dismiss it completely. It's your life, remember, and it's your choice.'

'I've thought about it, but can I face it? Can I walk into the doctor's surgery and tell him I don't want this child?'

'The embarrassment is the worst thought, knowing you.'

'Perhaps, but would it be worse than the way my father treated me? At least he gave me life.' She turned away and said slowly, 'My mother was murdered and that's a horrifying thought, but what I'm planning is murder too.'

'Emotive language won't help,' Sylvia said at once. 'It just clouds everything so you can't see clearly.'

Roma sat in her room for much of that night, staring into the semi-darkness trying to decide on her future. Should it include a child and, if so, how would she cope? What if this was her only chance of motherhood? As she grew older she'd regret not having the baby, wouldn't she?

She was miserable with the knowledge that she had no one to really talk it through with. No mother – surely she'd be sympathetic? No father. She wondered where he was and what his reaction would be. She knew there would be no sympathy, but she dreamed of him standing there, smiling and holding out his arms for her, until the shock of harsh truth changed the picture to one of him frowning disapprovingly and pushing her away.

Micky was out of his depth in this situation and Mal – she couldn't discuss this with Mal. She was on her own and the decision she reached would be hers to live with.

As dawn broke and made the light of her small lamp look drab and brassy, she made her decision. Losing the baby was something she would always regret, but her arrival was badly timed and she had to let her go.

*　　*　　*

Sylvia went with her when she went to see her doctor.

'I'd have made the same decision,' Sylvia told her as Roma prepared to tell the doctor she wanted an abortion.

'He'll try to talk me round,' Roma said fearfully. 'I don't think I'm strong enough to resist.'

'You've made your decision. Stick with it, Roma.'

'But is it the right one?'

'Now don't be swayed by emotional arguments and moral clap-trap handed out by people who've never been in this situation. This is your life, remember.'

Sylvia being with her gave her courage and she stood out against the doctor's well-meaning words. The appointment made, she went back to the Magpie to tell Micky.

She went to the clinic alone, refusing Sylvia's offer to go with her. She was shaking as she walked through the doors to be met by a smiling, sympathetic nurse. There was no last-minute pressure on her to reconsider and as she lay there after the operation, she felt calm and convinced that the right decision had been made. She had to put this tragic affair behind her and look forward.

When it was time to leave, she gathered her few belongings into her bag and went to the reception where they would book a taxi for her. The receptionist told her that wasn't necessary.

'Your boyfriend is waiting for you,' she said smilingly.

'I don't have a boyfriend.' Roma looked around her in dread. Surely Fletch hadn't heard and come to find her?

It was Mal who stood up and came to take her small case.

'Mal? What are you doing here? People will think you're—'

'Let people think what they like. I'm here to make sure you are all right,' he said gruffly.

Roma had heard nothing from Fletch. But when his parents realised what had happened, after Richie Talbot overheard a snippet of conversation and had pieced together the rest, they got in touch with their son to tell him. Fletch came straight back in the hope of stopping her.

For the few days she was unable to work, Ruby Gorse had kept everything going and it was business as usual when Fletch burst into The Kitchen to see Roma laughing at something Ruby was telling her as they packed the last of the left-over food ready for the Magpie.

'It's still all right? I'm not too late?' he said.

Roma frowned, presuming he meant the business. He couldn't know about the baby. 'Did you really think we'd let the business go just because you walked out on us?' she said. 'We're managing fine, thank you, and we haven't needed to cheat on anyone to do so! Now, if you'll excuse us, we have to finish cleaning up.' She walked briskly to the door and held it open for him.

'Leave us, Ruby.' Fletch pointed to the door held open by Roma.

'Stay where you are, Ruby!' Roma said threateningly.

Ruby went on washing the counters and packing the last of the food, while Roma held the door and Fletch fumed.

'Tell me it isn't true,' he said.

'What are you talking about?'

'You were carrying my child and you got rid of it. Please tell me my parents got it wrong?'

'It's true.' she said, avoiding his eyes. 'How did you find out?'

'Richie overheard and told my parents. But it doesn't matter how I found out! What have you done? It was my child too.'

'You weren't here, you left me, remember? The decision was mine.'

'But why? Why didn't you tell me? It was my choice as well as yours, wasn't it?'

'Hardly. You haven't contacted me once, I had no idea where you were or who you were with. Fiona, was it?'

'I've seen Fiona, yes. She was in a bit of trouble and I had to help her. But she and I aren't—'

'Stop trying to justify yourself, Fletch. You ditched me and I'm not giving you the chance to do that again.'

'I wouldn't!' Tears filled his eyes and the words were little more than a whisper.

Roma stared at him. Could he really expect her to believe that line? Grabbing a tray of sandwiches, leaving the cakes and pasties for Ruby, she went to where the mini-van was parked. He followed but didn't attempt to open the doors for her, but watched her struggling.

Clumsily she succeeded in loading the tray into the back, then, without looking at Fletch, she got into the driving seat and threw the kitchen keys to Ruby. Fletch stared at her as she started the engine, he continued to stare as Ruby locked the door of The Kitchen, loaded the rest of the food and got in beside her. As they drove off, he shouted, 'You bitch! You evil bitch!'

Eight

Roma was shaking as she drove away from Fletch. Humiliation and guilt vying for first place. His finding out what had happened would make it harder for her to put the tragedy aside. Damn Richie Talbot and his inquisitive nose!

She was torn with shame on the deceitful way she had treated Fletch. But how could she believe he would want a child, another person for whom he would have to take responsibility? It wasn't in his nature to have someone dependent on him. So why was he so angry? Cynically, she wondered if he had decided that if she were settled with a thriving business and a child, he would always have a place to return to when his career attempts finally faded out.

Then she felt ashamed. Why shouldn't he want a child? Most men did at some time in their lives. And for his parents it would have been something on which to build their happiness. If she had chosen to keep the baby she would have had their support. Her decision should have been discussed with Fletch. She had been selfish, even though she had believed she was doing the best thing for them both. Fletch should have been told.

But it was all too late. It was over and the decision made. Deep down, she knew that it had been the right decision for herself and everybody else. Producing a child wouldn't have magically changed Fletch into a caring, loving father and there were already enough children born without that basic luxury.

This sombre thought led her into wondering once again

about her own father, who had shown her no love in the brief time she had lived with him. He had been in her thoughts a great deal during the time she was making her decision. So when she stepped out of the van at the pub and began unloading the trays of food, she stared in disbelief when her father, with a small child holding each of his hands, walked towards her.

She knew him straight away and felt a pleasant warmth suffusing her face; a glow of happiness she would never have expected. He'd come to see her. The long years when he had shown no interest were forgotten. He was here. She could tell him everything that had happened to her and he'd listen and care.

'Roma,' he said abruptly. 'I need a place to stay.' No smile, no loving greeting, just the demand.

As the joy faded from her eyes, she asked, 'You what? Why are you here? Who are these children?'

'They are mine,' he said as if he had expected her to know. 'My daughters, Catrin and Melanie.' Neither of the girls moved or acknowledged the introduction, if it could be called that.

Of all the dozens of imagined scenarios she had dreamed up over the years, of a reunion with her father, this was not one of them. Not even a 'Hello, how are you?', surely that was the minimum she could expect.

'Dad – I – er – Where are you staying?' Frantically, she tried to remember what he'd said, and think what she should say. She stared at this gaunt man who was her only blood relation.

She wondered afterward how she had recognised him, but constant study of the few photographs she owned, had obviously kept her memory fresh. He was taller and thinner than she remembered, but the disapproval edging toward anger that darkened his aquiline features was the same.

She was holding a large tray containing sandwiches and pasties and suddenly aware of their weight, she nodded to the door of the Magpie and said, 'I have to deliver this food to Micky. Will you come in?'

'No.' The loud, abrupt word startled her and she stared at him again trying to see some sign that he was pleased to see her, and failing.

He was over six feet tall and probably weighed less than eleven stone. His coat hung on him and the belt was tied tightly round his waist as though holding him together. His trousers were well pressed and of good quality, but his shirt and tie showed more than a day's grubbiness. His hair was lank and rather greasy as if it needed washing. The little girls too were slightly less than immaculate and their faces were pinched with cold. She thought this scene would be indelibly printed on her memory, the forlorn group staring at her with unfriendly faces on the forecourt of the Magpie.

The girls were visibly shivering in the chill of the January afternoon and she suggested, 'Perhaps the girls will come in with me?' It had all been such a shock she couldn't remember their names. She handed them each a small packet of food and asked them if they would like to help. The oldest, who looked about six years old looked at her stonily without speaking. The youngest, aged three or perhaps four, half smiled and stepped forward, but her father's hand pulled her roughly back.

'We do not enter such places,' he said firmly.

Roma shrugged. 'Then you'll have to wait until I deal with the deliveries.'

The instantaneous thrill she had experienced on seeing him was fading. Memories flooded back, the enchantment she had sometimes imagined was cruelly stripped away. She went into the bar and called for Micky. Hearing the anxiety in her voice he hurried out of the back room.

'My father is outside,' she said abruptly and Micky ran to the door and looked out. There was no one in sight, then a movement caught his eye and he saw that people were getting into Roma's van. Mr Henry Powell was carelessly dropping the trays of food on to the ground while the two girls stepped over them to climb into the back.

Roma came and stood beside Micky and said, 'He wants somewhere to stay. What can I do, with a single bed-roomed flat?'

'D'you want me to tell him?'

'No, I'll take them back and he'll be able to see for himself.'

'Are you sure? Wouldn't it be best to tell them here? They can use the phone and get an hotel room for the night easily enough.'

'They don't enter places like the Magpie,' she said sorrowfully.

Micky quirked an eyebrow and said, 'How odd. He practically lived here once.'

Micky and Roma went to pick up the trays of food and carry them into the pub together. If Henry Powell saw them he didn't acknowledge them with the slightest movement. The two girls were in the back, their solemn little faces staring out through the small windows.

'Where d'you want me to take you?' Roma asked when she got in and started the van. 'I have to come back here, I'm afraid, I help Micky Richards most nights.'

'We need somewhere to stay.' There was that slight emphasis as if having to repeat himself was irritating.

'An hotel?'

'You have a flat, we can stay there.'

'Sorry but there isn't room. An hotel it will have to be.'

'Your place will do.'

This was getting more and more weird. Something about the cold words and the dead-pan face frightened her, and the little girls hadn't opened their mouths, or changed their expressions of disapproval. She wondered what they had been told about her.

'You can't stay with me, I have only one extra bed,' she

said slowly. She pulled in to the side of the road and turned off the ignition.

'Dad, you can't just turn up unannounced after almost sixteen years, and demand I find beds for you and your – my half-sisters. Sorry, but it's impossible. I can either leave you at Micky's, or somewhere in the town, but I can't find two extra beds in my flat.'

'I'm not your father. *THESE* are my children.'

She turned and stared at him. What had she done to make him hate her so, and why, if he felt that way, was he here begging favours?

'We'll go to your flat,' he said, 'and we'll discuss it.'

'I can't let Micky down. I have to go back to the Magpie,' she said firmly. 'You can come to the flat and use the phone to find somewhere to stay. That's all I can do.' Believing she had made it clear, she drove them to The Kitchen.

She couldn't resist boasting a little as she showed them in. Opening the door of the spotlessly clean food preparation area she said, 'It's from here that I run my business. I employ six people now, three full time and—'

'Can we do this later?' her father cut in.

'Well, yes, I was only telling you what I do. The business is mine you see and I thought—' she had been about to say, 'thought you'd be proud', but she knew that was a wild hope. 'I thought you'd be interested,' she finished instead. Without another word she escorted them up to the small living area above.

She watched his face as she opened the door on the cosy, attractively furnished room then chided herself for expecting a reaction or the murmurings of admiration. He looked round, opening the office, bedroom and bathroom doors then came back to where the silent girls were waiting.

'We'll stay here,' he said.

'But – it isn't convenient,' she protested.

'We stay.'

* * *

Fiona was waiting for word from Fletch. She had been upset by his hasty departure. On being told about Roma's pregnancy, he had caught the first available train and had left a brief note explaining what had happened. She had thought he was hers, then word of Roma made him dash off to see her. She just couldn't let him go. All this nonsense about a baby. It couldn't be true, Fletch had assured her it hadn't been that sort of relationship. Roma was just trying it on, hoping to get him back. Well, it wouldn't work. But it was unsettling.

They had a small flat, furnished from charity shops, with a shower room, and a balcony that sadly only overlooked the main road. What they earned just about covered their expenses, but Fletch worked at weekends on a market stall, where his patter brought the customers flocking, which provided them with money for food and an occasional treat. It wasn't much, but with the work in the theatre and sometimes a club booking, they were content. Until Roma popped up and caused him to run back home.

She telephoned his mother and asked her when he was coming home.

'I don't know dear,' was the reply. She didn't pass on the information that he had returned very drunk and had gone out again without saying when, or if, he'd be back.

'Will you pass on a message?' Fiona asked as she invented a story that would bring him back.

'He's out somewhere,' Mrs Morgan told her. 'I think he said something about meeting Roma Powell. I don't know when he'll be back.'

Fiona's heart slipped lower but she kept her voice light and cheerful.

'Just tell him there's an audition in the offing, for a part in the West End,' she lied. That should coax him away from that woman. It would be easy to tell him it was too late when he eventually got back. It was easy to lie, as easy as pretending to be pregnant when you want a man who doesn't want you, she thought, and a frown crossed her young face. She'd do anything to keep him away from Roma Powell.

Roma stood by and watched in disbelief, as the stranger who was her father settled the little girls on the couch and covered them with the duvet from her bed. 'I'll just give them some hot milk and they'll be all right until morning,' he said calmly.

'This is not convenient,' she almost shouted.

The telephone rang, startling her with its impatient demand.

'Hello.'

'Can I speak to Fletch?' a young woman's voice asked.

'He isn't here!' Rudely, she replaced the receiver without another word and at that moment, there was a wild knocking at the door and she gave a sigh of exasperation and went down to answer it. Fletch burst past her and shouting at her, ran up the stairs and into the flat.

'Who are these people?' he demanded. He was flushed and obviously more than a little drunk.

'My father and his – my step-sisters. Tell me your names again, will you?' she asked the subdued children, hoping to calm the situation by the girls' intervention. Again it was the younger who might have responded, but her father's hand on her shoulder hushed her.

'Who are you?' Henry Powell demanded of Fletch, as though he lived there.

'I'm only the poor sod whose child she's just aborted, that's who!'

'My father then gasped and stepped back like the offended goody in a Victorian melodrama,' she told Micky an hour later when she returned to the Magpie in tears. 'I suppose it was funny really, but then he dragged those poor children out of their makeshift beds and left.'

'Did he say anything else?' Micky asked.

'Just mixed up words, nonsense really. Wanton women had a mention and there were some quotes from the Bible, and remarks about how I was evil and from a child had been destined for a depraved life. How bad seed will produce bad harvests. What with him calling me depraved and Fletch standing there crying about the child he pretended to have wanted, a really began to believe I'd slipped into a very bad melodrama by mistake!'

She forced a laugh and Micky joined in but he was soon coughing, then she heard him being sick and it wasn't funny at all.

She stayed at the Magpie that night, unable to face the flat with the memory of her father's strange visit. She didn't expect to sleep but as soon as she cuddled into the familiar duvet she felt the tensions leave her and she was floating away in dreams.

Very loud banging on the pub door woke her; banging as only the police know how. Sleepily, she reached for a dressing gown and went down. Micky followed close behind her, coughing, and muttering complaints.

'All right, I'm coming!' Micky growled as he released the bolts on the heavy old door. He gestured for Roma to stand away, in case there was trouble on the other side of it.

'We're looking for a Henry Powell. Seen him have you?' the sergeant asked. Two constables went past him and with a brief, 'Mind if we check?' went into the back rooms and up the stairs.

'Come in, don't wait to be invited,' Micky said sarcastically as he waved his permission.

'He's my father and he came to see me earlier, but I don't know where he is now,' Roma said. 'What's wrong?'

'Did he have two children with him?'

'Two little girls, about three and six, yes.' She tried in vain to remember their names. 'They aren't hurt are they?'

The constables came back down and then they went outside to search the yard and sheds.

'What's happening?' Micky demanded. 'Henry Powell hasn't stepped foot in here.'

'You saw him though?'

'He didn't speak.'

Turning to Roma the detective sergeant asked, 'Did he tell you where he was going?'

'No, he didn't. He just took the children and left. I'm sorry but I didn't ask any questions. It was all so strange, him turning up like that. I told him I didn't have room for them to stay at the flat and they left. He wasn't very communicative,' she explained.

When the place had been searched and Micky and Roma had answered their questions, the police gathered ready to leave.

'At least tell me if they're all right,' Roma pleaded.

'His wife left him and he called at her parents' house and took the children. She's worried for their safety, that's all I can tell you.'

Roma gave them the key to her flat and told them to check there, 'Even though it's extremely unlikely he'd return.'

'Why is that, Miss Powell? He's your father, isn't he?'

'He disowned me years ago,' she replied in a wavering voice. She moved nearer to Micky and he placed an arm round her for comfort.

The silence, after the instant-response-unit van had driven away, was palpable. The rooms echoed with the footsteps of the men running through as they searched; their subdued voices hovering in the air and the anxiety for the safety of the children pulsing in the very walls.

'I'm frightened, Micky,' she whispered.

He went to the kitchen and made a pot of tea, sliced bread thickly and slid it into the toaster.

'Toast and jam and hot cups of sweet tea, that's what we need, even if it is only three a.m.!'

She was surprised at how hungry she was, but noticed that Micky only played with his snack and left most of it. She guessed he had only made an effort to encourage her to eat.

Later, when she was back in bed and trying in vain to sleep, she again heard him being sick.

Next day when her rounds were finished and she could leave the clearing up to Ruby and the rest of the staff, she drove to the police station to enquire whether there had been any news of her father and the children.

'He's back home,' the constable told her. 'They travelled through the night, thumbing lifts would you believe! They got back to his wife's parents an hour ago. No harm done, the children are tired but they'll soon catch up on sleep. He wanted to frighten his wife into taking him back, I think.'

'And his wife, she's there with the children?'

'No, she went looking for them and she hasn't been in contact so far. But I expect she'll be in touch before long.'

She was relieved that the girls were safe but there was a niggle of fear about the disappearance of his wife. She chanted the newspaper articles describing her mother's death in her head. She'd read them so often she could recite them word for word. Her mother died from a blow to the head before being left to drown. Where was her step-mother? Had a similar fate overcome her?

She drove to the pub to tell Micky the children were safe. Then she telephoned his doctor and made an appointment for him.

'You're going, Micky, and there's no arguments. You could have an ulcer or something and it won't get better by your pretending it isn't happening, will it?'

She prepared herself for an argument but none came. At four o'clock he set off while she stayed behind and began preparations for opening.

'Now you promise to mention your lack of appetite? And your sickness? And don't forget to ask about the cough.'

He laughed away her list of instructions. 'I've promised to go to the doctor, haven't I? That's more than I want to do.'

'Tell him everything,' she pleaded.

She was glad to have Micky to worry about that day, it helped take her mind off her father's strange visit and the revival of his dislike and disapproval of her.

Was she the daughter of a man capable of murder? She shook her head firmly. He was unbalanced and she feared for the loss of a happy childhood for those two little girls, but there was nothing more than that, was there?

Micky returned from the doctor with the worrying news that he had to see a specialist. A week later he told her with forced cheerfulness that he had to go into hospital for a biopsy as there was a constriction in his throat that needed investigation.

Roma's first thought was to reassure him and she said at once, 'Ruby can look after the kitchen for a week, I'll come here and run the pub. I know your routine well enough so it won't exactly be difficult, as long as you find me a cellarman to do the heavy lifting.'

Her efficient tone and the matter-of-fact planning was better than telling him how she really felt: that she was afraid it was something serious and was terrified at the thought of a life without him.

It was almost eleven that night before she had a spare and private moment to ring Mal. She was so upset at the news she had to impart, that she didn't react when the phone was answered by Susie Quinn.

'Is Mal there?' she asked and it was seconds before Mal spoke. It was only later that she wondered whether they had been in bed together and felt the unreasonable pain of it.

'It's Micky, he has to go into hospital, for some tests,' she said. That sounded innocent enough. 'He has a bit of a cough and his appetite isn't what it should be so they are going to investigate, that's all, but I'll be running the pub alongside a temporary manager and leaving Ruby to deal with The Kitchen. I just thought you'd like to know.'

'Thanks for telling me. I'll come and see him tomorrow. Everything all right?' he asked.

'Fine, except that my father turned up, told me I'm depraved and evil, and left.' She explained then, making a joke of it all, but she ended by adding her fears.

'It was rather odd, Mal. He had two little girls with him and they looked as though they had been given horror stories about me and were't allowed to talk to me in case I contaminated them.' There was a choking cough as she tried to hide her distress from him. 'And,' she went on when she had recovered sufficiently, 'there was no mention of where his wife was.' She paused again, then added, 'When I last spoke to the police, she still hadn't turned up. He's returned the children to his wife's parents but his wife hasn't got back from searching for them.'

It was another opening for him to tell her about his mother, perhaps add that mystery to this one, but all he said was, 'Don't let him upset you, love. He's the one with the problems, not you. Remember that.'

'What problems?'

But he wouldn't be drawn.

Mal came to the Magpie the following day and dealt with the deliveries, while Roma worked with Ruby at The Kitchen and arranged for her usual jobs to be covered by other members of staff. By midday it had all been sorted out and Roma was content to leave the day-to-day running of her business in the hands of Ruby Gorse.

As soon as Ruby had seen her drive off, there was a shout from one of the packers. A pipe had sprung a leak and water was pouring out across the kitchen floor. As Ruby picked up the phone to call a plumber and others searched for the stopcock to turn the water off at the mains, there was a knock at the door and Fletch came in.

'Where's Roma?' he asked, then, seeing the predicament, went to the point of the trouble and assured them he could fix it. Silently thanking the plumber who had given him a job during one of his lean times, he smiled confidently and told them to, 'Worry no more, folks, your favourite and mine, Fletch, is here.'

He ran off to borrow tools and buy what he needed and returned within an hour. As he worked, he sang to the young girls and cracked a few jokes, mainly about amateur plumbers, for the older women. They laughed and applauded and he felt his heart swell with the joy of it. There wasn't any greater thrill than performing, even to a bunch of kids and middle-aged mums like these, he thought contentedly. Even the cynical Ruby shared the enjoyment and there was a softness in her eyes as she smiled at him. Not her type at all, she admitted, but he certainly had something, sex appeal or little boy lost, cheeky little boy or dangerous professional. By one route or another, he seemed able to get to the hearts of all ages.

'It looks as though something got jammed behind it and wrenched it out of place and the plastic gradually split and gave way,' he explained to Ruby. 'It shouldn't give any more trouble. But you can get a plumber to check it if you wish. Now, where's Roma?'

'At the Magpie,' Ruby said. She told him about Micky's proposed visit to hospital and Roma's arrangements to run the pub while he was away.

'Don't go there and upset her, mind,' Ruby warned. 'She's got enough to think about without you starting on your complaining. What she did was for the best and it's over and done with.'

'I'll go and tell her about the pipe and see if I can help,' he said to an admiring audience of young girls. He departed to sighs and murmuring of, 'Isn't he fantastic?' and 'What a dream,' that warmed his heart.

Seeing Mal in residence at the pub, Fletch's hope that he'd be allowed to stay was dashed. He reported on the repair he had done, modestly accepted payment, then decided it was time to go and see Fiona. The information about an audition had been vague but it was worth going back to London for, specially as his mother had secretly handed him the fare.

On the journey he began to rebuild his outrage against Roma and the loss of his baby, so that when he walked in to Fiona's gratifyingly affectionate welcome, he at once began to talk about it all.

After an hour, Fiona said, 'Don't be sad about the baby, Fletch. The next time it will be perfect. You'll have the child you really want, yours and mine.'

'Oh, Fiona, I didn't think I wanted the responsibility of being a father, but knowing that I'd lost one has devastated me,' he said, opening his arms to her and begging for comfort. It wasn't true, but playing a part like this, when he was safe from having to face up to his fantasies was quite good fun.

Then the impossible happened and he was faced with the lie.

'Darling, Fletch, I haven't known how to tell you, but I think I'm pregnant. You and I, we'll be parents. Thank goodness Roma acted so selfishly, clearing the way for the child you really want. Darling, isn't it wonderful?'

The look he gave her was beyond description but she took it as disbelief that his prayers could have been answered so soon.

A week later they had visited Fiona's parents, Fletch had agreed to take a job in a shop selling men's fashion, and they had arranged to be married in a week's time by special licence.

'Now our life together really begins.' Fiona sighed happily. 'We'll go down and tell your parents, shall we? They'll be so thrilled to know you're settled and have your heart's desire, a baby on the way.'

Fiona wasn't pregnant, but she thought she soon would be now Fletch thought there was no point in taking precautions. The discrepancy could later be explained by an unannounced miscarriage and a new beginning.

* * *

Micky's stay in hospital was a worrying time for Roma. She worked long hours keeping everything running smoothly at the Magpie, often sitting up long into the night making sure the books were up to date. Anything to keep busy, to stop her thinking of the consequences if he died. She didn't try to sleep until she was exhausted, and sometimes it was as though she had only just closed her eyes before being woken by the strident demands of the alarm clock.

Mal helped, having left the running of the wine bar in the capable hands of Susie.

'We're so lucky with our staff,' he said as Roma displayed the leftover food brought to her by Ruby.

'We are,' she agreed.

'So is Micky!' he added, giving her a look of admiration.

During the first few days she tried to contact Leon. She had been given a couple of phone numbers but no one knew of his whereabouts. She left messages and hoped that one would eventually reach him. She knew how much better Micky's recovery would be if his son came to see him.

She didn't go to the hospital, as Micky had begged her not to. So each day she waited for Mal to come and report on his progress. 'It was simply a few polyps,' he told her on the third day. 'A problem often suffered by singers, so he has to promise not to sing for a while,' he joked, 'but he'll be fine once it's healed.'

'Singers? Micky doesn't sing, except to join in the choruses with the Finks!'

'Nevertheless, that's what the problem was.'

It was a relief to know it was nothing worse and she set about her tasks more cheerfully than since Micky's first visit to his doctor.

Roma was offered a large new contract, supplying sandwiches and other items to a small chain of cafes. The two dozen different fillings she could offer made it more practical for them to buy from her rather than give a smaller choice made by themselves or accumulate a lot of wasted food trying to offer the same selection.

Roma was no longer involved in preparation. The pasties she sold, meat and cheese and onion, were made by a full-time cook and her part-time assistant. They also made the ever-popular Scotch eggs and the cakes that were increasingly in demand. Handing over more and more of the routine work meant Roma was able to help full time at the Magpie. It also gave her time to think about her next steps, as the success of the sandwich round was threatening to outgrow The Kitchen.

When Micky came out of hospital he looked drawn and seemed to lack his usual energy, and, in her new authoritative manner, she suggested that he should go away for a holiday.

'In February?'

'Yes. Why not? You could go down to Devon or Cornwall and have a leisurely rest from it all,' she suggested. 'Devon is lovely at any time of the year.' The mention of the West Country, where his son Leon was likely to be, was the right thing to persuade him and a week after coming out of hospital, wearing a polo-necked sweater to hide the scar from the operation, which, he explained, had been necessary because of the awkward position of the polyps, he left to drive off and look for his son.

There was no news of Roma's father or his new family, but Mal spoke to one of the police officers and gleaned the information that Morfedd, Henry's second wife, had turned up after a week, explaining that she hadn't wanted her children to see the bruises on her arms and body, from their father's fists.

Mal wasn't sure about telling Roma this. There wasn't anything to gain, apart from warning her never to allow Henry into her home again. But working with her at the pub while leaving Susie Quinn to deal with the wine bar made it impossible not to discuss Henry's unexpected appearance from time to time.

'Your step-mother has turned up safe if not completely sound,' he said, having decided that he needed to warn her of the possible danger to herself.

'What d'you mean?' Roma demanded.

'Apparently your father lost his temper and hit her and she stayed away so her girls wouldn't see the bruises.' He reached out and pulled her gently into his arms when he saw the shock clouding her eyes. 'I'm sorry, love, I almost decided not to tell you, but you must promise me you'll never invite him into your home again. He's too unpredictable.'

Safely held in his arms, her head on his chest, where she could hear the loud strong beating of his heart, she asked, 'Why have you never told me about my mother's death, Mal? Don't you think it's time?'

'What d'you mean?' he asked to give himself time to think about his reply.

'She didn't die in a car crash, did she? She was – murdered.' The word filled her head, the pressure of the horror threatening an imminent explosion.

'How long have you known?'

'I went into the library to look up the death of Micky's wife. Fletch told me she had committed suicide and I wanted to find out what had happened.'

'Fletch!'

'He didn't tell me about my mother being—' she couldn't say the word murder again, it made it too real.

'He told you about Micky though, and in an unpleasant way no doubt.'

'He just said Micky wasn't the person to tell me how to live my life, something like that.'

'And you found the report of your mother's death while you were looking?'

'It's true? She was hit on the head and the police still don't know who did it?'

'Your father was questioned, but he had an alibi or at least they couldn't find any evidence to convict him.'

'You think he did it?' she gasped.

'Roma, I'm not psychic! I was nineteen and too involved in setting up my first business to delve too much into a local murder. Like most people I've learned about it from gossip and the newspaper articles. Your father wasn't likely to tell me, and he certainly didn't discuss it with Micky!'

'He disapproves of Micky, doesn't he?'

'Yes.'

'Because of the Magpie?'

'Let's talk about something else, shall we?'

'Coffee?' she offered but he held her a fraction more tightly and said, 'No, don't let's move.'

She lifted her head and looked at him, his eyes deep in shadow from the lights turned low, the occasional flame from the fire showing in their depths.

'Fletch is more than eleven years older than that silly young woman he lives with. The age difference between you and me is a bit less than ten.'

'What are you saying, Mal?' His lips were tempting and very close. A kiss hovered in the air and the tightness in her throat, the beating of her heart were intense. This was nothing like she had felt when Fletch had been as near. This seemed so right.

She remembered their previous kiss and the way she had run away from its implications, shocked by Mal stepping over that invisible barrier. This time there was a different kind of shock, the shock of wanting.

When the banging on the door startled them into breaking away, she couldn't decide whether to feel relief or dismay. With a curse, Mal moved her from his arms and went to answer the knock.

'Susie!' Roma heard him exclaim and she straightened her

skirt unnecessarily as she stood up and went to join him at the door.

'What is it? Is there something wrong?' she asked.

'It's so late,' Susie said. 'You promised to be back to help cash up and everything. I wondered what was wrong.'

'You came here to find out why I was late?' Mal shouted. 'Come on, what *is* this?'

'I'm sorry.'

'You're paid to manage Parry's Place. If you can't do that, well, let's face it, shall we, and I'll find someone who can!'

Roma had never seen Mal so angry and she went into the kitchen and filled the coffee machine. Not because she wanted coffee, but because she had to find something to do. Something to take away the look of hurt and disbelief on Susie's face.

That Susie loved Mal Roma could see clearly in her face – the hurt and disappointment, and the fear that she wasn't loved in return. Susie had expected a very different sort of welcome. The rejection was a worm eating into her heart. Roma had known rejection and a wave of sympathy flowed from her towards the unhappy woman.

'That does it,' Mal said when he returned. 'I am selling the wine bar and the cafes and from now on I'll concentrate on property.'

'Coffee?' she asked weakly, knowing that the spell had been broken. They would never be able to get back to the moment when they had been about to declare something more than friendship.

A glance at Mal's face convinced her he was already thankful for his escape. She thought his anger was directed not at Susie but at her. It was Susie he loved and his anger towards her was really anger with himself and the mistake he had almost made.

Nine

Susie Quinn ran from the Magpie and headed for her car, humiliated and very angry. The darkness was absolute, as the outside lights in the car park had been switched off and no light came from the windows of the pub. Running from a brightly lit room into the darkness had blinded her and she was careless of running into something; the pain would have been a relief. Bumping into an unrecognised figure in the darkness would have been frightening in other circumstances, but her blank misery made her hit out and demand he looked where he was going.

Two hands grabbed her wrists, and Jason said firmly, 'I was standing still and you bumped into me. Now, calm down and tell me where you're going in such a hurry. Is this your car?' Barely visible in the darkness, the bonnet of her car showed dully, and she fumbled with her keys, unable to speak for the fury bubbling inside her head. She lost her grip on the bunch of keys, juggled futilely for a moment, dropped them and wailed, no longer able to hold back tears.

Jason picked up the keys, found the right one and unlocked the door. 'You'd better not drive until you've calmed down,' he said.

'I'm all right,' she shouted at him as though he were the reason for her state.

'Allow me to disagree,' he said firmly. 'I left my wallet in the bar. I'll just get it then I'll drive you home.'

Taking her ignition key with the rest to prevent her driving off, he knocked on the door of the Magpie and, when a subdued Roma opened it, explained his problem.

She stepped back for him to go and find his wallet and he saw through the open door to the back room that Mal was standing near the table. Mal had his back to him and didn't turn to greet him. Jason sensed the tension between the two people, guessing that the woman in the car park was involved. He thanked Roma and went out and walked to where the woman was sitting in the driving seat of her car waiting for him. As the inside light flickered on, he saw her clearly and thought he recognised her.

'Don't you work for Mal in the Harbour Road wine bar?'

'Why do you want to know?'

'I thought I recognised you, that's all,' he replied. 'Now, where do you live? I think I should get you home.' It took a while to persuade her to let him drive but eventually she agreed.

'I could get a taxi,' she said as a last protest, but there was doubt in her voice and he guessed she didn't want to leave her car there and have to face coming back to collect it.

'Just slide over and let me get in and I'll get you home safely,' he said. 'You and your car.'

'Thank you.'

'Where do you live?' he asked again.

'I have been staying at Parry's Place,' she said and tears began anew. 'But I think I'd better go back to my flat.'

'You live with Mal Parry?' he asked, gradually beginning to see the triangle of Roma, Mal and this unhappy woman. He introduced himself and told her about his friendship with Roma, Micky and Mal. She said nothing. She was pulling apart some tissues and wiping her eyes on the resulting mess. He went on talking, her silence was making him edgy, and he began to wish he had ignored the woman's distress and driven away.

She gave him her address and he sighed inwardly. He would have a three-mile walk to get back to his own car.

'D'you want me to come in?' he asked when they reached the block of maisonettes, owned by Mal, where the woman lived.

'I'll be all right,' she said, 'sorry I was such a weakling.'

'We all have moments when everything looks impossibly dire, but they pass,' he said vaguely, hoping it might help. He got out of the car and handed her the keys and was about to walk away when she suddenly realised what he had done.

'Jason, how will you get back to your car?'

'It's all right, I'm not far from home, I'll pick it up tomorrow.'

'I can at least offer you coffee and thank you properly for your trouble,' she said. She opened her door and stood while he made up his mind.

He managed a surreptitious glance at his watch. It was past eleven o'clock, another half hour wouldn't make much difference. He went in.

Fiona knew the week when Fletch would guess she was not pregnant was only days away and to avoid being with him and her lie being discovered, she arranged to go and stay with her parents.

'You don't mind, do you, Fletch, darling? Mummy hates not seeing me and I haven't been home much since our wedding.'

A brief booking had just ended and on that Saturday evening they were eating a late-night snack in their cramped flat. One bar of the electric fire glowed bravely but it was bitterly cold and they sat on the bed with the duvet wrapped round them as they ate toast and drank hot chocolate.

'I'll miss you, darling, but it will be a treat to get out of this place for a while. If you'd taken that job in the clothes shop we could have afforded something better,' she said in a baby voice. Seeing the scowl forming around his eyes, she added quickly, 'But I know we decided to give it another year, and we never know what's around the corner, do we? That's what so exciting about the stage. Just imagine if you got a part in *Coronation Street*!' Her beautiful eyes sparkled at the thought.

'I hope your mother will make you go to the doctor while you're there,' Fletch said. 'You're much too thin. You should be showing a pleasing little bump by now and you exercise every day and eat nothing but rabbit food as though you're ashamed to show you're going to be a mother.'

'I'm fine, you worry about me too much,' she said affectionately. Perhaps she'd have an imaginary miscarriage while she was away, she mused. She couldn't kid him much longer. He had been touring during the last two danger weeks but her luck couldn't hold much longer. She should have told him long before this, but he'd been so sweet and gentle, spoiling her with luxuries and gifts, it had been hard to give it all up.

On the day before she was due to visit her parents, Fletch told her he had a last-minute booking for a show in Birmingham.

'Not much of a part, one of the chorus is ill and they want someone urgently. It's only for a week but I thought, as you'll be away and I'd be lonely, I'd take it.'

Fiona rang her parents and told them she wouldn't be coming after all and settled down to a nice, lazy few days on her own. The railway fare Fletch had given her would be enough to eat out once or twice, no work, no waiting around for Fletch to come home wanting a meal and clean clothes. She would see a few plays, get up late, catch some of her friends and enjoy a good gossip. She could ignore the cleaning and there would be no cooking. Bliss.

On the third day, she was watching television in bed. It was almost midday but she wasn't meeting her friends until the evening so there was no rush. It was very cold. The February weather was making it very tempting to stay in bed, the only place where she felt warm. She was feeling a bit impatient for the dreaded curse to begin. If it didn't start soon, Fletch would be due home and she'd have to go to her parents anyway. It crossed her mind briefly that she might be pregnant after all.

The dishes were all dirty and she was just thinking of getting up and washing a cup and making some coffee, when Fletch arrived. As usual his first thought was for them to go to bed, and he wondered why she was wearing protection.

Fiona cried and told him the baby had been lost.

'It happened a month ago when you were in Aylesbury. I was devastated Fletch and I couldn't tell you. I kept it to myself and pined all alone,' she said sobbing. 'I knew how much you wanted this child, and I just didn't know how to tell you.'

He stared at her lovely tear-streaked face and didn't believe her.

'It was just a ruse so I would marry you, wasn't it?'

'The thing is, Fletch, darling, I'm a few days late and although it wasn't true before, I think it is true now,' she said in a little-girl voice. 'Isn't it wonderful? You're going to be a father after all.'

'No I'm not! I want you to get rid of it.'

'What? You don't mean it!'

'Oh, I mean it. I didn't want to marry you. You tricked me into it. I don't want this baby, d'you understand?'

'Fletch! Remember how distressed you were when you heard that Roma had aborted your child? You can't want me to do the same thing, you can't!'

'That was different. That was Roma!'

'You love me, not Roma,' she wailed but he didn't appear to hear. He was walking round the small room, a wild expression on his face.

'I left the theatre to come home to you. What a fool I was. I was stuck in a sparsely furnished little room which I had to share with two others and there I would sit on my own, too broke to join the rest of the cast when they went to lunch or for a drink. On my own, cold and miserable, bored out of my skull, apart from when I was rehearsing or on stage, and I thought, what a life. I was thinking that I should have taken that job in the gents' outfitters that your father got for me and settle down, accept a bit of comfort in my life. That's a laugh, isn't it?'

'You still could,' she murmured hopefully.

'I made some excuse about a sore throat, went to your parents' place to tell you how I missed you, expecting you to be pleased to see me, and instead of that cosy little scenario I come home to this. Lies and cheating, and you sitting here in this mess enjoying the money I scrape together and pretending you love me.'

'I do love you. That's why I lied.'

'I don't love you! Think about that while you sit and daydream about us being the perfect little family!' He took the bag which he hadn't unpacked and left.

'But, Fletch. What if it's true this time and I'm really having our baby?' she shouted after him.

'Baby? What baby?'

He headed for Paddington and home.

Jason spent several hours with Susie that Saturday night after she had run out of the Magpie in tears. She talked about her relationship with Mal with regret for entering into it and allowing it to go on when she knew he would never love her.

'He's never been in love with me, in fact, he's so obsessed with Roma Powell I doubt he's capable of loving anyone.'

'Obsessed?' Jason frowned. 'I know he cares for her, but that's affection that goes back to when she was a child. Her mother died when she was just nine and her father abandoned her and left her with an aunt. In fact, she was brought up by the aunt for most of the time even before her mother's death. Mal was always there like a substitute uncle or a big brother. I think the habit of looking after her is hard to break.'

'It's more than that. Look at the way he tried to break up Roma and Fletch.'

'I'm not in love with Roma, but even I was glad when that affair ended. He's a user and she's been used enough in her life.'

'What is it about the woman? Mal with a mother-hen complex and you looking out for her, and Micky Richards treating her like a long-lost daughter!'

'She's hard-working, generous with her time, kind and thoughtful to everyone she meets. Why shouldn't people warm to her?'

'She's too good to be true!' she snapped irritably.

'What are you going to do?' he asked.

'I won't be going back to Mal's flat.'

'Won't working with him be difficult if you break off the relationship?'

'What relationship!' She sighed and added, 'I was only a substitute, a pretence to cover up his real love, Roma Powell.'

'And you can still work for him?'

She stared at Jason, her blue eyes softening with tears. 'I thought we had a future. I was wrong. I won't be going back, to the flat or the job. In fact, if you'll come with me, I'll put a note through his door now, telling him that.'

Jason watched as she wrote the note in large, flowing letters. It was brief and she signed her name, Susan Quinn, with a flourish.

'Are you sure?' he ventured. 'Perhaps now isn't a good time for you to be making decisions.'

'I'm sure.'

While Micky was away, Jason had been coming to the Magpie most evenings and, on the occasions when Mal wasn't there, he stayed and helped Roma clear up. The temporary manager, Gwyn Thomas, was always eager to leave as soon as the door was closed and locked behind the last customer. Micky had employed two other staff to make sure Roma didn't have too much extra work; he knew perfectly well how busy her own business kept her and didn't want her to have any more to do than was necessary.

As Roma closed the big oak door after the last of the help left, she would sigh with relief and head for the kitchen where Jason would have coffee ready to pour and a sandwich of her favourite salmon and cucumber, made by him exactly as she liked it. As Micky's week off drew to its close she said, 'Jason, I'm going to miss this spoiling. Most people think that as I make sandwiches for a living I don't appreciate them, but it's still the most comfortable and easy way to snack. Thank you.'

'All part of the service.' He smiled.

So when three evenings had passed since Susie had made her unfortunate appearance, and neither Mal nor Jason had come to the pub, she was puzzled and a little hurt. At closing time she went into the back room and left the staff to finish clearing up. Making a tray of coffee, she went in to offer them a drink before they left but they were in a hurry to leave, each one had someone waiting for them. The coffee was getting cold, so she took her own and stood it in solitary state on the table. Her business was doing well, but she was alone and lonely. Money and success weren't enough to compensate for that.

When the phone rang she picked it up quickly, wanting to hear Mal's voice, hoping he was going to explain his absence. It was Micky.

'I hope this isn't too late, love, but I thought you'd be sitting down with a cup of coffee and be free to talk,' he said.

'The two part-timers are just leaving, but yes, I'm sitting here with my coffee. How are you? Is the holiday going well?'

'Great. I feel much better, is everything all right at the Magpie?'

'Marvellous. We haven't had a single disaster,' she assured

him, crossing her fingers superstitiously to ward off quirks of fate. 'Have you found Leon?'

There was a pause before he said, 'No. But I haven't been looking. Not really looking. I suppose I hoped it would just happen. I've asked in a few places but no one has seen him.'

'Why don't you try the emergency number he gave us?'

'I don't want to do that. I promised I'd only use it in a real emergency, remember? My being on holiday is hardly that. If we meet, well that'll be great, but I don't want to give the impression I've been looking for him.'

'Ring him!' she said. 'Please, Micky. He won't be angry and anyway, what if he is? He'll hardly beat you up,' she said with a laugh.

'No, I won't ring him. I'll be home on Friday,' he said.

'Stay for the weekend. We're managing fine here. Come back on Monday.' It took a little persuasion but he finally agreed to stay the extra few days.

She lay awake for a long time that night, listening to the sounds of the house settling, wondering whether her life would continue in the way it was at present, or whether a change would bring her more or less happiness. She was aware of how fortunate she was. She had money and independence and while Auntie Tilly had lived she thought there would be nothing more she could desire other than those two precious things. Was contentment too much to hope for?

Far away in London in her chilly bedsit, Fiona also found sleep was evading her. In the three days since Fletch's unexpected return and angry departure, he hadn't been in touch. She had telephoned his parents but they told her they didn't know where he was. Even over the distorting effect of the telephone she knew they were lying.

With little money and the room so cold she never seemed able to think or plan her next move, she wrote a note to Fletch, assuring him of her love and her conviction that this time she really was pregnant. She packed and decided to go to her parents. He'd know where to find her. He would soon come back. He loved her really, it was just the worry of finding work, she told herself. She prepared a similar story to tell her mother.

The following morning, when she was free from her own business commitments, Roma telephoned the emergency contact number Leon had given her. It was a friend of the boys called Gaynor.

'I haven't seen them for a while, but I know where they'll be,' Gaynor told her cheerfully. 'In a farmer's barn they are. This weather! Can you believe these youngsters?'

'How do they manage? Are they safe?' Roma was concerned. 'Why do they accept such misery when there's an alternative?'

'They work in a cafe cleaning and washing up for very little money but all the food they can eat, and at their age it's probably quite a good deal.' Gaynor laughed. 'And from what I gather, the farmer is very good to them. Heaven alone knows why, but there you are. They must have a special angel watching over them.'

Roma gave her name and telephone number and asked the woman to try and pass on a message. 'Can you let Leon know where his father is staying?' she begged.

Gaynor promised to try.

Now the choice was his. If Leon didn't want to see his father he had the information he needed to keep out of his way but if he did want to meet, then he knew where to find him. Satisfied that her interference had been lightly done, she began preparing the bar for opening.

On Saturday evenings at the Magpie, the entertainment was still a popular event. It was one of the busiest times and as Roma still hadn't seen either Mal or Jason, she wondered whether she ought to find an extra pair of hands. She was very tired. Dealing with her own business and running the pub meant long hours on her feet and she longed for a few days off.

Several newcomers had joined the voluntary entertainers, some old hands and a few quite talented youngsters all bursting with enthusiasm. She thought of Fletch and wondered where he was and whether his enthusiasm had yet faded. There were still the regulars, like the Finks, who staggered through the door loaded with their instruments and still drew genuine and affectionate applause for their very dated performance.

As the clock moved round towards ten thirty and there was still no sign of either Mal or Jason, she resigned herself to facing another late night: followed by the emptiness of the rambling old building once everyone had gone. If either Mal or Jason were there for the hour after the noise of the bar subsided, the silence was never so oppressive. To suddenly close the big oak door on the last of the staff and turn towards the empty room to wind down on her own, was something she hated.

It is time, she told herself as she rinsed glasses and replaced them on their shelves, that my life took another turn. There has to be something better than depending on Mal and Micky to keep me from becoming depressed. Looking after Auntie Tilly had been a far from perfect life and she knew she would probably have begun to resent it by now, but she had at least been needed, and being needed was a good substitute for being loved, she thought sadly.

The Finks were singing their last 'cowboy lament', the audience were joining in the choruses, when the door swung back on its hinges and a familiar voice said, 'He's back! Your favourite and mine! Fletch is here!'

His arms wide open, slightly down on one knee, big smile, the build-up was corny and decidedly overplayed, but the Finks put down their instruments, abandoned the final verse of their song and joined the audience in welcoming him.

He nodded towards the pianist and began to sing and Roma watched the faces smiling their pleasure at his return. Whatever level he achieved in his career, there was no doubt about his popularity at the Magpie.

He went into a spiel about mothers.

'If your wife ever throws you out, or your girlfriend tells you goodbye, go home to mother,' he said. 'She'll feed you till you burst and lend you a pair of dad's socks, and even warm them first by the fire.' He looked round at the groups of young men and spoke specially to them. 'And she always gives you a pudding. Dad says, "A pudding? On a Saturday?" and Mam comes over all steely eyed and says, "It isn't for you, it's for the boy." If anyone else called me boy, I'd thump 'em, but when Mam says it I know I'm in for a bit of *maldod*, a bit of spoiling, a bit of, "that wife of yours doesn't feed you proper."' He spoke conspiratorially as he went on, 'Never approve of wives, do they, mothers? "She's never good enough for my boy". You get bigger helpings, much more than Dad gets – and he's the poor sod who's paying for it!'

Roma was warmed by the laughter that filled the air and when he told them he was home because it was his mother's birthday, and began to sing, 'It's my mother's birthday today, I'm on my way with a lovely bouquet', she felt the sting of sentimental tears.

Not having a mother to remember, or to run to in times of trouble didn't prevent her imagining how wonderful it would have been.

The place was slow to empty, as everyone wanted a word with Fletch, and as it was Saturday she told the staff they needn't stay as the cleaners would be in in the morning. At last she threw the bolt and turned to face the empty room. Standing in the doorway of the back room, was Fletch.

Reopening the main door, she demanded he left.

'It's all right, I'm not looking for a bed for the night,' he said in mock protest. 'But I'd like to help you clear up. I understand Micky's away and you're on your own.'

'I'll manage!'

'Easier with two.'

'No need, the staff will sort it out in the morning. Mal and Jason usually help but—'

'But Susie Quinn has walked out on Mal, leaving him to cope without a manageress and Jason, well, he's comforting Susie.'

'How long have you been back!' she gasped. 'I didn't know about Susie Quinn leaving her job. Or her being – comforted – by Jason!'

'It doesn't take long. Talking to Mam, who's head of the WI grapevine, then sitting chatting to the regulars, well, I soon feel like I've never been away.'

He began clearing the tables and wiping them down as she set about washing the glasses. He made her laugh with stories about some of the people he had met and the disasters that had happened during performances. She laughed at everything he said, realising how she had missed his light-hearted fun. It wasn't long before she was aware that all the time he was looking at her, with such longing in his eyes, that she knew she would have to be strong and make sure he left as soon as the work was finished. There was danger in the air and much of it was coming from herself.

As the last ashtray was placed on the last of the cleaned tables, she thanked him, trying to sound casual, putting into her voice that unmistakable dismissal tone that said clearly, here's your coat, there's the door, it's over.

'You didn't mind me staying?' he asked.

'After the lively Saturday crowd, I'd have hated being suddenly on my own. The contrast is numbing sometimes. I'll be glad when Micky is back.'

'The crowd gave me a good welcome, didn't they?'

'You were on top form tonight, Fletch. All that stuff about when the wife throws you out and going back to mother went down well, I think many recognised the truth in it.'

'I certainly did. I've just walked out on Fiona.'

'Oh Fletch, I'm sorry. What happened?'

He told her about the lies, the imaginary pregnancy to persuade him into marriage. 'She even lied again, saying that she is now really expecting and isn't it wonderful.'

'Perhaps this time it's true.'

'I told her to get rid of it.'

'You what? After the bad time you gave me when I did just that?'

'It was different with you, Roma. I wouldn't have needed persuading to marry you.'

She moved away, afraid of the look in his eyes and the desire growing in her own mutinous body. Then he said her name, softly, with a choking sob, and she looked at him and his arms opened and went round her, making her feel wanted and loved and very much a woman. The kiss was like the culmination of years of dreaming. She was floating in sweet warm air, weightless, purposeless and so blissfully happy she wanted never to come back to earth.

His hands began to explore her body and she relaxed against him, giving herself to him completely. His lips moved against her skin and waves of passion ebbed and flowed with increasing force. They were partly undressed when the loud banging on the door startled them and made her heart race with shock.

'Don't answer it!' Fletch hissed.

'I have to.' Sanity returned and she hurriedly fastened her blouse and patted ineffectually at her hair.

'Your lipstick,' Fletch said as she moved towards the door. A glance in a mirror revealed her tell-tale smudged and swollen mouth. She ran to the kitchen, washed her face quickly and took a deep breath before walking more slowly towards the door where the banging continued at intervals.

Then the telephone shrilled and she looked at Fletch, who was leaning against the door watching her.

'Answer that, will you, Fletch?' He didn't move, his eyes staring reproachfully, and the telephone went on ringing as she threw the bolts on the door and opened it.

'Mal!'

'Sorry I couldn't come sooner but I've been stuck without help in the wine bar and –' he nodded towards the phone behind the bar – 'are you going to answer that?' Then he saw Fletch. 'I'm sorry. I seem to have interrupted something.' He went to the phone and picked it up. 'It's Leon, for you,' he said and was about to leave, when she called him back.

'Please, Mal, wait while I talk to Leon, he might have seen Micky.'

She was trembling as she spoke into the phone and she could hear the tremble affecting her voice. 'Leon, what a lovely surprise. Look, can you give me your number and wait just five minutes? I'll ring you back in less than five minutes, I promise. Please don't go away I want to talk to you but there's something I have to do first.'

'Mal,' she looked guilty as she began to explain. 'Fletch came in, and when he realised I was on my own he stayed and helped. He doesn't deserve your rudeness.'

'What happened to the staff?' he demanded.

'Well, as it was Saturday night, I'd told them they could leave early . . .'

'I see,' he said ominously.

'No, you *don't* see!' she protested.

'It's all right, Roma,' Fletch said, moving from the doorway. 'I'm off back to Mam's.' He added quietly, for Roma's ears only, 'Then I'm going home, to Fiona. To end it. I'll call in before I go back, just to say cheerio.' He didn't look at Roma or Mal as he left.

Mal followed him in less than a minute, banging the door loudly. Roma ran and locked it, slamming home the bolts and hoping Mal would hear her vehemence in the clash of the metal. After taking a few deep breaths to calm herself, she dialled the number given by Leon and was pleased to learn that he and Micky had met, had had a meal together and spent an evening talking about their disparate lives.

'I said I'd come to stay for a while,' Leon told her. 'Got a job for me? I'm seriously broke.'

'I'll find something, I promise,' she said. 'And I'll try to get rid of Thunderbirds and Action Man from your bedroom!'

She was exhausted when she replaced the receiver. It had been an effort to sound cheerful after the traumatic evening. She went to bed but her thoughts wouldn't let her sleep. Was her father right about her? Was she a wanton woman, capable of having an affair with a married man? An old-fashioned label but the meaning hadn't changed. That Fletch's wife had cheated on him to persuade him to marry her wasn't an excuse. That was as blatantly false as, 'my wife doesn't understand me'.

With no sandwich round, her books up to date and little to prepare for Monday, Sunday morning was a quiet oasis in her frantic week. Roma rose early and went to talk to Sylvia, her confidante for all but her most private thoughts.

She found her at Dorcas, dressing the window and they sat and drank coffee and discussed their various loves.

'I don't love Fletch, and I know he'd ruin everything if I let him into my life again, but last night, I was ready to go to bed with him,' Roma confessed.

'So what?' the worldly Sylvia retorted. 'I don't love Daniel but I'm going to marry him in a few months.'

'You don't love him?'

'I like him a lot and we work together really well, but there's no great passion, no conviction that he's the one and only love of my life.'

'What I feel for Fletch isn't love, I know that, but I want him. I wouldn't consider marrying him, he'd ruin everything for me, I know that too. But I'm different from you, I'd have to love someone to give up my freedom and commit myself to them.'

'Love and desire sometimes go together, but not always. Sometimes your body doesn't have the common sense to separate the two, and people marry for the wrong reasons. That sort of common sense is down to your brain, not your body and your brain isn't always sensible, is it?'

'You and Daniel have been together for a long time and there's no sign of a wedding. Why the delay? What are you waiting for?'

'I won't marry him until he sees things my way. I won't give up my career and while he still has foolish dreams about my being a house-mother, it won't work. If anyone gives up a career it should be Daniel. Love isn't really blind, Roma, at least not where I'm concerned!'

'But if you don't love him enough to make some compromises, are you and Daniel going to be happy?'

'Oh, he loves me,' Sylvia said confidently. 'For my part, I'd never let him down and I know he makes me feel good enough in bed not to want someone else. That's a good basis for marriage.'

Roma went home confused by Sylvia's attitude. Was she hoping for too much? Should she be prepared to take her fun when it was offered? No, that wasn't in her nature. Or was it? she wondered, remembering her response to Fletch's kisses. Should she settle for less than a deep, loving relationship, marry someone she didn't really love? She sighed as she unlocked the door of the pub. She was so busy there was hardly a chance of finding out!

When Micky returned on Monday, he looked relaxed and well. Although February was hardly the month for suntans, he had a better colour from his long walks and seemed fully recovered from his health problems.

'Walks, meals and lots of sleep,' he told her 'and, a meeting with Leon. It certainly made me forget my worries.'

He smiled, pushing aside the books she presented for his inspection.

'Worries? What worries?'

'You're right, Roma love, I don't have any, do I?'

Was it her imagination, or was there an edge to his voice? He had been vague about the result of the biopsy.

'Everything *is* all right, isn't it, Micky? The throat problem has been cleared up?'

'As long as you're here in the Magpie and Leon is coming for a visit, everything is perfect,' he replied.

She noted with some alarm that he hadn't answered her question.

Ten

Leon arrived, but Roma didn't invite him to work at The Kitchen.

'If you help your father, that will be the best way of helping me,' she told him and he was soon making himself useful at the pub. She was delighted when father and son seemed to get on well, laughing, teasing and getting to know each other in a way neither had expected. But she was still struggling to do all the jobs she was committed to do.

The temporary manager was dismissed as soon as Micky returned but it was exhausting dealing with her double workload and Roma was very tired. Without Ruby Gorse she knew she couldn't have coped. She decided to offer her more responsibility and a generous increase in wages.

'But first,' Roma said, 'I think we should both take a break, we've worked extra hard these past weeks and we deserve it. You take a week off, then I'll go away somewhere to unwind and when I come back we can discuss the situation and decide where we go from here.'

'Micky was right, February isn't the ideal time for a holiday, so I don't think I'll look for something in this country. I'll grab a passport and search for some sun. Thank you. I will be glad to get away.' She went to the travel agents, determined to make the best use of the surprise break, and booked an eight-day holiday in Tunisia.

Ruby was a widow with grown-up children and it was Roma who took her to the airport and waved her off. She watched her dependable friend go with some dismay, wondering how she would survive another week of the exhausting double workload without her. The thought of flying off herself soon after Ruby's return gave a boost to her spirits and she drove back to The Kitchen with revived enthusiasm.

Things would have been all right but for the sudden onset of flu. Two of the girls who did the morning shift failed to turn up and a hurried phone call to the employment exchange brought three inexperienced and rather uninterested young people who were a disappointment her. She had seen nothing of Mal and wished she could call on him. He knew so many people and would certainly have found someone to help her out.

If only Leon were free. She would have enjoyed working with him again, but she didn't even hint to Micky how difficult she was finding it to cope alone. Sylvia came with Daniel one day and Daniel offered to help for a few hours, but Roma tactfully refused. Teaching him would take longer than doing the jobs herself. She didn't want to disappoint Micky by being unable to appear at the pub each evening and somehow she struggled on. She had to admit that part of the reason for going to the Magpie when she felt more like sleeping, was in the hope of seeing Fletch, and that thought made her feel guilty and ashamed. Some quirk in her nature made this shame a cause to worry about her father's poor opinion of her. She knew him well enough to know he would be pleased to be proved right, and be able to say hadn't he told her so.

She still slept at the pub and one morning, halfway through the week, she was woken out of a deep sleep by Leon banging on her door. At once she thought Micky was ill and she leapt out of bed in a panic. Then a glance at her clock increased the panic and she gave a shriek of dismay. She had overslept.

'I went down for a drink and could see you weren't up,' Leon said.

'Thank goodness you did! I'd have been there till opening time!'

The cook and her assistant were banging on the door waiting to begin making the pasties when she drove up. It was a bad start to a bad day: one of the mini-vans broke down halfway through its delivery round and she had to leave the work she was doing and go and rescue the two people and the load. Doing the rest of the round in her van, meant the morning had gone and she still had the accounts to settle and the ordering to do. Why did I choose this week to let Ruby go away, she groaned to herself.

It was just after eleven o'clock that evening when she excused herself from staying any longer at the pub and went back to The Kitchen. Not to sleep, but to work. She didn't like leaving Micky to clear up, he looked so tired, but there were two girls and Leon to help, and she really had to finish her day's routine or tomorrow would be worse than today had been.

She let herself in and ran upstairs to change into her overalls. It was as she was coming down the stairs from the flat that she thought she heard water running. At first she thought it was rain, then she realised it was inside and gave a groan of disbelief. The kitchen floor was flooded and the leak, supposedly repaired by Fletch, was oozing water at an alarming rate. She shut the water off at the stopcock and began phoning emergency plumbers. She didn't phone Micky. He would have come to help, and she didn't think he was well enough, so she struggled on alone. It was after one a.m. before a plumber finally came and two a.m. before she had paid his startlingly high bill and begun clearing up.

Mal walked past The Kitchen on his way to his car at midnight, having decided to go for a drive before bed. He saw the light, but didn't investigate. Finding her with Fletch after hours at the Magpie, he guessed this would be more of the same. Seeing them that evening had convinced him that

Roma would never turn to him. Fletch's attraction was too strong. Bitterly he thought that even the fact that Fletch was married and, he presumed, had a child on the way, wasn't sufficient to keep them apart.

Roma phoned Fletch, hoping it would be he who answered and the call wouldn't disturb his parents. Sleepily he told her he was catching the early train and couldn't come. The two girls who came early were still both stricken with flu and when she rang one of the temps and begged for their help she was told succinctly to 'get lost'.

At five a.m. she was boiling eggs, cutting up salads, and wondering when her staff would arrive. At six she rang a sandwich-fillings firm and tried to leave a message on the answerphone asking them to deliver an order as early as possible. It would save precious time buying ready-made fillings. The crackling sound gave her some doubts that the message would be received. She would have to go round there as soon as someone came to take over what she was doing. What a day!

At six fifteen there was a knock at the door, and she sighed with relief. At least the cook was on time. It was Mal.

'Is everything all right?' he asked.

'I've been here all night,' she said, and burst into tears.

Mal phoned the sandwich-fillings company and collected an order, then he helped her finish the sandwiches and prepare the pastry for the pasties. If they weren't the usual choices, there were sufficient to please most. The cook still hadn't arrived and, bleary-eyed, Roma looked through her files to see if there was someone else she could ask. But before she could dial the first number the cook walked in with her assistant – who depended on her for a lift – and confessed that she had slept through the alarm. But as the fillings and the pastry were already prepared, she got the first batch of pasties and sausage rolls in the oven within half an hour. By ten o'clock the van was filled ready to set off on the first round.

'I'll drive,' Mal said to Roma, 'you might fall asleep halfway through. Just tell me where we're going and do the deliveries.'

Roma was so tired her face felt puffy and her eyes seemed to be filled with sand. She had worked all the previous day from five thirty and all through the night.

'You'll have to get bigger premises,' Mal said as she picked up the basket for her last call of the day. 'You need more staff – reliable staff – not be dependent on finding last-minute temporary replacements who don't know what they're doing, and who don't care.'

'They do their best,' she said defensively.

'I'm sure they do, but knowing it's only for a week at most, how can they care?'

She knew he was right. She had been playing with the idea of the business, treating it like a hobby and it had outstripped her ambition by miles. She needed to take a good long look at what she was doing and build a sound base for further development.

'I think I'll make Ruby a partner,' she said sleepily.

'Why not me as well? I could put money in, be a sleeping partner, and it would enable you to get a good premises and the best equipment.'

Her eyes had been drooping, but now they opened wide. 'Do you mean that, Mal?'

'I think it would work – strictly on a business level,' he said, and she knew that he was still angry and hurt at her behaviour with Fletch.

'Fletch has gone back to Fiona,' she said, guessing his thoughts. 'It was only a tiff between them and he was talking it through with me,' she lied, then told him about Fiona's dishonesty in tricking Fletch into marriage.

'It's better than he deserves.'

When the deliveries were completed and the remaining food packed into trays to take to the pub, Mal told her to go to bed. 'Sleep all day, you need it.'

'But I can't, I—' she began to protest.

'Take the time to think about my offer. There are machines available that would make your life easier. Have you thought of adding doughnuts to your selection? There's a machine that makes them three dozen at a time.' Seeing her interested look he patted her shoulder and added, 'Don't think about it too hard, just get some rest and we'll discuss it later. I'll take these sandwiches and I'll help Micky in the bar this evening. Just sleep.'

'How can you do that? You have your own bar to run?'

'I'm selling up and the prospective owners are spending the evening seeing how it works and whether they like the business.'

'That's an odd thing to do,' she remarked. 'Can you trust them?'

'Oh, yes. It's Susie Quinn and Jason.'

At the end of the week Leon told Micky he was moving on.

'I have someone to see, and Joe and I promised to meet them in Salisbury,' he explained.

'You'll be back one day?' Micky asked, trying to hide his disappointment.

'I'm coming back, Dad. Probably quite soon.'

When Roma drove him to the coach station he said, 'Dad isn't bad, is he?'

Misunderstanding she said at once, 'Oh, he's much better now. That holiday did him good and seeing you helped too.'

Leon laughed. 'I mean he's not bad, he's a good bloke. I like him.'

'I'm glad.'

Roma's relief when Ruby returned was immense. She listened as her friend told her about the holiday and then admitted she had not booked one for herself.

'I feel better now,' she said untruthfully. 'Besides, I can't go away just now. Mal and I are looking at new premises, and I want you in on it. Your comments will be useful. We work together well and I hope a closer partnership will develop once we get rid of our shoe-string attitude.'

Ruby smiled. 'What about a new name? Perfection Pantry?'

'Mm. Sounds good. We'll see what Mal thinks, shall we?'

'I'd love to help set it up. Where do we start?'

Finding premises wasn't easy; with his contacts, Mal found several for them to look at, but it was March before they were satisfied that they had the best possible building. It had been a small factory making electrical goods, but the owners had cleared it completely and it was in excellent condition. The space was divided into a main room for the kitchen and several smaller rooms, which Roma and Ruby decided would make preparations rooms, a staff room and a good-sized office.

They went to see what equipment was available to help them and ordered a machine to make doughnuts and one to take most of the work out of pastry-making. They also decided on a larger dishwasher, a second oven and racks on which to stack the baking trays. It was very exciting.

Selling The Kitchen created a problem that Roma hadn't immediately thought of. She would lose her flat.

'Buy a house, you can afford it,' Mal suggested.

'You can always live here,' Micky offered.

With her new confidence she decided on buying a house.

Leon came home again at Easter and immediately became involved in helping her to find somewhere. He and Mal went to several to decide whether they were worth her taking a look, cutting down on her making wasted journeys, and what might have been a chore became a pleasant exercise.

Micky seemed brighter when his son was there and secretly admitted to Roma that he hoped he would stay, but after ten days, by which time Roma had chosen her new home, Leon's rucksack was filled and he said his goodbyes once more.

The property she had chosen was not far from the Magpie and two miles from the new kitchen premises, which they had named Perfection Pantry, with Mal's approval. It was a semi, built between the wars and had been maintained extremely well; all she needed to do was choose her curtains and carpets and move in. This had been a consideration in her selection of the property because she had little time to attend to building work and decorating.

It was the end of April 1983, when she completed on the purchase of the factory, and two weeks later she moved into her house. Longing for a few days to relax and settle in, she arranged for Ruby to manage without her and looked forward to getting to know her new house. Two days later, her father turned up and demanded she offer him a home.

'My wife has left me and taken our children,' he said by way of explanation.

'I'm sorry, but I run a business and I don't want a lodger. I need a place where I can come and go as I please without worrying about meals and the extra work an extra person would involve.'

She was angry. How dare he expect to walk back into her life and demand she help him? Where had he been when *she* had needed someone? It was hypocritical to say the least.

The house was filled with boxes waiting to be unpacked and in her frustration she began to open them and take out the contents. The result, after an hour of frantic effort, was a room filled with piles of objects without a place to store them. Henry Powell sat in the one chair relieved of its plastic cover and watched in silence.

'I have to go to the Magpie,' she said at four o'clock. It was far too early but she had to get out, get away from this strange, disapproving man.

'You should stay away from that place,' he said. 'It's an evil place run by an evil man.'

'I love it,' she said defiantly. 'I love the whole business; the atmosphere, the friendliness and I love Micky and his son.'

'His son? You mean Leon? I thought he'd left his father and disappeared?'

'He comes to visit,' she said, without explaining how rarely that happened.

'I won't have you helping Micky Richards. He's evil I tell you.'

'So am I, according to you,' she retorted. 'At least, until you needed a home. Well, I'm sorry . . .' she wasn't sure what to call him. How could she call him father or dad? 'I don't have to listen to your opinion. I've been on my own since Auntie Tilly died and I've survived quite well. I'm capable of making my own decisions.' She spoke quietly and calmly. 'Now, if you'll excuse me, I have to go.' She handed him his coat and stood, jingling her keys, waiting for him to leave.

'Your aunt left you the money to get started on this business of yours. You owe it to me to provide me with a home.'

'What money?'

'Tilly had a house and a good bank balance.'

'She did. But she didn't leave any of it to me.'

'Liar!'

She stared at him wide eyed with shock. 'How dare you call me a liar! She left all her money to a charity for rehousing unwanted animals.' She frowned. So that was why he had sought her out. He thought she had inherited money and property! 'She left me nothing,' she said slowly and deliberately. 'Nothing. I built my business by my own efforts and with help from Micky.'

He grabbed his coat from her and went out, muttering, 'Liar, cheat. Evil. Evil.'

She closed and locked the door after him and stood for a long time until she calmed down. Then she phoned Micky.

'Micky, I know I sound pathetic, but will you come and fetch me? My father's been here and, well, I'm a bit edgy.'

'On my way, love,' Micky replied.

Although outraged by his attitude towards her and more than a little frightened by his odd behaviour, there was still a part of Roma who was a child, wanting her father's approval.

Since seeing him when he had turned up with Catrin and Melanie, her step-sisters, Roma's thoughts had twisted from confusion to a need to understand, from clear dislike to an unclear curiosity, from hatred to a distantly recognised need for him to love her.

'Don't take him in, he's unbalanced and there's no knowing what he'll do,' Micky warned her. 'Promise me you won't let him over the doorstep if he calls again. Call me or Mal or the police, if necessary, but don't let him in.'

'I can't promise that, Micky. He *is* my father.'

'No he isn't! A father loves and protects his child. What has he ever done for you except tear away any confidence you've built? What man can call himself a father when he does nothing but try to destroy his child?' Micky spoke with an anger she had never seen in him before.

'I know all that, Micky,' she tried to explain. 'But I've never had a family, only Auntie Tilly. It's tempting to think he might learn to at least like me, give me a chance to get to know him and my step-sisters.'

That night she wrote to her father care of the hotel where he had told her he had been staying, offering a short stay while he sorted out something permanent.

A few days later, Micky told her, 'I'm sorry if I'm interfering, Roma love, but I got in touch with your step-mother, Morfedd. She told me your father is forbidden to see the girls except when there's a social worker present. Besides being violent towards his wife he's teaching those little girls that everyone is evil and forbids them to make friends. I really don't think you should see him again. Promise me you won't let him into the house. I'll make sure he stays out of here. If he calls, phone me or Mal and we'll come straight away. Better still, get someone to stay with you until he's given up and gone away.'

'I can't,' she said. 'I've told him he can stay for two weeks while he finds something permanent.'

'Fine, fine,' Micky said tensely. 'Then you come here. Your room is always ready for you. Stay here until he's gone, and make sure you tell him exactly when he has to leave. Right?'

She agreed although it was disappointing not to settle into her new home and have the pleasure of going back there every evening. But she did as Micky advised and returned to the back bedroom of the Magpie.

It wasn't as easy as they had imagined to find experienced and interested staff. They tried several girls and a couple of young men, but even those who seemed enthusiastic at first, failed to survive more than a couple of weeks. In desperation, Roma placed larger advertisements in local papers and in shop windows and even on the bar of the Magpie.

Fletch turned up one Saturday evening and Roma felt the usual tremble of excitement. Micky left what he was doing and came to serve him. When Fletch saw the notice, he asked, 'Will I do?'

Micky gave a snort of disapproval and moved off with a glance of amusement at Roma.

'No entertainers or fly-by-nights need apply,' she said flippantly. 'I want someone utterly reliable. Someone committed to staying and helping us build the business.'

'I'm serious, Roma,' he said, when Micky had reluctantly left the bar to clear a few tables. 'I've given up on showbusiness, for good. Fiona can't work because of the baby coming and I'm desperate to find a career I can give myself wholeheartedly to.'

He seemed sincere. Then she imagined working with him and was afraid of what might happen, so she shook her head. 'Sorry, Fletch.'

'At least give me an interview. Is Ruby still working with you? She's a good judge. If I can convince her of my genuine need for a steady job, will you give me a trial?' He smiled at her and added, 'Everyone has to grow up sometime, Roma. Even me. I owe it to Fiona and our child to stay loyal and bring in a regular wage. I'm really committed to her and the baby now.'

'Ruby, Mal and I are partners,' she explained. 'I leave most of the hiring and firing to Ruby.'

'Then you'll arrange an interview?'

'She's got too much sense for that, Fletch, so forget it,' Micky said, returning with empty glasses.

Next morning, Fletch went to Perfection Pantry and offered his services as preparation assistant.

'Where is your wife?' was Ruby's first question.

'Still in London, I'm afraid,' Fletch looked suitably sad. 'She won't come here until I have a proper job, and somewhere for us to live. I need this job, Ruby. I'll never give you cause to complain. My marriage depends on it.'

After a long discussion with Roma, Ruby decided that as they would be in serious difficulties unless they found help soon, they should give Fletch a month's trial.

'After all, there's no one else on the horizon at present,' Ruby reminded Roma.

Mal demanded to know when he, as a shareholder, was going to be involved in any decisions.

'Employing staff is Ruby's area of responsibility,' Roma protested. 'When your expertise is needed, you'll be able to make decisions. If we all have to go over each other's work, we'll never get anything done, will we?'

'Watch him!' he warned.

* * *

Micky went with Roma to her house to make sure her father was not staying beyond the agreed time. But Henry had gone and had left the house clean and neat. Roma was concerned to notice he had left a few belongings behind: clothes and some books, mostly religious tomes including a well-used Bible.

On Micky's recommendation she had the locks changed on the doors and made sure the windows were secure, but she still slept fitfully for a few nights, imagining him coming back into the house. She had not lived there long enough to get used to its strangeness before being forced back to the Magpie and now she didn't feel easy there. She wasn't even sure she still liked it.

Ruby offered to come and stay for a few nights and Roma gratefully accepted. Together they unpacked the last of the dreaded boxes, discarding much of what Roma had once thought important, and finding places for her few treasures.

They invited other members of staff for drinks, and Roma even found time to meet her neighbours and share an evening with them. When Ruby went back to her own home, Roma felt comfortable and content. For the first time she had a place she had chosen and furnished to represent her personal taste, a base that mirrored her, Roma Powell. There was no longer any need to search desperately for people whom she could pretend might love her. She was complete. Sighing contentedly she began planning the garden she would plant in the spring.

Leon came home again during the autumn and told his father he would be staying for a few weeks. He didn't work with Roma but helped his father in the pub. Young and strong, he was soon dealing with the cellar work, carrying bottles up and dealing with the deliveries when the cellar had to be rearranged to make sure the stock was rotated correctly.

After a couple of weeks had passed, he asked Roma to go for a walk with him. On a Sunday afternoon in early October, they set off to walk round the cliffs, their lunch in Leon's rucksack and binoculars and a camera in hers.

They chatted cheerfully for the first hour, Roma happy to be with him, Leon obviously enjoying her company. He knew many of the wild flowers and pointed out the different birds that lived on the cliffs and in the fields beyond. Roma felt tension easing away from her.

They sat amid the rocky foundation of the cliffs on a sandy beach and ate their lunch. Relaxing in the welcome sun of that late-autumn day Roma thought about her life and decided she was as content as she could hope to be. Then Leon spoilt it by saying something she had been pretending not to notice.

'Dad's ill, isn't he?' Leon said.

'I—'

'No fairy stories, eh?' he said as she began to make up some reassuring reply.

'I think his throat is still giving him trouble.'

'It's worse than when I saw him at Easter.'

'Is that why you're staying longer than usual?'

'I wish he'd talk to me.'

'I think he's afraid you'll stay out of sympathy and he'd hate that.'

'I'll stay because I like him.'

'I'm glad – for both of you.'

'I've an appointment with the doctor tomorrow. I want to find out what the trouble is. If there's treatment, why isn't he getting it?'

'He had an operation early in the year to remove a constriction in his throat.'

'I know, and when he was in Devon he looked really well. But what if it's something they couldn't cure?'

'Cancer you mean? I'd have thought there'd be more signs by now. Perhaps he's just too old to work so hard. Running the pub isn't easy. If he retired he might pick up, get strong again.'

'Fairy stories, Roma,' Leon said, standing up and putting on his rucksack. 'Fairy stories.'

* * *

At work the following morning there was a phone call for Fletch. It was Fiona's mother telling him the baby had arrived, a boy, whom they were going to name Laurence Olivier Morgan.

'I'll have to go to her, Roma,' Fletch said, 'but I won't stay away long, I'll be back and you'll be able to rely on me utterly. I have to work now and provide for him.'

He looked excited and she watched as he hurried off, and hoped that he meant what he said about supporting his wife and their child.

Fletch was back after three days, but things began to go wrong with his dedicated dad act. He was often late and he usually made sure it was a morning when he knew Roma would be there to cover for him. Nothing was said, but he knew she would make excuses for him. Occasionally he missed shifts altogether and then he complained about being ill; suffering a migraine was the usual excuse. That, or a bad back that made it impossible to get out of bed.

Roma thought he was going to see Fiona and the baby and even helped by rearranging the staff's hours to make it convenient for him to go home for a long weekend. One weekend he didn't get back until Tuesday, which meant an all-night session for her, and this time Roma couldn't ask either Mal or Ruby to help. The problem had been created by her and she had to deal with it.

She hadn't said anything to Mal, and Ruby – taking her cue from her – said nothing either. But both women knew something had to be done.

'I think he's back on the circuit,' Ruby said.

'He can't be. He promised he'd finished with all that.'

'Your friends the Finks saw him when they did a tour of the clubs around Swindon way.'

'Why am I such a fool where he's concerned, Ruby?' Roma groaned. Ruby just shrugged and said nothing.

'I suppose it's easy for him to accept bookings and the temptation of just one more try is too much for him. We don't often have to work in the evenings and that's when these things happen. It's just that late nights and early mornings aren't a good combination.'

'He'd find a way whatever the hours. It's like a drug, he can't give it up.'

'Perhaps they need the extra money.'

'If it wasn't money he'd find another reason. Being adored might be high on his list!' Ruby remarked cynically. 'He won't be young and handsome for ever.'

Now Mal had sold Parry's Place he was concentrating on property development. He unfolded his plans to Roma and Micky one evening after the Magpie had closed.

'I've bought a piece of land on which I have permission to build four properties. When they are sold, I'll buy more land build six and after those, who knows?'

'There's building land at the back of the Magpie,' Micky said. 'I hoped one day that young Leon might build there.'

'Perhaps he still might?'

'Too late.' Micky shook his head.

'What d'you mean, Micky?' Roma said with a glance of alarm at Mal. 'Leon's hardly too old to be dismissed as a potential house builder.'

'Leon isn't, but I'm too old to help him,' Micky said.

Micky was ill the following day. A serious cough and what seemed like the symptoms of a cold. Roma reassured herself that incubating a heavy cold and sore throat had been the reason for his depression. If she knew she was pretending, she couldn't bring herself to admit it, even to Mal.

She made Micky stay in bed, and called the doctor. She wasn't told his diagnosis but saw that he had left a prescription. Micky put it in an envelope and sealed it before asking her to take it to the chemist to have it filled. The chemist sealed it for her to bring back. It was all very worrying.

* * *

Mal found out about Fletch's unreliability from the younger members of Roma's staff. One of them announced he was leaving and Mal happened to be there when Ruby asked him why.

'Him, skiving while we have extra to do, that's why,' the boy complained, and a few enquiries soon revealed the cover-up.

'How long are we going to pay Fletch for work done by other people?' Mal demanded when he met Roma later that day.

'What d'you mean?' she asked.

'Fletch, that's what I mean. I suppose this is not my area of responsibility either?'

'I feel sorry for Fiona. He needs the money for her and I didn't know until last week that he was back doing his act and getting in too late to get up for work.'

'He hasn't been with Fiona. He hasn't seen her since three days after the baby was born.'

'What? Then where is he going?'

'He's staying with his long-suffering parents.'

'He sends Fiona money each week. He told me that.'

'I've spoken to his parents and it's rot! He's scrounging from them and on top of that they've had a letter from Fiona begging them to help her. She's taken as much as she can from her own parents and Fletch has contributed nothing, not even his presence! Roma! Wake up to the man!'

'I'll talk to him, make sure he does his share.'

'And in the meantime we let a capable and honest young man leave?'

'I'll talk to him too. Right?' She glared at him and he shrugged and walked away.

Eleven

Roma wondered why Sylvia and Daniel had yet to find a house, when they had made their intention to do so known so long ago. They had not yet made a date for their wedding either and when they called at the Magpie one evening she asked them why.

'There's no hurry, is there, Danny?' Sylvia said vaguely, and Daniel agreed, but with less conviction Roma thought.

'We're both happy enough, being engaged and planning the house we'll one day be able to afford,' he said, but Roma had the impression that the decision to wait was not his.

'It's better not to rush into buying a small semi if by waiting we can buy a super deluxe house in a decent area, something we both really want.' Sylvia covered her face with her hands in dismay and added quickly. 'Sorry, Roma. I wasn't criticising you for choosing a semi, for you on your own it's a perfect choice. It's just that we are both working hard to get something permanent, a place where we can build a home, put down roots, knowing we won't ever have to move.'

When Daniel went to order drinks, Sylvia whispered to her friend, 'Truth is, Roma, business excites me more than buying a house and choosing carpets and curtains. I did all that with my doll's house when I was seven!'

'I want both, but it's difficult to spare the time for a private life when there's work to be done,' Roma agreed, 'and I find building a business very satisfying too. But surely Daniel is worth finding some time for?'

She watched Sylvia through the rest of their stay and wondered if the romance was cooling and whether they would ever get to the altar or the register office to make their vows.

Although she had no idea where he was living, Roma knew her father was not far away. He often stood outside her house when she closed the curtains at night. He could sometimes be seen in the shadows near the Magpie and would turn his head slowly to watch her getting into her car. He moved away when she saw him, never said anything, and she began to feel quite spooked.

'I'll have a word,' Micky said, but whenever he opened the door to look for him, the man had vanished.

Micky was very tired and he spent less and less time in the bar. Leon had stayed on and between them he and Roma managed.

'What did the doctor tell you?' Roma asked after Leon had been to see him.

'Nothing specific, but what he did say makes me think something is seriously wrong with Dad.'

'I know something's wrong, but why doesn't he tell us?'

'Pretending it isn't happening is the way some people deal with things,' Leon replied.

'And you don't want to ask him and make him face it?'

'I've given him opportunities but he hasn't taken them. We have to wait until he's ready to talk.'

Fletch was still working for Roma and although he was unreliable she paid him his full wage, much to Ruby's disapproval.

'I know you say it's for his wife and the baby, Roma, but how much of it d'you think the poor girl sees?'

'I have to hope she gets enough.'

'Sack him. It isn't your problem and you won't change Fletch however much you pretend. He's a self-centered dreamer, nothing is more important than his ambition. He really thinks his retirement from the stage would be a loss to the world.'

'I wish I had some of that confidence.' Roma laughed. 'I'm too easily persuaded of the opposite.'

'You're doing a lot for the town. Employing people, providing a service that's appreciated by your customers.'

'And,' Roma said, neatly changing the subject, 'and, I have an idea for further expansion.'

'Tell me!'

'More and more people are buying microwave ovens and I want to experiment with the idea of providing ready-to-heat meals. What d'you think?'

'If it takes off it could be a real money-spinner and even if it doesn't, you still might persuade some of the larger offices and shops to buy one and give their staff the choice of a hot meal each day. Canteens are gradually being fazed out and I think this is the right time to try it.'

They talked enthusiastically about the project, made lists of people they needed to advise them, and even experimented with a few recipes containing rice and pasta. Roma was excited when she went to the pub that evening, impatient to tell Micky about her idea.

She took a couple of the meals they had made up for him to try. He ate so little, and she had noticed that he preferred easy-to-swallow food. So it was no surprise when he chose minced chicken and vegetables in a creamy sauce, with rice. To her delight, he ate more than half of it and approved of her idea whole-heartedly.

'A winner, Roma love,' he said. 'I think you're amazing and if you want any help getting it off the ground, just ask.'

'You take it easy and rest, get well, that's the best way you can help me.'

'I'm all right, it's just blues at the approach of another winter. I couldn't be happier, with you and Leon here with me.'

But Roma wasn't satisfied. She had seen him coming out of his bathroom one day and had been shocked at the weight he had lost. The surprising thing was that he looked quite well. No one but his closest friends noticed that anything was amiss. She said nothing. Leon was right, they had to let him deal with it in his own way. She decided to make up several of the new microwave meals and tell him she needed his opinion; perhaps that would persuade him to eat a little more.

Fletch was furious. A telephone call had offered a five-minute stand-up comedy slot followed by a song. It was seventeen miles away and he hadn't appeared at the venue before. He wanted it badly, but he was working that evening and, as it was an eleven-fifteen spot and he'd been given such short notice, there wasn't much hope of getting there – none at all if he finished his shift, and very little if he sloped off early. But he had to try. Just his luck to have one of the rare evening shifts.

Cheating on the evening's work he had been given, he ran to the car, hurried back to his parents' house and changed into his stage clothes. Then his car wouldn't start. He needed this job so badly that when his father refused to lend him his car he lost his temper.

Running down the street, intending to ask Roma officially for the time off and the loan of one of the firm's vans, he saw a woman getting out of a large Rover. Beautiful! She didn't stop to lock it and, unbelievably, she left the keys in the ignition. She was probably delivering Avon or something and was sure to chat for a while. He slid into the driving seat and with his foot hard down, he drove away.

He hadn't driven that model before and his eyes drifted across the dials as he headed out of town. There was so little time. All he thought of was the low level of the petrol tank gauge. Would it get him there?

* * *

The pub was quiet that evening and Roma stood near the bar working out a few more recipes ready to discuss with the consultant nutritionist the following day. When she drove home, her mind was on the new project. The journey was so automatic she hardly needed to think. As she approached the house she began to look out for her father. Her mind was not on the road because nervousness had her searching the shadows for the tall, silent figure.

The other car came hurtling towards her in a blur.

Both cars skidded across the road and up on to the kerb, where Roma's car tipped on to its side and continued to slide. The screech of distorting metal filled Fletch's ears and went on and on and on. Roma's car ploughed through the low wall of the garden on the other side of the pavement and ended up in the front garden. Fletch had no idea that it was Roma who he had crashed into and, when his car stopped, his first and only thought was to get out and away from the scene. He pushed and pulled at his door, which had jammed. Kicking and struggling, he failed to open it and began to panic. He couldn't get out! He'd be found here in a stolen car having caused an accident! Climbing into the back seat he tried to open the back door but that was stuck fast. Then he managed to roll down a back window and slid out of it. Staggering a little at first, his legs weak with shock, he ran back the way he had come.

He hurried home, using side streets and back lanes. Trying to speak calmly he asked his father one more time to lend him his car, and this time he agreed. Taking a different route to avoid the scene of the accident, he drove at a furious speed to his appointment and gave one of his best performances; the danger he had faced and fear of discovery giving him an extra edge.

Roma sat in the damaged car for several minutes before trying to move. She thought her arm was broken because every time she tried to lift it, the pain made her scream through clenched teeth. She was aware of a ticking sound and realised it was made by leaking petrol or water.

A motorist stopped and, seeing her in the wreckage, tried to pull her free. When he couldn't, he ran first to the house but there was no reply, then he went to the corner, where there was a telephone box, and dialled 999.

The first Mal knew of the accident was when Roma phoned him from the hospital. He went straight there.

'Roma!' He ran into the room where she lay and tried unsuccessfully to hug her. She was bandaged and badly bruised and he was afraid to touch her.

'My darling girl, what happened?'

'I don't know, Mal. All I remember was approaching the crossroads and then a sound like an explosion and the car was on its side and I was being pushed along by something I couldn't see.'

She felt weepy and somehow he found a place on her shoulders where he could put a hand and he slowly stroked her face.

'The police say the other driver must have been driving like a bat out of hell,' she said, trying to smile. 'But I must have been dreaming not to see or hear him.'

'The car was stolen and the driver ran off, I understand,' Mal said. 'There was a telephone box only yards away and he didn't bother to phone 999. I hope they catch him. He must have been driving like a maniac!'

'Perhaps I was inattentive too. I was thinking about microwave meals!'

When Leon arrived and saw her nursing a broken arm, he grinned.

'What's the matter? Jealous of the attention I got with mine?' he teased.

There were two witnesses to Fletch stealing the car. One of them was Roma's father, who had been making his way to Roma's house when he saw Fletch approaching. He had melted into a gateway and watched as the woman got out of the Rover and the man got in and drove off. He recognised Fletch easily.

'Evil,' he muttered as he made his way to where he could see Roma arriving home and note the disgustingly late hour. He waited until three and decided that she was sleeping with a man. Everything proved him right, she was evil. Micky Richards had taught her well.

Fletch called on Roma the following morning. He took flowers, orange juice and some chocolates. He was full of concern.

It had been a shock to realise that the accident he had run away from had involved Roma, but he soon convinced himself that accidents did happen and he could only be partly to blame.

He had hardly sat down and reached for her hand before a police constable asked to talk to him. 'Can we talk here, officer?' he asked. 'I don't want to leave Roma just yet. It's been such a shock you see.'

'Where were you last night between the hours of seven and ten, sir?'

'On my way to a gig,' he said, looking apologetically at Roma. 'Sorry love, but it was one I couldn't turn down.' He smiled at the constable. 'I should have been working, see, but Roma understands my ambitious struggles, don't you, love?'

'And you saw nothing?'

'No. I was using my father's car. I was late and I didn't see anything. Besides, I drove a different way. I didn't pass the crossroads.'

'Can you tell me why you didn't go by a direct route when you were in a hurry to get to your booking?'

Fletch looked at Roma again with an apologetic smile. 'I should have been working and I didn't want to bump into my boss.

* * *

The second witness to the accident in which Roma was hurt was Richie Talbot. He had been walking home and had seen Fletch by the car's interior light as he got into the Rover.

'Knew it was him and wondered where he was going. Drove off like a bat out of 'ell, he did.' The constable thanked him, and went to talk to Fletch again.

Pleading his innocence, Fletch spent several hours under questioning before admitting that he had stolen the car.

'But I didn't cause the accident,' he insisted. 'I drove it as far as the phone box and left it there. I tried to phone Roma to ask to borrow a van but there was no reply. Desperate I was, I had less than fifty minutes to find a car and get there. So, I left the car, feeling a bit ashamed, mind, and ran back to my father and pleaded for him to help. He agreed, and lent me his car and I got there just in time.'

Roma was allowed out of hospital the next day. She went straight to see Ruby.

'With an arm in plaster I can't do much,' she said, 'but I can deal with the new meals project. And I'll get the paperwork so up to date we'll amaze ourselves with our efficiency.'

'Why don't you spend a few days helping Micky? We can manage here,' Ruby said. 'Or, better still, what about that holiday you were planning last January? When are you taking that?'

'Soon,' Roma promised. The thought was tempting, but how could she leave Micky and Leon now?

Mal spent extra time at the pub and Roma began to rely on him to do much of the work. Micky still opened up and spent a lot of time in the bar, where he joined in the chatter and laughter, appearing to be well. It was when he went into the back room to relax that he showed how he was really feeling. Roma would sit with him and, while ignoring the fact he was ill, try to make him comfortable. Leon worked with Mal, but they never spoke about the failing health of his father.

Fletch had been charged with stealing a car, and it was clear from the attitude of the police that they hadn't completely ruled out his involvement in the accident. He pleaded guilty and had dark thoughts about the possibility of the extra charges of reckless driving and leaving the scene of an accident. He convinced himself that he was reasonably safe. Roma hadn't seen the car and was sure to be confused about the whole thing.

One evening Jason and Susie came to the Magpie. Jason asked Roma how she was coping with her arm in plaster, and offered to help if needed.

'I can pull a pint,' he assured her, 'and I'm a dab hand at washing glasses. Just call me if you need me.'

'Call and I'll come running!' Susie sneered. 'That's all she has to do, isn't it?'

'Susie?' Mal frowned. 'What's the matter? You and Roma haven't quarrelled, have you?'

Susie began shouting at Roma, accusing her of heaping the blame for the accident on Fletch when she was really its cause. Jason looked alarmed and tried to persuade her to leave and Mal demanded to know what she was talking about.

'Roma was with Fletch that night. They were fooling about, driving like idiots and the accident happened because of her. Then she tries to blame it on Fletch. The pair of them, carrying on while his wife is at home looking after his child. She's a disgrace.'

Mal was alarmed at how bitter Susie was, and how much she disliked Roma.

'She wanted Fletch and she took him. His being married to a young girl he'd got pregnant didn't matter to her. She thrives on excitement. Being in the car, chasing each other along the road, the risk, the danger, it's what she needs.'

'This is nonsense, Susie,' Mal said sharply. 'You're talking utter rubbish. Take her home, Jason, please.'

'Nonsense is it? She took you away from me, didn't she? She only has to look helpless and every man she fancies goes to her like fish on a line. Fletch offers irresistible excitement. She'll never let him go.'

Jason took her back to her flat and begged her not to repeat her outburst.

'The police know how it happened and it wasn't as you describe it,' he said firmly. 'There's no point upsetting Roma or Mal because you hope that it involved Roma more than Fletch!'

'Mal is besotted! He needs shaking out of it.'

'Maybe, but it's not for us to decide.'

He held her while she calmed down and she said, 'Sorry Jason. I was just getting Mal out of my system I suppose.'

'Not before time,' he murmured as he kissed her.

With her father ominously present on the periphery of her life Roma often stayed at the Magpie, avoiding going home to see him silently watching her. During this time she rarely gave a thought to her step-mother or her two half-sisters, so it was a surprise therefore one evening to receive a visit from Morfedd and her daughters.

The second Mrs Henry Powell walked in close behind Richie Talbot, the girls cowering behind her nervously.

Roma was unsure how to address her. What title should she use? Mother? Step-mother? Or her Christian name? She settled for, 'Hello! This is a surprise. Would you like a drink? Would the girls like some crisps?' She was completely thrown. Should she be formal or friendly? Welcoming or cold? Did this visit mean trouble? Her smile felt stiff and trembly as she waited for Morfedd to speak.

'Can we go somewhere private?' Morfedd eventually asked.

Roma explained briefly to Micky and took her visitors into the back room.

'Can you tell me where my husband is? He hasn't been seen and, although he's been forbidden to visit the children except when accompanied, I do need to talk to him.'

'He's staying round here but I don't know where,' Roma told her. 'He . . .' she hesitated, trying to word it carefully. 'I sometimes see him when I go home from here at night, but I've no idea where you'd find him. All I can do is ask him to phone you if I get a chance to talk to him.'

'What d'you mean, have a chance to talk? You said you see him often when you go home?'

'He's – well, to be honest he hovers around, watching, but never approaches me. When I've tried to speak to him, to ask him what he wants, he turns and hurries off. To be perfectly honest, he frightens me a bit.'

'Henry wouldn't harm anyone,' Morfedd said confidently. 'His anger was short-lived and only towards me.'

Roma wondered at the truth of this when the courts had forbidden him to see the children without a chaperone.

'I do think he's having some sort of breakdown though,' Morfedd went on. 'He seems to believe you have the devil in you. He talks a lot about the devil, and the wickedness of women.' She looked at Roma and added, 'He hasn't been paying the mortgage you see, and if we don't get something sorted very soon, we'll lose our house. I don't think he understands how near we are to being homeless.'

'Haven't you tried to explain?'

'He hasn't been near us for weeks and the financial problems began months ago without my knowing.'

Roma went to the bar, gave Micky and Mal a brief update on the conversation and went back into the room with sandwiches and lemonade.

'The bar is filling up,' she said. 'I'll have to go and help. Stay here and eat and I'll pop back when I get a chance.'

After an hour, Morfedd asked her to phone for a taxi and took the girls home.

Mal insisted on driving Roma home that night, and when they reached her house, she saw her father standing against the hedge across the road. She got out of the car and ran towards him, but he turned away and with long, impatient strides disappeared into someone's garden.

'Dad!' she called. 'Please come back. Morfedd is in trouble. She's going to lose the house if you don't go back and sort things out. They'll be homeless! Dad!' But there was no sign he had heard.

Mal parked the car and came to join her. He ran through the garden into which Henry had disappeared but found no sign of him.

'I wish you'd come back and stay at my flat tonight,' he said. 'I know Morfedd said he isn't a violent man, but there's more than one way to be violent. And anyway, I don't think anyone can be certain about another person's potential behaviour.'

'Are you thinking about my mother's death?'

'No, of course not.' Mal tried to sound convincing. 'I mean he's mentally ill, and I don't want him to upset you. That's all.'

For three days Roma tried to speak to her father. When she was close enough she shouted for him to get in touch with his wife, but whether he heard or responded she had no idea.

Fletch was still being questioned periodically about the accident, and Henry heard about this after seeing Roma's arm in plaster when he looked through the windows of the Magpie a few days later. Remembering seeing Fletch steal the Rover, he went to the police station and told them what he had seen, adding that Fletch had been driving furiously and had seemed to be in a temper.

'From what subsequently happened, I'd think he was out to get Roma,' he confided quietly. 'She was driving him crazy you know. Wouldn't leave him alone to get on with his marriage. In fact, although I'm giving evidence against the man, I feel sorry for him,' he told the sergeant. 'Women drive you to do terrible things, don't they?'

Asked what he meant, he rambled on about the wickedness of woman and original sin, until the police began to wonder about the accuracy of his statement. He sounded as though fact and fantasy were inextricably mixed.

Further enquiries revealed that he had abused his present wife, that he had been forbidden to go near his daughters, and that his first wife died an unexplained death. They decided not to act on what was probably false information.

After talking to the police about Roma, Henry's anger became uncontrollable. He walked and walked, thinking about his disappointments. Why should Micky have a good business and the friendship of Roma and Mal and so many others when he was evil? Why should he have his son sharing his life when he'd done nothing to deserve him? All Micky had done for the boy was drive him away, send him out into a world full of danger and evil. He didn't deserve to have a son.

He dwelt on the fact that he had only managed to have daughters, women born to wickedness. Like Roma. Micky didn't deserve a son.

Micky sat with Roma and Leon one evening after the pub was closed and told them he wanted to transfer the licence of the Magpie to Roma.

'But why?' she asked. 'I have a business of my own, and besides, why would you want to give up the licence? What's the point?'

'No reason, except I've been thinking of the accident that happened to you, Roma love. I began to realise that if something like that happened to me, there'd be all sorts of problems for you two to sort out. This would make things simpler.'

Roma began to think this through and finally said, 'You want me to take the licence in case you die before Leon is ready to take it on?'

'I wouldn't want to run a pub!' Leon protested.

'Perhaps not now, son. But in a few years you could change your mind,' Micky said. He turned to Roma. 'You're right, I did think you could hold it for Leon, but my dream is for you two to run it together. Is that too way out to be a possibility?'

'I'm not free, Micky,' she said kindly, 'and Leon can't know how he'll feel in the years to come. It's too soon. Just stay well and keep everything going, then, when you decide to retire we can think again.'

'But in the meantime? Just as a precaution?' he pleaded.

'All right, I promise that if anything should happen and you can't run the pub, I'll take over until Leon decides whether or not he wants it.'

'I'll start proceedings to transfer the licence tomorrow, shall I?' Micky looked so relieved that Roma couldn't argue any further. She looked towards Leon for approval, then simply agreed.

Roma received an invitation to an engagement party in early December.

'Jason and Susie are going to be married next Easter,' she told Micky. 'They're having an engagement party and want me to go. D'you think I should, after her outburst the other week?'

'Yes, why not? It's probably her way of saying sorry.'

The news had given Roma a jolt of dismay. Easter 1984. How the years were rolling by. She was past the age at which most people married and all she had to look back on was a distressing affair with Fletch, a lost baby and a brief friendship with Jason which was now completely over.

'I like Jason and enjoy his company although it would never have developed into anything stronger, but now I won't even have his friendship,' she told Ruby Gorse later. 'Susie Quinn will be a jealous wife and won't allow even an innocent friendship between her husband and me, I'm certain of that.'

Not for the first time she regretted the years spent looking after Auntie Tilly and suffering the boring job with the two glums, Mr Graham and Mr Pugh. Why hadn't she struck out earlier and made a proper life for herself?

'Perhaps I'd be married with children by now, and suddenly I'm aware of the loss.'

'Are you sure you'd have been happier?'

'Perhaps not. Perhaps looking after my aunt gave that part of me which enabled me to build this business a chance to develop. Once Auntie Tilly died and I was free, I think a part of me that had been lying dormant suddenly woke up.'

'Your strength and independence might have stayed hidden if you'd married early.'

'Yes, and if Auntie Tilly had lived longer, it might have soured, causing resentment and poisoning everything I did. And if she'd died sooner I might have settled for some mundane existence, another office with another pair of Glum brothers. I might not have been ready to achieve what I have, and resentment might still have grown, children might not have been enough.'

'That's right, Roma,' the sensible Ruby said. 'There's no guarantee that what we want is the best thing for us. You can be proud of your achievements and you should be happy with the work you do.'

'I am. Although,' Roma admitted ruefully, 'just now I could do with a lot less of it!'

The plan to create microwave meals was showing great promise. Already Roma had been approached by a firm of manufacturers offering a deal to supply microwaves to businesses large enough to be interested in taking her products. They planned to start delivering their meals in a freezer van by Easter.

* * *

The engagement party for Susie and Jason was held in a function room on the outskirts of town. Roma arranged to attend, although it was not an occasion she thought she was going to enjoy. She made sure Micky had plenty of help, offering an evening's work to Matthew Rolands, and Leon promised to make sure his father didn't tire himself.

Mal called for her and as they drove to the venue they talked, mostly about Micky.

'He looks fine and while he's in the bar talking and joking with the regulars no one would think he was ill,' Roma told him. 'It's when the door closes and the work is done that he collapses into a chair and shows his exhaustion.'

'And he isn't eating?'

'Watching him, swallowing seems to be an effort.'

'Let's try and forget him for this evening and enjoy a rare evening out. Tomorrow I'll make him talk about it.'

'Promise?'

'Without fail.'

'And you'll tell me?'

'Yes.'

'Everything?'

'Everything.'

They smiled at each other, content that after all that had happened, their friendship remained intact.

That evening, Fiona arrived at the home of Fletch's parents with her small son and demanded to see him. A flustered Mrs Morgan invited her inside, found a place for the baby on the couch and offered tea.

'Where's Fletch?' Fiona demanded, and calling from the bottom of the stairs, Mrs Morgan succeeded in persuading her son to surface. He wore a dressing gown over underwear, his hair was tousled as though he'd been sleeping and his face was unshaven.

'Darling! What a wonderful surprise!' He went to hug

Fiona but she stamped on his bare foot and made him stagger back.

'You are coming home with me. *Now*!' she said, as Mrs Morgan backed out of the room.

'Love, I can't. I have a performance to give tonight, that's why I've been resting. And there's another tomorrow. I've been busy, and without sufficient time between jobs to come and see you but oh, I've missed you.' He limped to the couch and looked down at his sleeping son. 'He's all right, is he?' he asked.

'Fat lot *you* care!'

'But I do care. I've been working for Roma and cheating on the hours she pays me for so I can do my act and make extra money. All for you, love. You and Laurie.'

'There's a train at five thirty. We are going to be on it.'

'But I can't let people down. I've got two spots tonight, ten o'clock and eleven thirty. Please, love, be reasonable.'

'You can choose here and now. Your precious bookings or Laurie and me.'

'Mam?' he called. Mrs Morgan came into the room carrying a tray of tea. 'Will you mind your grandson tonight while I take my wife out for the evening? We have something to discuss, and,' he added with a wink, 'I want the ambience to be just right.'

They argued while Fletch prepared himself for his evening. Fiona explained to an excited Mrs Morgan the cleverness of her new grandson. Fiona took a lot of persuading but she finally agreed to stay the night and go out with Fletch that evening. He didn't tell her he would be the cabaret.

Not far away another couple were discussing their future and each was trying to persuade the other of the advantages of the way they saw that future developing.

Daniel wanted Sylvia to sell off part of her business and become, at least, a part-time wife and eventually, mother. While Sylvia asked Daniel once more to resign from his job and become a partner in her business. She planned a further expansion, having found three very small premises, each only one small room, in which she intended to sell cheap but fashionable clothes for young teenagers. Cheap, short-lived fashions which, she told Daniel, were a typical example of today's throwaway society.

They ended up quarrelling and Daniel stormed off and went for a walk, not planning any particular route but heading towards the fields and woods where he might find peace and quiet to consider where he and Sylvia were heading.

Susie and Jason were standing at the door greeting their guests when Roma and Mal arrived. Small tables were filled with flowers and waiters hovered with trays of champagne. Susie greeted Mal with a kiss but only offered a limp hand to Roma, who shared a smile with Mal, amused rather than offended by the slight.

They found a table and noticed for the first time that there was a small stage on which a microphone stood. As she watched, a man stepped forward and tested the microphone. She recognised Fletch. He waved at someone sitting behind them and, turning, Roma saw a pretty young woman. She guessed she was Fletch's wife from photographs and descriptions given by Fletch. She went over and introduced herself and Mal, but there was no welcoming smile, just politeness and a faint air of disapproval.

'Oh dear, another woman who considers me a femme fatale,' Roma whispered.

Henry Powell was searching for Roma and getting more and more anxious because he couldn't find her. He wanted – needed – to know where she was every moment. She wasn't at Perfection Pantry and she hadn't returned to her house. Her car was parked outside, but there were no lights showing, and peering through the windows revealed that the place was empty. Where could she be?

He walked to the Magpie and looked through every window, including a bedroom window reached by means of climbing on to a convenient shed. She wasn't there. He slithered back down and, frowning deeply, watched for a long time as Micky and his son laughed and joked with their customers. Leon wasn't allowed to serve, but he collected glasses and reached for things his father needed when he could save him stretching or lifting anything.

'Devoted son,' Henry muttered bitterly.

That Micky and his son got on well was obvious, and every time Micky touched his son's shoulder and shared a joke, or Leon smiled happily at Micky, Henry felt the agonising pain of envy. 'Three daughters I had. He gets the son I should have been given,' he muttered resentfully. 'He's evil, yet he's been given what should be mine.'

Climbing again on to the shed and stretching across, he could see into another bedroom window and, from the contents, he guessed it was one used by Leon. He was tall and quite strong, and it wasn't much of an effort to climb up by means of a drain pipe and get in through the window. He made hardly a sound as he walked across and stood waiting behind the half-open door.

Pulling three tables together, Jason arranged for Susie and himself to join Roma and Mal, leaving room for Fletch and his wife to join them. It was an uneasy gathering. Roma felt waves of dislike emanating from Susie towards her and Fiona was edgy too, looking at Roma with some disapproval.

'What have I done to these people?' she whispered to Mal with a forced smile. 'Susie looks as though she's hoping I'll drop dead.'

'Nonsense.' Mal laughed.

'You do know she blames me for you two splitting up? She believes I stole you from her.'

'Nonsense,' Mal repeated. 'If you'd stolen me, I'd have noticed.'

'In fact,' Roma went on, 'she stole Jason from me. His friendship I mean.'

'As long as they're happy now.'

Roma watched the two couples sharing their table and wondered. Neither pair was acting like happy lovers. Fiona had been upset when she realised that the evening out was so Fletch could do the acts he'd been booked for. She sat there, head down while he did his patter, obviously wishing she were somewhere else.

Roma felt waves of sympathy for the young woman when Fletch sang the Nilsson number, 'Without You', singing not to his sad-looking wife but to her. 'Can't live, if living is without you . . .'

She turned away and looked at Susie and was startled by the intensity in her expression. The words of the song seemed to come from her silent face and were directed not at the man she had agreed to marry, but Mal.

Susie was still in love with Mal, Roma realised with a shock. No wonder she hates me! Mal seemed unaware of what was going on, Fletch was still singing to Roma, making sure everyone in the room realised it.

Susie loves Mal, Fletch is still half in love with me. What a mess, Roma thought with growing panic. No one is with the right person.

She was not alone in this knowledge. A glance at Jason showed her that he too had noticed Susie's expression as she gazed at Mal. His own face was grim.

Unnoticed by anyone Jason left the celebration and went out of the building. He got into his car and drove a little way out of town, parked, doused the lights and sat, staring into the darkness. It was a mistake. He knew it was a mistake. He loved Susie, but Susie's love for Mal was greater than her love for him.

In the silence of the night he heard footsteps approaching

and he slid down in his seat not wanting to talk to anyone. Two men passed him and he wondered curiously why Roma's father was taking a late-night stroll with Micky's son, Leon. But such was his misery the facts drifted from his mind, forgotten in the gloom of his miserable thoughts on his future with Susie. Still undecided about what to do, a few minutes later he returned to the soured celebration.

During Fletch's final spot he chose a light-hearted song to finish and, this time, ended by taking his wife's hand, leading her on to the stage and dancing with her.

Susie didn't watch Fletch's performance. She moved her chair closer to Mal and began talking to him, making him laugh, giving him glances that would leave him in no doubt of her feelings. There was promise in the dark eyes and in the body language. Roma felt sick.

Fletch returned to the table amid applause and at once Fiona began talking to him. Although the words were low and sibilant it was easy to see they were quarrelling. The tension around the table was building until Roma could stand it no longer. While Mal and Susie were still involved in their intimate conversation and Fletch and Fiona glared at each other, face to face, she felt herself receding from them. She didn't belong here. Gathering her shawl and bag, she left.

The sounds in the hall became muted, distant, alien. She was no longer a part of the scene. No one had noticed her leaving, she might as well be invisible.

Loneliness fell round her in waves, chilling her, spreading like icy water over her whole body. There was no one in the world who cared whether she lived or died. Only Micky, and he was only a friend. She knew in that moment that when Micky died and Leon moved on, she would be completely alone in the world.

A few minutes later, Mal turned to raise his glass and ask the others to share a toast to the happy couple, and saw the empty chair. No handbag, no coat. Roma had gone.

Making his excuses, he hurried out of the building, hoping

to catch Roma and make sure she was all right. Where would she go, home or the Magpie? Aware of her concern for Micky he decided on the pub and caught up with her taxi just as it reached the car park and saw at once that something was wrong.

Roma stepped out of the taxi, and paid the driver as Mal reached her and held her hand. Together they looked at the gaudily lit facade of the Magpie.

All the lights were on, including the car-park lanterns, the floodlights and the coloured garlands that were sometimes used for garden parties on summer evenings. Their first thought was that something had happened to Micky, but then he appeared in the doorway and stumbled towards them and said, 'Thank God you're back. It's Leon, he's missing. Someone broke in, there was a fight, over-turned furniture, blood.' His distress caught at his voice and what should have been a shout came out an agonising whisper, 'Someone came in and took him and I didn't hear a thing. I didn't hear a damned thing and now my son has gone!'

Twelve

The scene outside the pub was one of chaos: people milling about; police cars pulling up with their lights still flashing; voices shouting instructions; conversations at a loud level as ideas were expressed and groups formed to search for Leon. Roma hugged Micky and asked what had happened.

'Nobody knows,' he said, looking round in anxiety. 'Leon went up to his room to fetch a book on fishing that he was lending to Richie Talbot and he didn't come back down. When I went to look I found his room empty, the window open and –' his voice broke as he went on – 'there were ornaments smashed and blood and broken glass on the floor. Furniture had been tossed round, the curtains had been pulled down. I called and several customers came running up and we rang the police.'

Mal telephoned to the function room where Jason and Susie were celebrating their engagement and begged Jason to come. Surely Susie wouldn't object at a time like this? He immediately promised to come and help search. Fletch came with Jason, who began talking to the rest of the customers who had been about to leave when the abduction had taken place. Some of the locals ran to gather others, as Mal, Jason and Fletch organised people into groups under the instructions of the police. A van pulled up and a dog-handler jumped out with a German shepherd. Micky phoned as many people as he could think of, begging them to look round for a sight of his son.

'I know it's Henry Powell,' Roma was startled to hear him say.

'He might have taken him, but he won't harm him,' Mal comforted him.

'Of course he will. Why would he attack him and take him away if he doesn't mean to harm him? It's hardly a blackmail or kidnap for money!'

'He does need money,' Mal told the police. 'His wife has been here trying to find him, they are in danger of losing their house if he doesn't sort out the arrears on the mortgage.'

Mal looked at Roma who looked stricken.

'Don't worry, we'll find him,' he said, hugging her. He took off his coat and wrapped it around her trying to stop her shivering. 'With the police here so promptly, he'll be found.'

It was more than fear for Leon's safety that terrified her. It was overhearing Micky's conviction that her father could physically harm him. 'D'you really think my father could hurt him? Kill him?' she whispered.

Mal looked at her strangely and replied, 'Your father? No I do not.'

She sighed. It was some small comfort at least.

She didn't go with the searchers although she wanted to, standing and doing nothing except waiting was harder than she could ever have imagined. Comforting Micky, she helped by manning the phone and passing on any information through the long night as people reported on places where they had looked. Several people said they had seen two men but most of the reports were explained by discovering that the people were innocent passers-by. Hopes rose and were dashed and the night slowly passed.

Rain began to fall as dawn broke, icy cold rain that seemed set in for the day. Roma's eyes were heavy and she was dropping with fatigue but she wouldn't leave Micky. She watched him and saw that the shock of his son's disappearance had aged him years in the few hours since discovering the abduction.

Fletch was with a group sent to search Saunders' farm. It had been Micky's idea, not that he thought his son had gone there voluntarily, but it was somewhere with lots of places to hide and not too far from the Magpie. The group set off and divided the area between them. Fletch was told to go into what had once been a barn for storing wood. He had a torch which was fading, but as it was nearly dawn it was thought there would be sufficient light to search.

Weeds had grown and died year after year since the place had been abandoned, and mounds of debris and rotting foliage had built up at the bottom of the wooden doors. Pushing against them, Fletch looked round and, finding he was alone, began to feel the atmosphere of the eerie, unwelcoming place send shivers of fear along his spine.

The doors opened with a groan of protest against the now muddy ground. There was more light than he'd expected and he realised that what had been a window frame in the back wall, had fallen away and taken some of the stonework with it. Around the walls were stacks of wood. Mostly cut to the same length, and with the bark still on it, obviously once intended for fencing. A roll of barbed wire lay close by, dead grasses and sawdust caught in its jagged spikes.

He stepped inside but then hesitated. No one could be hiding in such a place. The door had needed too hard a push for one thing, making it obvious it hadn't been moved in a long time, and no one could have climbed in through that weakened window. Behind the piles of wood, and the lengths propped up, tent-like, against the old walls, were dark places which his imagination filled with inhabitants like mice and beetles and spiders, perhaps one or two snakes. He shuddered and went back outside. He shouted back to the policeman in charge of the search party, 'No one there and no sign of anyone being there.' The party moved on. Against the wall, Henry smiled. By his feet, the prostrate figure of Leon Richards struggled ineffectually.

The police found the bedsit where Henry had been living but no one could say where he might be. One of the other residents reported him as being, 'A quiet, polite sort of chap. Keeps to himself and seemed very respectable.' Another said he often went for a walk at night. 'Couldn't sleep, poor man, and a walk helped to settle him.'

A constable was left to watch the house for his return and the search went on.

Every empty house, every barn and shed in the vicinity was examined but by the following day, there had been no sign of Henry or Leon. The police were convinced of what Micky had insisted all along, that Henry Powell had taken his son.

Roma was questioned and gave details of every place and every time she had seen her father.

'He was talking in a strange way,' she admitted when they asked about his state of mind. 'I seem to bring out the worst in him. When I was a child he told me constantly I was not a beauty like my mother, that I was evil and unworthy of sharing her name. I have no idea why he hated me so much. And,' she added fearfully, 'he hated Micky too.'

'You think he could harm the boy?'

'No, of course not. He's a little mixed up and I know he needs help, but harm someone? I can't believe that. He's my father.'

'Yet he hit your –' he referred to his notes – 'your step-mother, didn't he?'

A need to defend her father rose in her and she said, 'So she tells us. We haven't heard his story yet.'

'You think she might be "a little mixed up" too?'

'I don't know what to think. I can't sort this out in my mind. Leon is missing and there's reason to fear for his safety. But why are we concentrating on my father? It might be someone else. If my father *didn't* take him, then we're wasting time investigating him, aren't we?'

'Sorry, Miss Powell, but I don't think we are.'

In the semi-derelict barn, Henry released one of the ropes binding the boy to the piece of wood, lifted Leon and tilted him forward, until he was sitting up. He took the sticky tape from his mouth and gave him a drink.

'Promise to be quiet and I'll give you some chocolate,' he promised gruffly.

'What are you going to do with me?' Leon asked.

'Shut up. I haven't decided.'

Encouraged by being given food, hoping it meant he was not going to be killed, Leon promised not to make a noise. The chocolate was fed to him piece by piece. His hands were still tied and his feet and legs were fastened to a length of wood.

He wanted to pee but held on, determined not to succumb to the temptation of wetting his clothes. Somehow that would be a victory for Henry Powell and he wouldn't give him that satisfaction, but he wondered how long he could survive with his dignity intact.

Henry knelt down beside Leon, watching as the boy lay lightly dozing, moving fitfully as though trying to change his position and get more comfortable. Could he kill a nineteen-year-old youth? It was easy to kill an adult; someone who had grown and revealed their evil character. This was different. He knew Leon would grow up to be evil; with a father like Micky how could he be anything else? Yet he had run away, he reasoned. Perhaps he too had sensed the wickedness in his father and didn't want to become tainted by it?

But it was too late now. Leon was here, already a victim. Henry looked away from the sleeping face and tensed himself for action. 'Henry Powell,' he told himself in a harsh whisper, 'You have to be strong. Micky must be punished. You are doing God's work.'

Sympathy softened his features as he stared down at the restless boy. As Leon began to rouse from his brief sleep, Henry eased the tape from his mouth and gave him some chocolate and a drink. Leon looked at his captor and tried to smile.

Henry pushed the tape roughly back into place.

Roma phoned Ruby at her home before her friend set off for work on Monday morning, the second day of Leon's disappearance, and explained why she would not be available that day. Ruby promised to prepare extra food and bring it with the surplus, as soon as the rounds were completed.

'You might be glad of extra to feed the searchers,' she said.

Grateful for the support, Roma replaced the phone and began clearing up after the evening before.

'I'll do that,' Mal said, when his small group returned from yet another futile search of gardens and sheds.

'I need to do something,' she said. 'I can't stop looking at Micky. This is killing him.'

He put his arms around her and she sank gratefully against his warmth and strength. 'Mal, what will he do if Leon doesn't come back? He's all Micky has in the world.'

'He will. With so many people looking, he'll be found before dark, I'm sure of it.'

'The police seem determined to blame my father.' She was thinking of that newspaper cutting and the suspicion surrounding her mother's death. 'You really don't think he could harm Leon, do you?'

'Henry Powell is sick, I'm sure of that, love, and that's why we're so anxious to find Leon before anything does happen.'

'Then you *do* think my father's dangerous?'

'Hush, my darling. Try to concentrate on positive thoughts. Keep an eye on Micky, try to get him to sleep. Leon will be back before dark. Cling to that fact, believe it and convince Micky of it. It's the best way to help him now.'

Places already searched were searched again. The dog, given some clothing to give him the scent had been led off in every direction but so far had not found a trail. Lunchtime came and the bar was open. The food arrived from Ruby, and the searchers came and went as new ideas occurred and old places were checked again.

Fletch went out with the group and appeared to search diligently, although, in truth he was too nervous of what he might find and on several occasions, failed to do what he was asked as thoroughly as he should. He really couldn't cope with finding a body, so he only looked superficially into the areas he'd been asked to check.

In the barn, Leon tearfully released the pressure in his bladder and felt ashamed and less of a man, and as though he had let his father down by his weakness. A duvet that smelled of mildew had been wrapped round him, but he was shivering as waves of cold air and despair spread over him. A cut on his arm caused when he fell on to a broken vase, was stinging and his head hurt where Henry had struck him as he entered his bedroom to look for the book for Richie Talbot. The blow to the side of his head had been swiftly followed by a stinging punch to his mouth and nose and it was this that had created the startling amount of blood.

He'd been confused by pain, and Henry had quickly and easily tied him up.

Most of the time Henry stood quite still and rarely spoke. Occasionally, when Leon slept fitfully, he left the barn for brief periods. When Leon asked what was going to happen, and whether the plan was to demand money, he was told to, 'Shut up,' and Henry taped his mouth again.

Evening approached, and with the rain still pattering on

rusted corrugated iron and dripping to the muddy floor, and the stones throwing out the dank chill of winter, Leon began to sink into depression. He was going to die. He'd never be found. They'd searched the farm once and hadn't found anything and they wouldn't be looking here again.

Henry offered more chocolate and another drink. He didn't eat or drink anything himself. It was almost dark when Leon was startled to hear Henry move out of the barn, and he listened hopefully for the approach of another human being. But it was as though a thought had just occured to his captor, and Henry came back quite soon with a couple of blankets, one of which he threw across Leon, tucking it in round his sides. The other he put over his own shoulders. Then he went back to standing silent and unmoving, barely seen in the gloom of approaching night.

Sylvia arrived when her shops had closed and began helping with the continuous demand for cups of tea and coffee. Daniel soon joined her. Roma was exhausted with worry and with having been up throughout the previous night but she noticed with pleasure how well they worked together. Perhaps their relationship would survive in spite of Sylvia's fascination with the business.

To take Roma's mind off the situation, Sylvia talked to her about her latest expansion ideas.

'I've taken three small shops – no more than small rooms really, and having sectioned off a small kitchen-cum-office, there's hardly room to breathe. In fact the fitting room is so small it's little more than a cupboard and my poor clients will even have to share that with a vacuum cleaner and a mop bucket.' She laughed.

'Are you using the name Dorcas?' Roma asked, trying to keep her mind on what her friend was saying.

'No. These three are called the Hideaway and my advertising is simply "Sylvia's Hideaway! You MUST find this place!" What d'you think?'

'I think you're amazing.' Roma smiled. 'What does Daniel think?'

'I've given up all thought of a quiet life of domestic bliss and accepted that I'm marrying a remarkably clever business woman,' Daniel repied. 'And what's more, I know how fortunate I am!'

Roma was glad they had sorted out their conflicting ideas for the future, but every time someone returned, or spoke loud enough for her to hear she was distracted as hope revived and quickly died. She even added one or two intelligent comments to the conversation but was relieved when the couple went away to deal with dishes and more coffees, leaving her to think. It was as though, by thinking of Leon, she was helping him to survive.

As the day drew to its close, Micky asked several times whether Saunders' farm had been searched. 'I keep seeing him there,' he told Roma.

She thought it was because that was where they had found Leon on a previous occasion, when Micky and Leon had fallen and both had ended up in hospital, but she went to the policeman in charge of the investigation and asked, 'Who searched Saunders' farm? Was it a police search?'

'The police would have been in charge, yes.' He looked through his notes, asked questions on his radio and added, 'It was led by two policemen but early on, so it was mostly locals. It included Frank – Fletch I believe he's called these days. You know him, don't you? I'm sure he'd have been thorough, knowing how worried you are.'

She wondered uncomfortably how much was known about her affair with Fletch and she also wondered whether Fletch would have been as assiduous as the constable believed.

Soon after this brief conversation, someone called in with a description of two men walking in the direction of Saunders' farm late on the Saturday evening.

'One was tall and he appeared to be limping,' the informant said. 'I remember the tall one particularly, because I've seen him there before. I've seen the other one there too, back a few months, he was with another young lad then, but I'm sure it's him. Dangerous place. Should be demolished before someone gets hurt.'

'We've already searched there and we are working further afield now,' the constable told Roma when she excitedly relayed the message.

She found Mal and asked him to go with her to the farm.

'It's dark. What d'you think we could find that the police experts couldn't?'

'Then you won't come!' she said flatly.

'I'll come, but don't get your hopes up.'

'Thank you.'

'I don't think we should go alone. Pick one or two others to go with us and I'll tell the police what we're planning to do.'

'Micky,' she said. 'Could you keep an eye on the bar while Mal and I go and take another look at Saunders' farm?'

He looked relieved. 'I know it's been searched, but I'd be very grateful if you'd look again.'

'Mal and I will go now.'

'Thank you both.' He touched Roma's arm. 'Stay together. He could be dangerous.'

That darting fear that her father might be a dangerous man was quickly swallowed and she smiled reassuringly.

'There are several others who'll come with us. We need the police too, with their powerful lights. Don't worry, we'll be back before you know it.'

'Be careful, love, and, thanks,' he whispered, his voice failing him again.

When they reached the road leading to the ruined farm buildings, Mal and the two policemen he'd persuaded to come with them got out.

'We're going to walk up on our own in the hope that if they're there, they won't hear us coming,' Mal told Roma.

'I want to come.'

'Sorry love, but this is a job for no more than two people and you simply aren't big enough,' he teased.

Henry heard the car pull up even though it was at the furthest end of the farm lane. The night was still, there wasn't a movement of air. No creature explored or searched for food, not even an owl disturbed the silence. The old buildings had long since settled and gave out no sound apart from Leon's breathing behind his taped mouth.

He moved slowly and with caution away from the still form hidden behind a row of planks and tied almost immovably to a length of wood.

Leon listened to his departing footfalls and felt a greater fear knowing he was alone. Was he going to be left here to die? His mouth felt slimy with the sickly taste of chocolate and he longed for a drink. Knowing Henry was no longer there to offer him one, his thirst increased. Then he heard sounds.

At first he thought it was Henry back, but the sounds came from a different direction and whispered voices approached. He struggled to move, make a noise, knock something over, anything to attract their attention. He dreaded them coming then walking away without finding him, as before.

Mal shone the beam of light around the barn and called softly.

'Leon? Are you there. It's Mal.' No sound. Hidden by the sloping row of wooden poles, Leon struggled to sit up, but only achieved a couple of inches before falling back, hoping the small sound would be enough.

Mal moved closer, and, as he held the powerful torch, the policeman who was with him moved oddments of wood. Carefully they cleared spaces, moving the wood behind them, working their way across the floor. When they reached the broken window space they had found nothing and Mal sighed.

'The other buildings were practically empty and there's so

much rubbish in this one I really thought we had a chance of finding him, but he doesn't seem to be here.'

Leon felt sweat pouring out of his forehead. They were going to walk away again! He tried to raise himself so the wood to which he was tied moved, but it was hopeless. He flopped back soundlessly, cushioned by the duvet and blankets, and tears ran down his cheeks until he tasted the salty wetness.

Mal shone the torch over the stone walls and the untidy piles of wood one last time, then stopped and aimed the beam on the row of cut fenceposts.

'Those fenceposts leaning against the wall don't seem to leave enough room behind them to hide someone, but I think we should look anyway. You never know.'

With the policeman helping, they began moving the lengths of wood propped against the barn wall, throwing them carelessly aside. The torch was on the floor, its light shining towards the end of the slanting posts.

Leon worked at the ropes holding him, the one across his chest was the one preventing him for raising himself and making even the smallest sound. It had been tied and eased several times as Henry had given him a drink, and now, feeling the rope slacken, he was urged to greater effort. But as he struggled, the movements he could manage gave no sound, muffled as they were by the blankets and duvet.

Mal was working fast and was soon panting. His face and hands were filthy. Both he and the police officer were practically unrecognisable, their faces disguised by streaks of dirt as they had wiped sweat from their faces.

Slowing down as exhaustion numbed their muscles, they reached the end of the row and as they did, Leon suddenly sat up, his face also unrecognisable with its patch of sticky tape, the eyes bulging with the effort of trying to talk. The apparition made Mal and the constable stumble and fall backwards.

'Bloody Hell!' Mal gasped. 'You gave me a fright, young Leon!'

Without pausing to still his racing heart, he leaned forward and carefully removed the tape from the boy's mouth and the first words Leon spoke were a warning.

'Look out, Henry Powell's behind you!'

The two men turned, crouched, as if to stave off an attack, then they laughed with relief as another policeman appeared out of the darkness to join them.

'My name's not Henry Powell, lucky for you,' he said, easing the tension with a laugh.

Mal unfastened the ropes that bound Leon to his prison of wood and half lifted him and half carried him back to the waiting car.

Mal drove and Roma hugged Leon on the journey back to the Magpie. They said very little; Roma crying softly with the relief of finding him relatively unharmed and Leon still shocked by how close he had come to being killed.

When Leon walked in and hugged Micky she turned to Mal.

'Thank goodness—' she began but she was still ridiculously tearful and although she tried to hide the fact, she couldn't say any more. Mal opened his arms and she clung to him, glad of his strength as on so many occasions in the past.

It was sometime later, after the ecstatic reunion of Leon and Micky, and after Leon had been examined by a doctor and declared fit and unharmed, that Leon told them of the near rescue of the previous day.

'It was Fletch. I couldn't see him but I heard him come and saw the light as he shone a torch round. Henry Powell was standing holding a heavy chunk of wood to hit him as he came in, but he didn't come. He took one step inside, then backed out and shouted to the rest of the party that he'd looked but there was no one there. He shouldn't have told them he'd looked, should he? Standing within fifteen feet of me and he didn't search.' He shrugged then. 'I can't really blame him for being scared to go inside, but he should have told the others and made sure someone else did.'

'Are you certain it was Fletch?' Roma asked. She was conscious of Mal's head turning to look at her and guessed he was angry at her attempt to relieve Fletch of blame.

'I recognised his voice. It was Fletch all right,' Leon said.

The police continued their search for Henry. A group of men examined every inch of Saunders' farm, while two constables went to the bedsit he rented, and there they found him, sitting reading the Bible and looking surprised when they asked what he knew about the disappearance of Leon Richards.

He was very convincing as he explained that he had been there all day and all the previous night. Indeed, he had left Leon sleeping and gone back to his room, where he had made a noise and disturbed other lodgers to make sure they saw him. It had been easy for him to avoid the solitary constable at the front door. He had entered the garden and climbed in through a window. It had been such an amusing trick that once he had almost fallen when laughter at the simplicity of the evasion overcame him. Fingerprints and other evidence soon confirmed to the police that Leon hadn't been lying, but one of the officers remarked soberly, 'Henry Powell is so believable, that in an earlier time, before the forensic evidence we can now collect, he might have easily convinced us that the boy was lying and not he.'

Before the bar opened for business the following day, Micky sat with Mal and Roma and listened while Leon told them of how Henry had managed to take him from his room.

'I went up to fetch the book for Richie Talbot and he was waiting behind the door,' he began. 'He hit me, hard, in the mouth and again at the side of my head. I was dizzy and confused. I put my hands up to cover my face, hold back the pain, and he grabbed my hands and pulled them behind me. He was frighteningly strong and as I took a deep breath to yell he held my wrists with one hand and slapped the other across my mouth. He had a piece of sticky tape ready on the door and he put it over my mouth. My lip was bleeding and it wouldn't stick.' He grinned then adding, 'I did manage to land a satisfying kick on his shin and was pleased to see he was limping as we walked away.'

'Why did you go with him?' Mal asked. 'He couldn't have got you out of the window without your assistance.'

'He said you were hurt, Roma, and you needed help but didn't want Micky to know and be upset. He had a hand over my face and warned me to be quiet. I remember I nodded agreement and he released me, but still held my hands behind me.

'I suppose I could have struggled free at that point, but I believed what he said about you being hurt and not wanting to worry my father, so I didn't try to get away. I believed him, and went along with it,' he said, shaking his head at his own stupidity.

'A blow to the head when you aren't expecting it scatters your wits,' Micky said. 'And why wouldn't you believe him?'

'I should have guessed when he took me to Saunders' farm though. Why should Roma go there?'

'Did he explain?'

'He said Mal was considering a barn conversion and she had been to look at it.'

'Clever, and plausible,' Mal said with a glance at Roma.

'He was very quick. You'd never believe how quick! He had a rope around my hands and twisted it round and round my legs until I fell, then he easily tied me to that length of wood. My mouth was painful but had stopped bleeding by this time, and he wrapped that tape across my face and draped a duvet round me and stood watching me for what seemed hours.'

'And you heard the police and the others as they searched?' Mal said, with another glance at Roma.

'I couldn't believe it when they stopped at the door and didn't come in. Henry was there then, he stood in the shadow of some rotting planks and had a heavy piece of wood raised ready to hit anyone who came close enough to find me. But no one did.'

Roma could see Leon was distressed as he relived that first disappointment. His Adam's apple rose and fell in his young throat and his eyes were glistening as he fought back tears.

'Well,' she said, getting up and giving him a hug. 'You are safe now, Henry is in police custody and nothing like that will ever happen again.'

'Why did he do it?' Leon asked.

'That's my fault,' Micky whispered, his breath uneasily drawn. 'I'll tell you about Henry and me one day, but not now. I think I'll go back to bed, nights up worrying about you, young man, have taken their toll.'

Roma and Mal agreed. 'We're all exhausted,' Roma said. 'Electric blankets are on, there's a hot drink on the way.'

Fiona phoned the Magpie that evening and asked to speak to Roma. Her voice was high, she was shrieking with distress.

'Where's Fletch?' she demanded. 'Why don't you leave him alone and let him come home to Laurie and me?'

'I'm sorry,' Roma replied, startled at the accusation. 'He's been helping in the search for Leon, who was missing for two nights. But I don't keep him here, how dare you suggest it?'

Fiona burst into noisy tears then and, between sobs, explained that their baby was ill.

'I want him here. He persuaded me to go back to London and promised to come home the next day, after the last of his blasted one-night stands!'

'All I can do is promise that if I see him, I'll tell him about Laurie and tell him you need him there with you.'

'Will you though?' she said contemptuously. 'Or will you say nothing so he stays where you can pick him up and drop him at will?'

Too weary to try and explain, Roma asked the nature of the baby's illness and promised to try and get a message to Fletch. She put the phone down on more of Fiona's wild accusations.

Fletch came in later that evening and smilingly shrugged off any guilt about his failure to find Leon on his abortive search. He made a joke of it and assured anyone listening that, scared as he had been, he had honestly believed that others would be following who would search with expert thoroughness, policemen who knew how to cope with the fear.

'Fair play, Fletch, you should have told someone that you didn't actually go inside,' Richie said.

'I know, I should have made sure, but with people milling about the place it seemed impossible that no one else would go through that particular barn. God, I felt awful when I realised what had happened. I couldn't sleep last night worrying about how it might have ended for the boy if Mal hadn't thought to go back and take another look.'

Roma saw the expressions on people's faces change to sympathy as he bowed his head in apparent shame. Whatever else he was, he was certainly a fine actor, she thought with growing disgust.

'Fiona called,' she told him, biting back her anger. 'Your son is ill and Fiona wants you with her.'

'Poor little chap, what is it, d'you know?'

'Bronchitis she said. She's very worried. You should be with her.'

'It's impossible,' he said, with a groan of apparent despair. 'I can't go, not for a few days. I've got bookings and I can't let my fans down.' Again he lowered his head, seeking sympathy. 'That's one of the tragedies of being a performer. Pagliacci crying behind the painted smile and all that, hiding your sorrow and putting your audience first. I want to be with my son but I can't go.'

It was at that moment that Roma knew that Fletch was out of her system for good.

Henry remained under arrest and a brief court appearance ended with a request for a medical report. His wife was told and she arrived at the Magpie once more, this time asking Roma to find her and the two girls somewhere to live.

'Henry told me you inherited a lot of money from his sister and thinks you should at least share it with us as we're in such trouble,' Morfedd said.

'I had nothing from Auntie Tilly! You can easily check that!' Roma said, exasperated with her father for not believing her. 'I told my father this but he obviously prefers his own version of what happened, to the truth!'

In the back room of the pub, as she was making drinks for Morfedd and the two girls, she began to suggest lending them her house.

'Perhaps I can let them use the house and I could—'

'Don't get involved,' Micky interrupted warningly. 'She really isn't anything to do with you. There are plenty of people to help her, and you can't risk being landed with more of Henry's disasters.'

'But those little girls,' she said sorrowfully. 'They need someone to help them. I feel responsible.'

Mal agreed with Micky. 'Don't do it, Roma. You could give up your freedom for many more years of your life, and for what? To prop up your father's second family from a sense of guilt? Why are you guilty about them for heaven's sake?'

She didn't reply but her reasons passed painfully through her head.

I behave in a way that makes him angry, she told herself. I've done something terrible to him and the girls are suffering because of it. Because of me he is ill and they are in trouble. I don't know how, I just know the fault is mine.

It was Mal who rang Social Services and put Morfedd in touch with organisations who could help. Micky flatly refused to offer them a room, even temporarily, and Roma didn't argue. Why should Micky help them? Her father had never shown Micky anything but animosity.

When the sad little family left in a taxi paid for by Mal, to go to accommodation found for them, she felt unutterably ashamed. She had a thriving business and home of her own besides the room provided by Micky. She had so much and she wasn't willing to share it. Guilt attacked her mercilessly. Micky and Mal hadn't talked her out of helping them: the truth was, she had been relieved to accept their intervention and do what they advised, she hadn't wanted to take on the unhappy and disapproving family. That made her conscience pain her even more.

That evening, while she and Mal were finishing up in the bar, they heard a noise upstairs and found Leon, kneeling beside Micky who had collapsed. Micky protested weakly, but Roma insisted on calling an ambulance.

He died the following day, four months later than the prediction of the surgeon who had found an inoperable growth.

He had been suffering from cancer of the oesophagus and had been determined to hide it from everyone. The shock of Leon's kidnap had been more than his weakened body could cope with.

Roma held back her tears and tried to comfort Leon. It wasn't until later, in the early hours of the morning, when Leon finally slept, that she turned to Mal to be held in his comforting arms.

'This is becoming a habit,' he whispered and she looked up and smiled through her tears.

'What would I do without you?' she said.

'You'll never have to,' he said. 'Unless you tell me to go away and never come back.'

'I'll never do that. I need you too much.'

'That's something I suppose. Not enough, but better than nothing at all.'

She looked at him and saw, not Mal, who was always there, but an adorable, wonderful man whom she had never really seen before. Mal stared in wonder at the discovery of love that shone in her eyes. 'I've loved you for so long, my darling Roma, but for you it's been such a slow awakening.'

Thirteen

The following hours were strange ones for Roma. She hardly had time to cope with the realisation that she was in love with Mal, or marvel at the wonder of it. As they prepared for Micky's funeral and discussed what would happen once it was over, she seemed to be living through a strange dream from which she would soon awaken.

Forcing herself to calm down and deal with the moment instead of dreaming of the future, she said to Leon, 'If you wish it, I'll continue to run the Magpie until you're ready to take over. My business is up and running in such a way I'm hardly needed any more.'

Leon looked up hesitantly, afraid of offending her, then said, 'I don't think I want to stay.'

'Don't worry, I'll give it a few years, you'll have an income – or a savings account to startle your friends and, only if you want it, you can take over when you're ready to settle down.'

'I might never be ready.'

'Well, you don't have to worry about it now. Let's give it a while and then rethink, shall we? The Magpie can be sold any time you want, it's just that I feel that this moment in your life isn't the time to make long-term decisions.'

'Thanks. But let's get the funeral and the will reading over first, shall we?' He smiled and added, 'Dad might have despaired of me and left it to an animal charity like your Auntie Tilly!'

'Heaven forbid!'

*   *   *

'In fact,' she said to Mal later, 'I'll be glad of a year or so running the pub. I'm seriously thinking of selling my business. Perhaps later, when Leon is settled, I might start something new.'

'Don't tell me you're giving the next few years of your life to Leon! When will you start thinking of yourself?' he asked a little impatiently.

'But I have to, you must see that? Leon can't do anything at present, he's not ready to settle down, and he needs a home. I already have the licence and—'

'You what? Since when have you been the licensee of the Magpie?'

'For several months. My name is over the door but I didn't want to bring anyone's attention to it. In fact, only Richie Talbot has noticed and I asked him not to say anything.'

'Why didn't you tell me?'

'I preferred to treat it as unimportant. Micky would have been questioned, there would have been speculation about his health and that was something he clearly didn't want.'

'All those things apply to other people. Why didn't you tell me?' he demanded. 'Am I so unimportant?'

'I owed it to Micky to do what he wanted.'

'And what about me? What d'you owe me?' he asked.

'Mal, I love you and I realise that I've loved you most of my life.'

'Then let's discuss our plans, shall we?'

'I have to see that Leon is all right first.'

'You won't give me a moment, will you?'

'Just a few years, Mal, then I'll give you every moment of every day for the rest of my life.'

'That's second best!' he snapped. 'I won't settle for that!'

He walked out of the back room of the pub as Leon came down the stairs.

'You haven't been rowing because of me, I hope?' he asked

anxiously. 'I won't be staying, Roma. I'll wait till after the funeral, then I'll be off.'

'Do what you have to do,' she said forcing a smile. 'I'll make sure the Magpie is here when you want it and if you want it. We'll give it a few years, shall we? Then you can decide.'

'What about your life?'

'Go on with you, I'm not that old. I can put it on hold for a couple of years.'

'And Mal? Will he agree?'

'We'll discuss it properly when we're over the shock of losing Micky,' she said dismissively.

During the days between Micky's death and his funeral, life went on. Matthew Rolands and the rest of the part-timers worked as usual and Matthew, who was broke, begged for an advance on his wages. The promise of extra hours to make up for the loss of Micky seemed to please him as he thanked Roma profusely.

Ruby Gorse ran the kitchen with her usual efficiency and Roma went ahead with the preparations for the new microwave-meals project. The logo was to be a microwave with a smiling face and arms stretched out offering a steaming plate of food. Two days before the funeral, on December 16th, she had booked a day of interviews for staff for the new enterprise.

'Mal, I know it's inconvenient, but will you help?'

'What d'you want me to do, sit in on the interviews?'

'Well, I think Ruby and I can manage those, it's the lunchtime opening. Would you and Matthew deal with it for me?'

'For you?'

'It has to be me until we know what Micky's will contains.' She reached up and touched his unresponsive lips with her own. 'Please, Mal, help me over these next few weeks.'

'And then?'

'And then we'll be clearer about what the future holds.'

'I'm clear now and I thought you were.'

'I want it to include you, you know that.'

'Do I?'

Sylvia and Daniel had moved into a furnished flat although they were still unmarried. Roma was surprised, it seemed rather a comedown from Sylvia's original plans for a spendid detached house in the expensive area of town. Perhaps she was still reluctant to commit herself to Daniel without his full commitment to her?

Sylvia had seemed rather subdued when she told Roma about the place she and Daniel had decided to rent, and Roma wondered whether everything was all right. Usually she would ask, but in this instance there was something about Sylvia's mood that forbade it. Perhaps she had been persuaded by Daniel into taking a step for which she wasn't ready? Although that was completely out of character for her strong-willed friend.

Sylvia's promise to meet and chat about where their lives were going sounded false, but Roma pretended to look forward to it and they made a tentative arrangement to phone and fix a time later in the week. Roma thought Sylvia was unlikely to make the call but also knew that, given time, she would learn the reason for her troubled mood.

With Ruby sitting beside Roma, they met and questioned twenty-four people for jobs in the new enterprise, and these were shortlisted down to twelve, from which they needed seven. They were employing the nutritionist on a short-term contract and a marketing manager had been given the task of setting up the whole organisation.

Extra freezers and ovens were bought. Microwaves were ordered in bulk and delivery promised for the beginning of January. All these happenings, which had once been so exciting, were nothing more than burdens and worries now Micky had died.

Roma knew she hadn't been putting her mind fully on interviewing prospective staff and apologised to Ruby, thanking her for her continuing enthusiasm. They had each written comments about the interviewees' responses and they photocopied each other's remarks and went home to mull them over.

In fact, Roma only glanced at the papers and decided to leave the final selection to Ruby. Micky's death had cut the tie that had held her to her business. She had lost the joy of it, and wondered whether she would ever get it back. Even thoughts of Mal seemed to take second place to her worries about Leon and the Magpie.

'Try not to take on too much responsibility,' Ruby warned. 'You can't make any decisions until you know Micky's wishes and when the will is read, you might even find it has to be sold.'

'I don't think so,' Roma replied. 'I feel certain he wanted it to be a home for Leon when he finished his wanderings.'

'He'd at the very least have given the boy a choice.'

'If he has to choose, Leon will keep it, I know he will.' She wondered if that was her true belief or wishful thinking.

She was very thoughtful when she went back to the pub in time to open the bar for the evening session. Mal was still there and one glance at her face told him he wasn't the main subject of her thoughts. A brief nod of recognition was his only greeting.

Seeing that they were short of mixers she went down to the cellar. It was still a place she feared but if she were to take on the running of the pub, that was something with which she had to deal. And soon.

She stood looking at the door of the cupboard and wondered why it frightened her so much. Hearing footsteps behind her she turned to see Mal watching her.

'Do you still have a memory of that cupboard?' he asked softly.

'I don't know. I seem to half remember something, something that was terrifying when I was a small child, but the fear has no form. I can't remember why I don't like it. I just don't.'

He came and put an arm around her shoulders. 'You were found hiding there one day, just before your mother died. Hiding from your father you were, and when he followed you down, you hid.'

'And he found me?'

'No. Your mother came to look for you and she and your father started quarrelling.' He tightened his grip to reassure her before going on. 'Your father was out of his mind with jealousy. You must understand that. He hit your mother repeatedly. She still had some of the bruises when she died.'

'And I heard it and couldn't help her?'

'You heard it all, but could do nothing, you were only a child. What could you have done? You were too afraid of being beaten yourself. You stayed there until Micky found you and took you upstairs.'

'My father knew I was there?'

'No, he didn't know anyone was aware of what was going on.'

'So it doesn't explain why he hates me?'

'No, only why you're afraid of the cupboard.'

Interviewing Henry Powell, the police quickly realised he was out of touch with reality. He spoke with great authority but what he said made no sense. He described Micky Richards as the evil one and his own daughter, Roma, as wicked. He mumbled about original sin and of her tainting the family, and bringing ruination to him and even touching his new family with her destructive powers. He described himself as, 'God's hand, doing God's work', and was upset as he explained that he had failed Him by allowing Leon and Roma to live, to spread the tainted seed.

'They're weeds that are destroying God's wonderful harvests,' he said with an oddly shamefaced look. 'I should have dug them out and destroyed them, but I failed Him.' He brightened up as he told them, 'I didn't fail when I was called to help Micky Richard's wife to kill herself,' he said. 'I didn't let God down then. She didn't have the guts you see. I had to lock the car door, then go back and unlock it. She was weak and Micky needed to be punished.'

'And your wife, Henry?'

'She was the worst of all. She had to die. You do understand, don't you?'

While Henry was in a secure prison hospital, the police went back over the death of his wife and Micky's wife's suicide and wondered whether, amid the ramblings, there were a few pearls of truth.

Because of Henry's confusion between reality and fantasy, caused by his deeply felt and inexplicable hatred of Micky and his imagined need for revenge, the police took no notice of Henry's insistence that he had seen Fletch in the car heading for the scene of Roma's accident. Fletch was interviewed one more time and told that, although he wasn't in the clear, they had no evidence – as yet – to hold him.

'Fiona, please forgive me for not coming when our darling baby was ill,' Fletch said when he phoned her after leaving the police station. 'I've been so frightened that the police were going to fit me up for the accident to Roma. I want to come home.' There was a choking sob in his voice as he said, 'I'm giving up everything and coming home, to you and Laurie.' He put as much love and emotion into his voice as he was able, he even allowed his voice to break again as he added, 'I love you both so much.'

'I'm leaving the flat and going to live with my parents,' Fiona replied matter of factly, untouched by his words. 'If you want to come back to me you'll have to accept that. And I won't let you in until you have a job.'

'A job? Of course, love. Of course I want a job and to work for you and little Laurie. Just as soon as I find something suitable.'

'My father has work for you, and unless you take it you don't come over the door.'

The slam of the phone deafened him and he sighed. How could she expect him to live the life of an ordinary fellow-in-the-street, content with a mundane existence? He had been born to be an entertainer.

As he slowly walked back to his parents' small, soulless house, he wondered whether he could give it a go. Could he cope with Fiona's demands? A nine-to-five job with boring people? It would be a comfortable home and regular food, no more travelling lonely roads and killing time in lonely pubs and lonelier guesthouses, or sitting round in launderettes reading yesterday's paper. And he'd have a chance to prepare a brand-new act.

He thought of the alternatives: to try again in London, starting from scratch on his own, or to continue living with his parents who didn't want him, travelling miles late at night in the hope of a booking leading to something better. He decided he would have to try the first option. I'll take a step back, he told himself, in the hope of it leading to a jump forward.

It isn't as though I'll have to give up on my career completely, he mused. Once I'm settled in with Fiona's parents, it will be easy to persuade them I can earn extra money by playing the clubs. Then, when I've built up my reputation with an exciting new act, I can leave the boring job they have in mind for me and really fly.

The decision made, he began planning his new, rather daring act. Then he thought about how he would greet Fiona, how he would play the loving husband and father. Of course, he'd have to ask his mother to lend him the fare.

Sylvia was pregnant. She stared at the doctor as though he was making a hilarious joke when he announced it oh, so casually.

But there was no laughter in his eyes when he assured her it was so. Four months pregnant? How could she be? There had been no signs. Or had she been so busy she hadn't noticed? She left the surgery in a daze. There was no one to talk to, certainly not Daniel. Not even Roma. She remembered how easily she had advised Roma to get rid of her child. How simple it was to solve other people's problems.

Abortion wasn't such an obvious solution now. She loved Daniel and that made the difference. Her mind whipped through the difficulties and considered them. The businesses wouldn't be a problem, each unit was small and staffing wasn't a difficulty, there were plenty of young girls who would enjoy the grand title of manageress at one of them.

The biggest problem was deciding whether she was ready for motherhood. And what about Daniel? What would he think of becoming a father with no proper home and a wife dedicated to expanding a business to the possible detriment of a home life?

'What a mess,' she said aloud. 'Just when everything is working out. What an ill-timed disaster.'

Another couple were having difficulties too. On Thursday, the day before Micky's funeral, Roma drove along Harbour Road and noticed that the wine bar, still called Parry's Place, was closed. She rang the bell at the flat and spoke to Jason.

'Susie and I are separating, the wine bar is for sale,' he told her.

'What happened? I thought you two were happy working together?'

'So did I, but I think she realised she doesn't love me enough. I couldn't kid myself any longer either. You've seen the way she looks at Mal.'

'What will you do?'

'Go back to insurance. In fact, I've applied for several vacancies, including Daniel's job.'

'Daniel? He's been promoted?'

'He's giving up and joining Sylvia as a partner in Dorcas fashion shops. Can you believe it? I never thought she'd persuade him. Apparently they are extending the shops on two levels, inexpensive clothes and accessories for the young and luxury garments for those who can afford them.'

'Abandoning his career and working with Sylvia? That is a surprise.'

'I don't know why it is. Women get what they want one way or another, don't they?'

'Sylvia certainly does!'

Choosing a moment when Daniel wasn't doing anything, Sylvia asked, 'How d'you feel about children, Daniel? It's something we ought to discuss, don't you think?'

'I suppose I'll want a child one day, but at the moment we have enough on our plates just dealing with the business. After all, you've persuaded me to change my life rather drastically, don't you think that's enough for now?'

She detected a sharpness in his tone that startled her. She had been forceful in her persuasions, but she hadn't thought he was harbouring resentment about giving up the insurance business. Now, looking at the rather set expression on his face, she began to have doubts. Alarm bells rang as she wondered for the first time whether he might not want her to keep this child. Without another word she left the flat and went to her parents' house.

The early morning of the funeral was clear and cold. Frost glittered on the tarmac in the car park, and the grass in the field behind the pub was as white as if it was covered with snow. Roma glanced at the clock and saw it was only five o'clock, but knowing she wouldn't sleep any more, she had dressed and gone out to look up at the stars; so many, so clear, in the frosty air, she marvelled at their numbers.

She and her problems were minimal by comparison. A blink of an eye in time's real scale and she would be gone and forgotten, she thought sadly. Death made one think of death; she remembered Auntie Tilly telling her that.

Cold though it was, she went out to the back of the pub and looked at the yard with its tables and chairs on concrete that ended in a straggly hedge with a rather neglected garden beyond. The space would be ample for a new building, and she envisaged a smart new restaurant, traditional food and an atmosphere similar to the Magpie, olde worlde but clean and with popular food of the eighties. But that idea was no longer a possibility. The place would belong to Leon after today, and he was too young to want to bother with such things.

The food for the mourners was prepared, Ruby was bringing the sandwiches and, for the rest, there were only ovens to light and everything would be ready when they returned from the service. How many would come she had no idea, but she had catered for the regular Magpie clientele as well as to friends.

She sat on her own, remembering Micky's kindness and determined to help his son in return. At eight o'clock Mal came, and together they went up to wake Leon.

When Leon joined them for breakfast at eight thirty he had his old rucksack over his shoulder and he brought his surf board to rest against the kitchen wall.

'I'm leaving straight after the funeral,' he explained. 'I can't stay, not now.'

'You need to wait until the reading of the will,' Mal reminded him. 'Your father wanted it read after the service, remember. Then, if you tell me the time of your train, I'll drive you to the station.'

'Thanks.'

Once breakfast was over the place began to be busy, people coming with condolences, flowers, offers of help and deliveries of various foodstuffs from Ruby. Ruby herself turned up at twelve, having left the kitchen in the hands of the staff and she offered to stay and help serve food when the mourners returned. Roma was glad of her company.

Roma and Mal both felt an atmosphere of unease between

them, of things unsaid, but there was no time to talk. In fact, they both tried not to look at one another, so great were their misgivings. Leon, the innocent cause, went back to his room and when Mal looked in to see if he needed anything, he was sitting looking out of the window, deep in thought, so he didn't disturb him.

Mal watched Roma's face as the solicitor, who had been instructed to attend and read the will, began to speak. If she looked at him, sharing the revelation about to unfold, he would know they were together, but if she looked at Leon, then he would know there was no future for him. He silently begged her to give him that glance of togetherness.

Only Mal and Roma and Leon were in the room.

'I have to tell you firstly that Michael Richards has made several small bequests for friends including Maldwyn Parry, but that the bulk of his estate goes to his daughter and his son.'

'His daughter? Who is she?' Roma whispered to Leon. '*Where* is she?'

Leon frowned, curiously waiting for the solicitor to continue.

'Michael Richards, Micky to his friends, wishes me to tell you that he is the natural father of Roma Powell.'

The shock made her reel, and after a second during which her mind seemed to somersault, she looked at Mal. He saw not love but fury glittering in her eyes.

'You knew! You knew and didn't tell me! You accuse me of not sharing things with you and you kept this huge secret.'

Mal said nothing and the solicitor asked for quiet so he could continue.

'I loved her mother, Mary Anne Rees, before she married Henry Powell. After they were married, that love continued until our daughter was born. My biggest regret in life has been not acknowledging Roma and being able to give her my name.' The solicitor paused and explained that they now come to the legacies. 'The Magpie I leave to my beloved son Leon and to my daughter Roma Powell to do with as they wish, but my hope is that they will continue to run it together.

'Any money in my various accounts, I leave to be equally divided between my aforementioned son and daughter.'

There were other smaller bequests to friends, including Micky's collection of antique china and glass to Mal. But Roma heard nothing after the shock of knowing Micky was her father. Relief that Henry, with his confusion and dangerous impulses, was not a blood relation came soon afterwards, and guilt, for feeling that relief, closely followed.

Mal watched as mixed emotions crossed her features, and waited for her to look at him with understanding. She did not. She was dazed and tearful, although she wasn't sure who her tears were for, herself or Micky or even poor Henry Powell. She had a swift understanding of how the deceit of his wife had distorted Henry's thinking and made him blame her, his small daughter, for ruining his life.

There was a letter from Micky in which he asked Mal to support Leon in whatever he decided to do. At this point Roma did glance at Mal to share a look of tacit approval.

When everything had been explained and understood, Mal came and stood beside Roma, but she ignored his silent offer of support and comfort. Automatically thanking the solicitor for coming, and giving Leon a trembly smile, she walked away and went to see Sylvia.

'It's such a shock, Sylvia. Suddenly I'm not who I thought I was, I'm someone else.'

'You're self-made like me. Who your biological parents were is irrelevant now. You are Roma Powell entrepreneur, successful business woman.' Sylvia smiled widely and added, 'Just like me. Did you know Daniel has agreed to work with me building up Dorcas into a national chain? What do I mean, "national"? I mean international!'

'How did you persuade him?' Roma asked. 'He's been unwilling to give up his career, hasn't he?'

'Most people get what they want, if they really want it. Whether it's a business, a man, or a new carpet for the spare room. Expectations vary as much as the means people use to achieve them. Take Micky. He wanted you to provide a home and business for Leon, didn't he? Well, I wanted a partner I could trust, and finally Daniel could see the sense of it.'

'I wish I had the knack!'

'You have. Mal gave up running Parry's Place so he would be free to help when you extended your sandwich business, didn't he?'

'I didn't ask him to.'

'Not in words, no. But he did it. When the search for Leon began on that awful day when he went missing, Susie, who is pathologically jealous, asked Jason not to help you, but he did.'

'Are you saying I manipulate these men?'

'We all get our own way in varying degrees. Some do it subtly like you, some by giving no alternative, like me. Then there are poor demented people like Henry Powell who never succeed in getting their own way, ever, and he, poor man, went off the rails.'

'It's a terrifying thought. I might have caused Mal to give up something he enjoyed.'

'I doubt it. You ask yourself what you want and then you go for it.' She looked at Roma with a half smile. 'Mal wants you.'

Realising how difficult the day had been for Roma, Sylvia avoided mention of her own shock, that of discovering she was four months pregnant. Besides being the wrong time to tell Roma, she hadn't accepted it herself. The realisation kept showering over her in a flood of disbelief, startling her as if with new discovery. Instead she talked about her business plans now she had Daniel to support her. Although at the moment with his obvious desire to remain childless she didn't think support was the right word.

* * *

Leon didn't leave after the reading of the will as he had intended. He hung on, working through the revelations. He made it clear that he was thrilled to discover he had a sister, and one he knew and liked. But Roma had the impression something was still worrying him.

'Why did Mum have to die, Roma?' he asked one day when they were preparing the bar for opening. 'Was it really Dad's fault? Was it because Dad made her so unhappy, d'you think?'

'Can you remember a moment when you thought death was a way out?' she asked, expecting him to say, no. In his short life, even living the way he had lived, there surely couldn't have been moments so dire?

'Yes, once,' he surprised her by saying. 'I was travelling with a bloke called Greg. I trusted him. We shared everything. Then one day I came back from an unsuccessful begging session and found he'd gone, taking my money, my bedding, spare clothes, everything. Even the tent. It was pelting with rain, had been for days. I was soaked, broke, and there was nowhere to shelter.' He smiled. 'For a moment then I thought I'd be better off dead.'

'That's the point, you felt that everything was impossible – for a moment. Despair is usually short lived.'

'Mum was temporarily insane you mean?'

He looked alarmed and she quickly said, 'No, I don't. She was deeply unhappy.' She smiled at him. 'After my relationship with Fletch, I can understand that.'

'You mean if Mum had waited for a while, the desperation would have eased and she'd have pulled through?'

'I would like to think so, wouldn't you?'

He nodded.

'I feel like a cheat,' Roma told him then. 'I'm robbing you of half your inheritance. If you want me to I'll hand over my share now.'

'No!'

'I'll be wealthy enough when I sell Perfect Pantry and the microwave business.'

'There's nothing that could have pleased me more than knowing you're my sister,' he repeated several times.

He helped with some of the work round the pub, which was still empty without the presence of Micky. He even painted the walls of the cellar and Roma let him, understanding that physical, tiring work was cathartic. When she went down to admire his efforts, she saw to her surprise that he had taken the door off the cupboard that frightened her and had filled the resulting space with deep, useful shelves.

'Mal told me about it,' he said when she thanked him.

One morning she went to Perfect Pantry and did a shift with the staff, enjoying using the new machinery in which they had invested.

Doughnuts were a very popular addition to their range and the machine cut the dough into correct-sized pieces by means of a lever, while a second lever made each of the thirty-six pieces into rounds which, after being left to prove were cooked in a deep fryer, thirty-six at a time.

Something that worked like an old-fashioned mangle produced neatly cut pasties from a large portion fed into the rollers. She wondered whether she would regret leaving the business to others and decided not. Once the microwave meals were established and doing well, it would be time to move on.

Sylvia and Daniel were waiting for her when she got back to the Magpie.

Smiling, they said in unison, 'We are pregnant!'

'What? Oh, how marvellous – er – isn't it?' Roma said, trying to read their faces. 'Oh, I knew something was up but I didn't expect this!'

'I couldn't tell you at first,' Sylvia said as Roma kissed them both. 'After recommending that you didn't keep your baby, I felt a bit of a fraud.'

'That was different,' Roma said seriously. 'And it's a decision I've never regretted.'

Roma and Mal both avoided any opportunity to talk to each other. Then, on December 20th, as she and Leon were belatedly putting up the Christmas decorations, forcing themselves to add cheer when they felt a serious lack of it themselves, Mal came in and immediately began to help.

'I'm glad you decided to go ahead as usual,' he said, addressing the remark to Leon.

'We know that Christmas is for other people not ourselves,' Roma replied for him. 'Leon and I know we can't expect our unhappiness to be shared by our customers. They expect everything as normal, and that's what they'll get.'

Leon went into the kitchen on the pretext of making coffee, leaving Mal and Roma struggling with a balloon pump that refused to work and was sending partly inflated balloons whizzing across the room.

'Did you know that Daniel is giving up insurance and going into the business with Sylvia?' she asked.

'She's always known what she wants and has refused to let anything get in her way.'

'She said most people do that, get what they really want, only some have greater expectations than others.'

'And what about you, Roma. What do you really want?' He was looking at her quizzically. His expression was strange, almost cold, and she wondered whether he had changed his mind about loving her, was regretting the words that had passed between them.

She was relieved when furious banging on the door announced the arrival of their first customer for the evening. It had to be Richie Talbot, who still arrived dead on time for opening. Any subdued behaviour after Micky's death had quickly reverted to normal once the funeral was over.

Christmas was an uneasy few days, with the bar filling up

noisily for every session and the silence that followed threatening to unnerve Roma with its reminder of her lonely life.

Leon seemed subdued and she guessed he was thinking about leaving. She dreaded him going and leaving her alone in this old, creaky house. But she was determined not to hint at her fears or utter a word to persuade him to stay. He had to do what he wanted with his life and she would not add even the slightest weight to one side of the scales as he made his decision. He might have seen through her forced gaiety but she hoped she was convincing him she was content. She intended to buy a dog for company and have security locks put on the doors and windows but decided to wait until he was gone before dealing with those things. She would not show how much she dreaded being alone.

The new microwave meals began to appear in the middle of January and at once Roma knew they were going to be a success. Their sales of microwaves surprised the suppliers and there was even a waiting list for the machines by the end of the month.

To her relief, Mal dealt with most of the organisation once the professionals departed. He came into the Magpie each evening and reported the day's happening and showed no sign of being anything other than an efficient partner. It was sometimes more than she could bear.

Leon left as March showed one of its surprisingly calm and mild days.

'Deceptive,' she warned Leon as he packed his clothes and wet suit, and picked up his rucksack and surf board.

She gave him food for the journey, handed him a very healthy bank book and wished him well. Mal had agreed to drive him to the station and, as they opened the door and stepped out, she thought she would never be happy again. Seeing Mal and Leon walking away from her towards the car, was like seeing the two people who were most important to her leaving for ever.

The need for something to do made her telephone about the security locks and the firm promised to send someone out the following day. Now for the dog.

But first she had an unpleasant job to do. One she couldn't have dealt with while Leon had been there. She went into Micky's bedroom and began packing his clothes into boxes to take to a charity shop. Good quality and much of it hardly worn.

Checking the pockets she found a small photograph album and was brought to tears when she saw that it was filled with snapshots of herself, through babyhood, school days and several each year since. He had been watching over her, loving her without being able to tell her.

She didn't hear Mal come back and he found her sitting on Micky's bed looking through the photographs, her eyes heavy from crying.

'I wish I'd known before he died, Mal,' she whispered. 'I could have told him I loved him too, and not because he was my true father but because he was a wonderful and generous friend.'

'I think he knew how you felt about him, and that made him very content. All he'd ever dreamed of was seeing you and Leon together at the Magpie and he had that, for a time at least.'

'Why, in all the years you've been my friend, didn't you tell me? It explains so much. Why Auntie Tilly kept his birthday cards from me. Why my father hated me.'

'I promised him. He didn't want to risk upsetting you. And he didn't want Henry hurt any more.'

Roma flipped the pages of the album and stared at the face of her mother.

'Micky never saw her again once you were born, you know. He married a few years later and was completely faithful. But he never stopped loving her – or you.'

'I should have been told.'

'You were, when Micky decided the time was right.'

'And that was after his death?'

'I think he was afraid you would be disappointed, angry, hurt, humiliated.'

'How could I have been any of those things?'

They went outside and with no lights on, stood in the back garden staring blindly into the dark evening.

'I've envisaged a restaurant out here,' Mal said and she turned to stare at him in surprise.

'But so have I! Can you read my mind?' She spread her arms encompassing the area she had in mind. 'I want to build an extension and the decor will be just like the pub. Stone walls and white paint, big fireplace, friendly atmosphere. Not chips with everything but good-quality meals at a reasonable price, and – can you really read my mind?'

'Oh yes,' he said, his voice gritty and low. 'And right now it's telling me not to interfere, not to come close, that you don't want any commitments. You want to do this all on your own, you want to show everyone that Roma Powell can cope, that she doesn't need anyone.'

'Mal, I—'

'Come on, we'll have Richie knocking the door down any minute.'

They went inside, both unhappy and neither able to explain how they really felt.

Mal didn't stay to help clear up that evening. He seemed restless, anxious to be off, and when she suggested he leave, he agreed with unflattering haste. Matthew, the part-time barman, was working and Roma knew he would go as soon as he could possibly escape without losing any of his wages, and leave most of the final clearing up to her.

She was right, Matthew made an excuse to finish early and it was almost midnight when she settled into bed. She usually read for a while, but tonight she was tired and turned off the light straight away. But sleep wouldn't come. So many thoughts filtered through her mind, so much to take in.

Mal and she had been friends all her life and they had always been companionable, easy with each other, but now – now she had fallen in love with him nothing was right. It was as though they had torn down the friendship and couldn't find anything with which to replace it. After the strength of that friendship, love was insecurity, a feeling that it could fall apart any moment. What had gone wrong?

The sound, when it came, was so slight she thought at first she had imagined it. Just a scraping noise as though a branch was rubbing against a window, but there was no wind. The night was frosty and still after the day of pale sun and clear skies.

She relaxed as the sound stopped, but a moment later she heard something more. A window was being opened, she was sure of it. Reaching for the telephone, she dialled Mal's number and when he sleepily asked who was calling, whispered that someone was trying to break in.

'Don't go down!' he warned her. 'Don't leave your room. Very quietly, lock your door.' The phone was replaced and she did as he told her.

She stood at the window for what seemed hours, and tried to see into the yard. She heard the occasional sound and watched her door handle, dreading to see it move. Then outside, a torch showed briefly in the darkness, and she guessed rather than saw that a figure was leaving by the back door.

Then shadows left the walls and police torches showed bright beams and the man was surrounded. He threw the bags he was carrying at the police but was soon overpowered.

Unlocking her door she ran down the stairs, straight into Mal's arms.

'Are you all right, darling?' he asked anxiously.

'I am now you're here,' she said breathlessly. 'Mal, please stay.'

'Of course I will. I couldn't leave you after this.'

'Not because of this, because I want you here always.'

There wasn't time to say any more as the police came to ask a few questions and to see if she could identify the intruder.

'He was after cigarettes,' the sergeant confirmed. 'And I reckon he's one of your barmen, miss.'

To Roma's further dismay the thief was Matthew Rolands. Always broke, always trying to win a fortune on the race track, he had resorted to stealing from her to pay his debts.

As he was being led away, the constable said, 'You must like having us around, miss. Your accident, then young Leon going missing, and now this.'

'In future I hope I see you often, but only as customers,' she said seriously.

The following morning, while Roma and Mal were eating a late breakfast, they heard the sound of a car slowing down and when Roma looked through the curtains she saw a taxi.

'A taxi. Who can that be?' She frowned.

'It wouldn't be Henry's second wife and her little girls coming to ask for a home, would it?' Mal queried. 'If it is, don't let them in. Right? No more lame ducks.'

'No more lame ducks,' she repeated. No one came in and she said, 'Perhaps it was just someone turning around in the car park?'

'Thank goodness for that!' He sighed happily. 'Now, come here and let's remind ourselves who we put first from now on.'

As they drew closer to kiss, there was a cough and they turned to see Leon standing in the doorway watching them.

'Thought I'd come home. Just as well I did. Seems you'll be needing a best man.' He grinned.

The kiss and all it might lead to was postponed. A loving embrace was shared by three.